Combust the Sun

A Richfield & Rivers Mystery

What Reviewers Say About Bold Strokes Authors

~

Kim Baldwin

"*A riveting novel of suspense* seems to be a very overworked phrase. However, it is extremely apt when discussing Kim Baldwin's [*Hunter's Pursuit*]. An exciting page turner [features] Katarzyna Demetrious, a bounty hunter…with a million dollar price on her head. Look for this excellent novel of suspense…" – **R. Lynne Watson**, *MegaScene*

"*Force of Nature* is an exciting and substantial reading experience which will long remain with the reader. Likeable characters with plausible problems and concerns, imaginative settings, engrossing events, and a well-tailored writing style all contribute to an exceptional novel. Baldwin's characterization is acutely and meticulously circumscribed and expansive. It is indeed gratifying to see a new author attempt and succeed in expanding her literary technique and writing style. Kim Baldwin is an author who has achieved both." – **Arlene Germain**, reviewer for the *Lambda Book Report* and the *Midwest Book Review*

~

Rose Beecham

"…her characters seem fully capable of walking away from the particulars of whodunit and engaging the reader in other aspects of their lives." – *Lambda Book Report*

"When Jennifer Fulton writes mysteries, she writes them as Rose Beecham. And since Jennifer Fulton is a very fine writer, you might expect that Rose Beecham is a fine writer too. You're right…On the way to a remarkable, and thoroughly convincing climax, Beecham creates believable characters in compelling situations, with enough humor to provide effective counterpoint to the work of detecting." – *Bay Area Reporter*

❧

Ronica Black

"Black juggles the assorted elements of her first book with assured pacing and estimable panache...[including]...the relative depth—for genre fiction—of the central characters: Erin, the married-but-separated detective who comes to her lesbian senses; loner Patricia, the policewoman-mentor who finds herself falling for Erin; and sultry club owner Elizabeth, the sexually predatory suspect who discards women like Kleenex...until she meets Erin." – **Richard Labonte**, Book Marks, Q Syndicate, 2005

"Black's characterization is skillful, and the sexual chemistry surrounding the three major characters is palpable and definitely hot-hot-hot. If you're looking for a more traditional murder mystery, *In Too Deep* might not be entirely your cup of Earl. On the other hand, if you're looking for a solid read with ample amounts of eroticism and a red herring or two, you're sure to find *In Too Deep* a satisfying read." **Lynne Jamneck**, L-Word.com Literature

❧

Gun Brooke

"*Course of Action* is a romance...populated with a host of captivating and amiable characters. The glimpses into the lifestyles of the rich and beautiful people are rather like guilty pleasures....[A] most satisfying and entertaining reading experience." – **Arlene Germain**, reviewer for the *Lambda Book Report* and the *Midwest Book Review*

"*Protector of the Realm* has it all; sabotage, corruption, erotic love and exhilarating space fights. Gun Brooke's second novel is forceful with a winning combination of solid characters and a brilliant plot." – **Kathi Isserman**, *JustAboutWrite*

❧

Jane Fletcher

"*The Walls of Westernfort* is not only a highly engaging and fast-paced adventure novel, it provides the reader with an interesting framework for examining the same questions of loyalty, faith, family and love that [the characters] must face." – **M. J. Lowe**, *Midwest Book Review*

Lee Lynch

"There's a heady sense of '60s back-to-the-land communal idealism and '70s woman-power feminism (with hints of lesbian separatism) to this spirited novel—even though it's set in contemporary rural Oregon. Partners Donny (she's black and blue-collar) and Chick (she's plus-sized and motherly) are both in their 50s, owners of the dyke-centric Natural Woman Foods store, a homey nexus for *Sweet Creek*'s expansive cast of characters.…Lynch, with a dozen novels to her credit dating back to the early days of Naiad Press, has earned her stripes as a writerly elder; she was contributing stories to the lesbian magazine *The Ladder* four decades ago. But this latest is sublimely in tune with the times." – Richard Labonte, Book Marks, Q Syndicate, 2006

Radcly*f*fe

"…well-honed storytelling skills…solid prose and sure-handedness of the narrative…" – **Elizabeth Flynn**, *Lambda Book Report*

"…well-plotted…lovely romance...I couldn't turn the pages fast enough!" – **Ann Bannon**, author of *The Beebo Brinker Chronicles*

Ali Vali

"Rich in character portrayal, *The Devil Inside* by Ali Vali is an unusual, unpredictable, and thought-provoking love story that will have the reader questioning the definition of right and wrong long after she finishes the book.…*The Devil Inside*'s strength is that it is unlike most romance novels. Nothing about the story and its characters is conventional. We do not know what the future holds for Emma and Cain, but Vali tempts us with every word so we want to find out. I am very much looking forward to the sequel *The Devil Unleashed*." – **Kathi Isserman**, *JustAboutWrite*

Visit us at www.boldstrokesbooks.com

Combust the Sun

A Richfield & Rivers Mystery

by

ANDREWS & AUSTIN

2006

COMBUST THE SUN

ISBN 1-933110-52-X

This Trade Paperback Original Is Published By
Bold Strokes Books, Inc.,
New York, USA

First Printing: June 2006

Credits
Editors: Cindy Cresap and Stacia Seaman
Production Design: Stacia Seaman
Cover Design By Sheri (GRAPHICARTIST2020@HOTMAIL.COM)

Acknowledgments

We thank the Bold Strokes Team, and Rad in particular, for recognizing and supporting our particular style of lesbian fiction and affording us unfettered creative freedom.

Dedication

For Camilla Parker Bowles

Who proved unequivocally that love does, indeed, conquer all

PROLOGUE

It would be months before I would learn of Sterling Hacket's desperate late-night call to Robert Isaacs regarding the too-perfect Italian boy whose exquisitely carved body lay naked on the floor of Sterling's palatial Bel-Air estate, threatening to expire and take with him Sterling's hard-won motion picture career.

Sterling apparently thought the youth had merely passed out from erotic exhaustion and designer drugs, until he felt for a pulse in his neck. Panicked, he tried to haul the boy out of his living room but, for all of his lithe beauty, the lad was far too large for him to handle. Sterling dropped to his knees beside the boy and began CPR. I could envision Hollywood's action-adventure idol, infamous for never being able to remember the most elementary dialogue, shouting, "Four breaths, two pushes, or two breaths, three pushes? Shit!"

That's when I imagine Sterling rang for help. The booming voice that had enthralled women by the thousands, scaling up to high C in near hysteria, "He's not breathing! We were partying and I gave him a little Ecstasy. That's all. You gotta do something, Bobby!"

"I warned you about this!"

"You're wasting time!" Sterling shouted.

"Try to get him breathing. Do CPR or something. I'll get someone over to your house right away. Do whatever she says."

Moments later across town, another phone rang in Barrett Silvers's Los Feliz home. Naked to the waist, she propped herself up in bed on one elbow and tried to sound awake when she picked up the receiver.

The voice on the other end of the line was loud and firm. "Barrett, get over to Sterling Hacket's house right away. He's got a kid over there who's not breathing. See if you can get him going. If you can't, I don't want any trace of that kid ever having been near him, you got that?"

"I'm not dressed—"

"I don't give a fuck what you're not! Be there in two goddamned minutes and get that kid breathing! Then call me." The phone went dead.

Shaking, Barrett dove into the pants hanging over the chair in her bedroom, slung on a shirt, slammed her bare feet into her loafers, and ran to her car, now fully aware that "she who rides on the tiger's back must go where the tiger goes."

CHAPTER ONE

My feet landed on the treadmill in time to the shriek of violins and a country singer proclaiming that the devil was down in Georgia trying to make a deal.

If he thinks Georgia's tough, he ought to try Hollywood, I thought and cranked the treadmill speed up a notch, out of frustration. The music was shattered by my own voice in the distance—"You've reached Teague Richfield. Leave your name and number and I'll call you back"—then a shrill beep signaling the caller to talk.

"Teague? Barrett. How about lunch at Orca's, one o'clock? I really need to talk to you. Unless you call, I'll assume we're on."

I shut off the treadmill and reached for the cordless phone just in time to hear the line go dead.

"Why didn't you get it?" I panted to Elmo, who lowered his long basset ears and let out a disapproving groan.

Staggering to the kitchen counter, I deposited myself on a bar stool in a palpitating heap and replayed Barrett's message. Whatever she wanted to tell me was obviously important. I'd known Barrett for years. The common denominator of our friendship was our studio ties, and the fact that she once fucked my brains out, but we rarely lunched.

I scanned the trades to be "au courant" for my lunch with Barrett, who knew more players in Hollywood than a gossip columnist. Half the women screenwriters in town owed their careers to her, and the other half were afraid of her. Barrett confided in me precisely because I wasn't afraid of her—occasionally attracted to her, but not afraid of her; and in Hollywood, that alone could constitute friendship.

I glanced at an article on Marathon Movie Studio's CEO, Lee

Talbot. Next to it was a smaller article about Marathon's star, Sterling Hacket, and the ongoing investigation into Hacket's alleged procuring of young boys for sex. I tossed the trade magazine aside as the phone rang again. It was Mom, in Tulsa, calling to tell me to turn on CNN immediately.

"Channel forty-one!" she shouted, persistent in her belief that the entire U.S. was on her cable system. I located the channel carrying CNN in L.A.

The crawl running along the bottom of the screen read "Dateline Oklahoma," over a scene of several homicide investigators and coroner's assistants loading a body into a morgue van while a reporter announced that in Tulsa, Oklahoma, prominent businessman Frank Anthony was found murdered and police were still looking for leads. I turned up the volume. Frank Anthony was a legend when I was growing up in the Midwest. I was ten years old when I saw him step out of a truck in the middle of an oilfield. He was wearing a pair of boots so highly polished that the cow who gave up the leather must have been able to see her reflection every time she scratched her ass. I asked my dad if Mr. Anthony was rich.

"Richer than three feet up a bull's butt," was my dad's colorful reply.

Frank Anthony owned everything from oilfields and car dealerships to shopping malls and movie theaters and was now apparently one of the richest dead men in Oklahoma.

"Do you see it?" Mom yelled through the phone line. "It would make a great movie! Maybe you could stay here and work on it. Diane Sawyer said the next earthquake could sink all of California into the ocean, so you should come home."

"If Diane Sawyer wants me home, I'm there," I said and told Mom I'd see her in a couple of days.

❖

At noon, I donned my new tweed faux riding jacket, looking a bit like I'd taken a wrong turn at the fox hunt, and drove through Coldwater Canyon to Beverly Hills in high spirits over my lunch with Barrett Silvers. If Marathon had a project for me, I could leave for Tulsa secure in the knowledge that work and money awaited my return.

As a screenwriter, I vacillated between the certainty that I would never be able to write the stories I was given and the fear that I would never be given any stories to write. And of course, there was my history with Barrett, which made me doubt I could write at all.

Dozens of stately palms lined Beverly Drive, stretching their elegant trunks toward a blue and balmy heaven, their leafy tops blowing in the wind like great pom-poms cheering on the row of multimillion-dollar homes. Hollywood might be violent, rude, and expensive, but she was still the woman with whom we all wanted to be intimate. Even I had succumbed to her allure, receiving my Hollywood initiation at the Beverly Bungalows that infamous Friday night when I learned that no one's ever too old to be naïve.

I went east, then south, taking a right on Third, and pulled up in front of the Sante Fe–style restaurant. Only a few small European letter tiles embedded in the adobe designated the building as Orca's. It was an address one could easily miss, which seemed to be a criterion for Hollywood hot spots. I entered the building, looping around the adobe wall, down a short and narrow unmarked path.

Inside, studio executives, directors, writers, and agents were huddled in twos and threes eating overpriced pasta in a room with so much reverb only Marlee Matlin would be able to make out what anyone was saying. I could see Barrett seated on the coveted patio enjoying the beautiful summer day. The light sliced through the vine-covered trellis overhead onto her Greco-carved curls, which lay flat against her head like an olive wreath, crowning the beauty and power and grace I remembered from that day I'd first stepped foot into her office on the Marathon Studio lot. I'd gotten the appointment by virtue of the script I'd submitted entitled *Sveltiana*, based on the true story of New York's top fashion model caught up in the runway rituals of binge-and-purge perfectionism.

It was exactly four p.m. when Barrett's gracefully gay male assistant led me to her office for that memorable meeting. From the moment I saw her, I realized I was looking at the most captivatingly androgynous creature I would ever see in my lifetime, her DNA seemingly able to morph kaleidoscopically from X to Y chromosome and back again, daring me to settle on a gender. When I entered the room, she rose to her feet, tall and washboard smooth from her chest down to her pleated slacks. Lifting her French-cuffed arm, tan at the wrist where the expensive gold watch dangled loosely, she shook my hand. “I’ve enjoyed reading your script,” she said with a genuine smile. Her phone rang before I could speak and she excused herself, picking up the receiver and showing the muscle definition of a young man who worked out at the gym. She pivoted, to profile her chiseled features framed by the Adonis curls, and stared out the window as she spoke. She could only be described as smashingly handsome.

“What time is it now?” she asked the caller and gave me a “this will only take a moment longer” look. Her light brown eyes were smart and cunning, going slightly soft in the center, if anyone could ever get to her center. Just looking at her left me short of breath and, of course, she knew that. She traded on that.

“All right then, six,” she assured the caller and hung up. “I’m sorry, I’ve just learned that I have to get over the hill and be at the Beverly at six to meet Talbot.” Name-dropping in L.A. was always effective, especially if the name ran the studio. “I wanted to talk about your script today because I’m leaving town next week…” She paused in thought. “Tell you what, if you want, we could meet this evening around sevenish at the Bev, if you’re not tied up.”

“That would be great,” I said.

“Good.” She bounced to her feet and shook my hand again. “Then I’ll see you shortly. If I’m not in the bar, ask Amanda, the redhead behind the desk, where I am and she’ll get us hooked up.”

“Perfect,” I said and left, elated that Barrett Silvers, head of development at Marathon Studios, enjoyed reading my script and delighted that I was going to get to see her tonight, script or no script.

❖

Promptly at seven, I entered the Beverly lobby and scanned the bar for Barrett. My quizzing the redhead behind the desk led me to bungalow 42, where a heavyset, matronly woman wearing a hotel uniform opened the door. She invited me in, saying she was Teresa, the massage therapist for the hotel, and this was Marta, who was in training. From across the room, Barrett, lying facedown and naked on a massage table, spoke nonchalantly, inviting me in. “My meeting was short. Talbot offered me his suite for the weekend, and of course, I never pass up pleasure.”

Her long, well-proportioned frame was tan from the nape of her neck to the soles of her feet. No white sock or panty lines for Barrett.

"Teague is a very good writer," Barrett told the masseuses, who oohed appropriately and offered me a free massage because "Marta is in training." Barrett laughed and asked who could turn down a free massage. I was ushered into the bathroom to hang up my clothes, shower off, and have a glass of wine, all the while believing this was the most So-Cal studio pitch I'd ever encountered.

After my second glass of wine, I decided that, in fact, this was the way all studio pitches should unfold; then, even if my story were turned down, I would be too relaxed to care. Marta gave me a forty-five minute going-over that made me question whether or not she was really in training. When I was as relaxed as a boneless chicken, she helped me up and placed me on the bed on clean towels and covered me with a sheet.

Assuming Barrett was still being massaged, I closed my eyes and was in a dream state when I heard the click of the latch as the door softly closed. Barrett and I were alone as, of course, I had suspected we would be, even hoped we would be. The massage therapists had been dismissed so quickly that they left behind their tables and the obligatory New Age waterfall music. Barrett slid onto the bed beside me, wasting no time on preliminaries, and rubbed her tan, fully lubricated, frictionless form against my own.

"On page thirty-six," she began flatly, as if she were sitting behind her desk and I were fully clothed, "when he first kisses Colette, he says, 'This is just a prelude.'" She leaned into me slowly and kissed me warmly on the lips. My mind registered disappointment that Barrett couldn't kiss. Being able to kiss, followed closely by being able to dance, were two key criteria in lovers, and oddly, I'd never found anyone who could do either satisfactorily. I reached up to encircle her with my arms, but she pushed my arms back to my side. It was clear that this was Barrett's motion picture, and she was directing it.

"The first thirty minutes work beautifully," she said of my screenplay, her hand stroking my inner thigh. "Then there's that moment when he suddenly sees her alone for the first time, and he wants her so badly"—her lubricated fingers, slick with coconut oil, slid gently into the pathway she'd created—"so badly that he literally slams himself into her," and Barrett entered me with an unexpected force that was both frightening and exciting. She retreated slowly. "It sets up a nice character arc for him later that pays off in the last scene. Very smart, very sexy." I moaned, and she slid on top of me, but for Barrett, the person beneath her was no longer me, it was the screenplay. She was making love to the words I'd written. She knew the dialogue and the silent act breaks and the characters. I felt as if I were merely the stage on which she'd chosen to perform her soliloquy. I told myself that I didn't care that she didn't care. She was technical perfection and my heart pounded, almost out of my chest, in testament to her skill. I perspired and pulsated in her hands in streaming applause. I was so emotionally high from her artful combinations of touch and taste and sound that my body could no longer take the intensity. It had to end.

"What would you say the climax of the movie is, Teague?"

"Tell me," I whispered, my mouth open, my head back, and my body screaming.

"It's your movie, you tell me," she said provocatively.

"It's your movie," I panted, giving up my screenplay, and in one explosive wave, giving up myself.

"The climax is when Colette lets go, really lets go." It was Barrett climaxing now, with no further assistance from me, just flailing and screaming and sobbing and all the while in me, finally falling forward on me and whispering, "I want to make your movie."

I had no idea that this show in bungalow 42 had been playing for so many years it could have gone on tour, that Friday night at the Beverly had been a rite of passage for women writers for a decade, a drama replayed time and again with Amanda and the masseuse, and that Barrett's Friday-at-four, sex-at-seven appointments with unsuspecting screenwriters were legend. I thought I was the star, because that's how naïveté works, when in fact, I was just an extra. New to Hollywood, I had not yet heard the cocktail party joke, "Barrett Silvers first makes you, and *then* she makes your movie."

After *Sveltiana* was green-lighted, I was no longer a struggling writer. I could finally say I was making a living in the business. How much of that was due to Barrett, and not me, remained the gnawing question. Did Barrett only sleep with real talent, or was my real talent that I had slept with Barrett? I was determined now to write a script that would forever set me apart from that sea of writers who would happily sleep with Barrett if someone would just give them her address.

❖

The maître d' at Orca's interrupted my reverie to ask if I was meeting someone. Barrett had sent him to retrieve me. He escorted me past the bar and through the double doors where Barrett's boyish figure rose to give me a Hollywood air kiss. She still epitomized the studio power broker: tall, fit, trim. Sort of a Jewish All-Star. With pants creased, shirt starched, shoes buffed, and jewelry gleaming, she made me feel like I'd gotten dressed in the dark.

"You look fabulous!" I surveyed her top to bottom. "You've lost weight."

"If you're ten pounds too heavy, the rumor is you've gone to seed. Ten pounds too thin, and the rumor is you're dying. There's this very narrow five-pound window you have to hit."

"Well, you're there." I flashed her an appreciative grin. There was still a small electrical current that pulsated between our lower extremities, vibrating now like a plucked guitar string. I had to remind myself that age and power are seductive, but in this day of STDs, I didn't need a relationship with a woman who slept with everyone in town.

"Got any more high-concept scripts?" she asked, looking deep into my eyes.

"Like Arnold Schwarzenegger is pregnant? Or *Pretty Woman*? Prince Charming marries his hooker."

"Made millions."

"I'm tired of movies conceived out of men's sexual fantasies."

"I prefer a good female fantasy myself." She shot me a smile. "Unfortunately, the studio likes women in jeopardy."

"I brought you *Haunted,* and it went nowhere. How much more in jeopardy can you get than a woman whose husband had her raped, beaten, poisoned, and then tried to shoot her?"

"Too much jeopardy."

The berries from an overhanging tree plopped into my salad nicoise, threatening to poison me, as Barrett recounted the latest list of ridiculous movies that had been green-lighted. She summarized the current buying trend with, "Find me a good true crime story, and I'll get it up for you," which bore an appropriate double entendre, albeit accidental I was sure.

"I've got a lead on a story. I'll let you know," I said, thinking of the Frank Anthony murder.

I told her I'd just seen the latest Marathon hype in the trade rags about Lee Talbot, Marathon's tall, vibrant, silver-haired septuagenarian CEO who had done the impossible, turning around a studio that, only six months earlier, had Credit Lebanc breathing down its back, threatening to close the studio's doors. To complicate matters, there was that nasty rumor about someone skimming money off the top, studio books that didn't reconcile, and nervous accounting types scurrying about trying to explain where the money was going.

"So what's really going on over there?" I asked, wanting the insider scoop.

"People are nervous. I'm nervous. My job puts me in a lot of… odd places at odd hours." Barrett shifted her weight as if getting more comfortable in her chair, but I noticed she was also checking out the room to see who was listening. She settled back down and ran her long, slender fingers around the rim of her coffee cup, in an unintentionally seductive moment of contemplation, before deciding to share what was bothering her.

"Talbot's success with Marathon makes good PR—silverback-CEO-still-has-what-it-takes kind of rhetoric—but it's Robert Isaacs, the motion picture division's president, who's the real brains behind Marathon's resurrection. He's working barter deals with Hollywood's A-list, getting them everything from desert islands to permanent police protection in exchange for signing with Marathon." Barrett swallowed her pronouns as she tried to talk and eat simultaneously.

"Not talking about stuff like 'keep the wardrobe.' Isaacs got Lola Landon's kid—straight-F moron—into the best prep school in New England. Built the school a new gymnasium in exchange for one scholarship per year. Guess who gets the scholarship? The cost of the gym was less than the cash Premiere Studios offered Lola for a three-picture deal. She chose Marathon over the cash. Isaacs tapped into the fact that, while Lola's a big star, she's also a mother. Getting the best for her son is what she wanted and what Marathon gave her. It's all about delivering that one thing a person wants more than anything in the world. Talbot was so happy he gave Isaacs a corner office the size of the Hollywood Bowl."

"And you?"

“I’m his new executive vice president of talent acquisition worldwide.”

“Congratulations! And what do you do?”

“Whatever needs doing. I wrangle the big talent and keep them happy. I’ve delivered a birthday yacht to a mooring in Malibu for a big producer, kept drug charges off the record of a prominent director, smuggled prostitutes into the bungalow of a well-known actor every night of the shoot without his wife’s knowledge.”

“So you’ve taken a job as a studio pimp?” I asked.

My remark seemed to curb her appetite as she put her fork down, placed her hands against the edge of the table, and pushed herself back slightly in the chair, her gold-embossed cuff links winking at me from under her designer jacket. Barrett had always looked like an ad for a gentlemen’s quarterly, but the cuff links looked more expensive than I remembered.

“You know, if I disappeared tomorrow, no one would notice for days.” She spoke cautiously, as if she were working up to something. “I don’t have anyone…”

“Because you have everyone.” I realized it was an uncalled-for jab.

“You’re smart, Teague. That’s what I’ve always liked about you.” She paused to smile at me.

“Not smart enough to stay the hell away from you.”

She waved me off, indicating that what she had to say was more important than rehashing old hurts.

“Suppose you knew that a studio was sending a messenger around to its top producer with, let’s say, a kilo of coke and …”

“Did that happen?” I asked, and she ignored my question.

“…no one at the studio reports it, because if the agents, directors, and stars are happy, better deals get made. But if you knew it was happening, would you…do anything, say anything?”

“Depends on if they’re going to knock me off,” I replied flippantly, trying to chalk this increasingly worrisome conversation up to Barrett’s predilection for good plot.

“Suppose your boss calls you in the middle of the night to—let’s just say for discussion’s sake—go help out a big superstar, and you get there, and there’s a body.”

“A dead body?” I put my fork down and gave Barrett my full

attention. It was evident from her tone that this wasn't just for discussion's sake.

"Almost dead, but you do CPR on the body and you get him breathing."

Barrett was leaning over the table now, whispering, "And you realize this was a fucking big near miss and that you could just as easily have been on a murder scene."

"You gotta tell the police right away. Listen to me"—I found myself leaning in—"No job is worth this shit. You've got to report it."

"I have reported it, to someone I trust on the Marathon board. But now I'm convinced the phone was tapped. These are big players, Teague. You don't think they can muzzle the police? They can muzzle anybody!"

"Who's involved in this?"

"You don't want to know that. I don't even know. To know is to be in some real fuckin' danger."

A dark, muscular Latin man leaning against the wall as if he were waiting for someone suddenly approached our table. His head was strangely shaped, wide and round at the cheeks, narrow and flat at the top with a dark blemish by his left eye.

"Barrett Silvers?" The thick Latin accent sliced through Barrett's sentence.

When Barrett nodded, the man locked eyes with her, laid his fist on the table next to her hand, and deposited a one-by-two-inch stone with petroglyphs on it. Barrett apparently recognized the object and began shaking uncontrollably. The man reached over to retrieve the stone, but Barrett quickly covered it with the palm of her hand, knocking over a coffee cup and sending a wave of cappuccino across the layers of pink and white tablecloths. The man grabbed Barrett forcefully by the shirtfront and pulled her up from her seat, giving her a rough kiss on the side of her face. I jumped up from my chair, realizing she was in danger.

When he let go, Barrett teetered back and forth on her heels for a moment, her face paralyzed in an expression of surprise. I grabbed her by both arms, trying to steady her. Her hand banged awkwardly against my jacket as her mouth opened grotesquely in an attempt to tell me something, but only moans came out. She sagged to the floor like a rag doll, excrement seeping down her pant leg, her eyes frozen open like a carp's in a fish case. The dark man had disappeared, and I felt my insides turning to putty. My hands shaking, I reflexively rolled Barrett onto her side so vomit wouldn't get into her lungs and shouted for someone to call 911, thinking all the while that it was too late to save her. A young male waiter hurried over, knelt down beside her, and began CPR. Despite being grief stricken, I could still appreciate the irony of Barrett Silvers leaving this world with her lips on a man.

Chapter Two

The paramedics were there in only minutes. They took Barrett by ambulance to Cedars Sinai a few blocks from the restaurant. I followed in my car.

Twenty minutes later, still shaken, I scurried through the ER and located a nurse who told me Barrett was alive. If she could be stabilized, they would take her to intensive care. No visitors allowed. I expressed shock that Barrett could even be breathing at this point.

"Your friend's lucky the paramedics got oxygen on her right away. That's probably what saved her," the nurse said.

"What could cause something like that?" I asked.

"An overdose of muscle relaxants, a severe allergic reaction. Could be a lot of things," she said before disappearing in a blur of white.

A patient's advocate approached me, a young woman trained to deal with the confused and the frightened. She introduced herself, patted me on the arm reassuringly, and said she had Barrett's notebook and would notify her family and the studio. Barrett had been assimilated into the great medical machine, and there was nothing for me to do now but go home.

Dazed and upset, I stopped by the ladies' room to wash up. *What will happen to Barrett?* I thought sorrowfully. I could not bear the thought of her being less than the beautiful creature she was, and yet, I could not bear the thought of her dying. I was emotionally and physically tied to Barrett in some strange way I couldn't articulate. *Did someone try to kill her? Was it the husband of some woman she'd slept with? Was it a drug deal gone bad? Was it somehow related to her bizarre activities on behalf of the studio?*

A young, sandy-haired cop intercepted me as I left the ladies' room to ask if I was the woman from Orca's. He introduced himself as Detective Curtis and said the ER nurse had pointed me out. He'd spoken with the waitstaff at Orca's, who'd described what they'd seen. He wanted to know from me if Barrett used drugs of any kind, had she complained of feeling ill, did I know the Latin man, and what if anything had been left on the table. Apparently the one-by-two-inch stone wasn't found on or around Barrett. He scribbled notes as he grilled me. I gave him a solid description of the guy and offered to help a police sketch artist with a drawing. He smiled wryly, saying my attacker would be on Social Security before an artist could get around to sketching him. They were so backlogged at the LAPD that they'd made the decision to do sketches only in murder cases. I told him that Barrett came within seconds of qualifying.

We exchanged business cards. I told him I'd be leaving for Tulsa in the morning and would be gone for a week but I could be reached if he needed me. It was a futile gesture, since I knew from Detective Curtis's tone that he wasn't going to follow up on this case unless Barrett Silver's body turned up dead in his bathtub.

I rummaged through my pants pockets for my car keys as I headed out into the bright sunlight and over to the parking garage. As I reached over to unlock the car door, a man came at me from behind a concrete abutment so quickly I had no time to react. With one body slam, he threw me backward against the cold, gray slab, knocking the breath out of me, and then quickly pulled me forward up against his chest, which was as hard as the concrete pressing up against my back. His breath came in snorting sounds through his nose. He was the man who'd delivered the small stone to the restaurant. He leaned in to get his mouth on my neck, and I thought he was going to try to rape me. I tried to break his hold, but he was skilled at grappling and, with only one hand, he managed to lock up my arms. I was beginning to panic and yanked my knee up to get it between our bodies and put some distance between his head and mine.

His dark hair, worn in a fifties flattop, smelled of old-fashioned styling balm. His puffy jaw was clamped shut. His eyes were a dark brown, accentuated by a spider tattoo at the left corner. This was the ugly face of death.

Suddenly two college-aged boys rounded the corner of the parking garage headed for their car. I let out a shrill yell for help. They ran toward me, shouting at the man. With his body strength, he could have incapacitated us all, but maiming three people was apparently a messier day than he'd bargained for. He let go of me and took off. Saved by two adolescents in USC sweatshirts. I would forever be a Trojan fan.

As I sagged to the ground from fear and exhaustion, the boys lifted me up by my arms, asking if I were all right and wanting to call the police. I told them I'd report it and thanked them profusely for their help. They were reluctant to leave me and watched me drive out of the garage, alive but shaken. My hands still trembling, I fumbled for Detective Curtis's card and dialed my cell phone.

He answered on the second ring. I told him that I'd been attacked in the hospital parking garage by the same man who'd attacked Barrett at the restaurant. He said they'd get a unit over to the hospital immediately and that I should stay out of the area. I told him I wanted to make sure that no one got to Barrett. He said he'd call hospital security and alert them. I hung up, then, fearful the attacker could already be in the hospital, I called hospital security myself, telling the lead on duty that Barrett Silvers's room needed a guard posted. I called the nurses' station as well to warn them that all visitors needed to be screened.

Exhausted, I sank back into the seat and ran a frame-by-frame of the day back and forth through my mind, trying to piece together a story that made sense. By the time I was halfway over Coldwater Canyon, I knew the Latin guy wasn't trying to rape me, he was trying to kill me in the same way he'd tried to kill Barrett—with his mouth. There was something in his kiss that was lethal. I needed to tell that to the police. I rang Curtis again, but this time got no answer, so I left the information on his voice mail.

❖

Back home, still worried over Barrett, I began preparing for my trip, promising the nervous Elmo that two days in a car would ultimately be rewarded by limitless eating for both of us. He sighed, rolling his basset eyes farther back into his head and looking nearly suicidal.

I collapsed onto a floor cushion for a little zazen meditation. My inability to concentrate and center myself was a clear indication that my encounter in the parking garage at Cedars had shaken me more than I wanted to admit. I'd spent a few years studying self-defense techniques, beginning in college and continuing into my brief and ill-fated stint as a police officer: one year and eight months of murders, suicides, wife beatings, and child abuse before I finally had to admit I couldn't take man's inhumanity to man. Today had brought up a lot of "stuff" for me, centered mostly around the disconcerting truth that in a heartbeat one can go from dining on fine linen to being wrapped in it.

"Life is short, Elmo. I don't want to die before I find that special person, you know?" From his roachlike position on the kitchen floor, Elmo briefly opened one eye just to be polite.

By nine p.m. I could no longer put off packing. I yanked a navy blazer and a tan jacket out of the closet and hung them in a dress bag, then threw jeans, socks, shirts, and four pair of Ferragamo flats into a suitcase. I'd already packed Elmo's dog food, dishes, leash, his Flagyl for colitis, Benadryl for allergies, Butazolidin for leg pain, and Ascriptin for arthritis. Elmo was proof positive that anyone who lived with me would ultimately end up on drugs.

I stood in front of the full-length mirror viewing my five foot seven inch frame and sucked in my stomach. The unflattering light seemed to highlight the laugh lines around what were, even I had to admit, not-bad green eyes. I brushed my punked auburn hair straight up. When gravity takes the body south, brush everything north.

I made the rounds, checking doors and windows and setting the security alarm system. Fully barricaded, I turned on the ten o'clock news. After the sixth murder story, I punched the Off button on the remote control and lay still in the dark.

This was when I missed living with someone, this time just before sleep when I wanted to discuss what had happened during the day and what would happen tomorrow. Sort of a nocturnal debriefing in the spoon position. That moment in the night when fears and frailties take over was the reason God created coupling. It was why the passengers on Noah's Ark didn't proceed up the plank single file. God didn't create couples merely for procreation, because mankind can too easily circumvent the Divine plan with petri dishes and test tubes. God created couples for that moment between "news and snooze," that moment when there is comfort in an icy bottom up against a warm belly and the sounds of rhythmic breathing in the night. Elmo must have sensed my sadness at being alone because he curled up in the small of my back, and we both went to sleep.

An hour later I awakened to one long ring of the fax startling my heart nearly out of my chest. Too tired to even turn on the light,

I stumbled into the office, where the machine was printing out its message. The metallic chunk-a-chunk of the fax paper spewing out made an eerie sound in the quiet room as the machine printed out the message, OPEN YOUR FRONT DOOR.

I froze. There was something about an anonymous fax that was more terrifying than a burglar. This stalker could slide into my home at any time of the day or night on optic fibers, threaten me, and then hide in a tangle of technology. I looked at the fax again. The remainder of the page was blank, the return fax number obliterated.

I pressed my back against the cool stucco of the living-room wall and tilted a wooden slat on the bay window shutters just enough to catch a glimpse of the porch steps. No one was standing there. Lowering the shutter again, I tried to get control of my nerves. I fumbled around on the desk for Detective Curtis's card and quickly dialed the number he'd left me. It rang ten times and no one answered. There was always the option of dialing 911, but how could a fax telling me to open my door be construed as an emergency, even by me?

Oh, hell, I'll have to open my door sometime, I thought. *If not now, then in the morning. Is there a bomb, a note, a package I can't see from here?*

"Well, shit!" I whispered to Elmo.

Slipping open my desk drawer, I pulled out my loaded .38 and peered through the slats one more time. Total serenity outside. Forcing myself to move to the front door, I took a deep breath, then pressed down on the latch suddenly and kicked the door open with the sole of my foot, hearing it reverberate against the wall of the house. Elmo launched himself from behind me, through the front door and into the courtyard, baying wildly.

As the door swung toward me, something flung itself at me from overhead, batting against my face. I jumped back and screamed as two large, dead rats dangling from cords dripped blood onto my doorstep. My scream got Elmo's attention. The sight of the rats swaying in the doorway sent him into another round of barks. He stood still, staring at the grotesquely dead animals. I flipped on all the floodlights around the house to illuminate anyone who might still be prowling around. Seeing no one, I located scissors in the hall table and cut the rats down. One had its mouth taped shut with silver duct tape, the other had its throat slit.

"Silence or Death. What is this, death threats for dummies?" I asked loudly to steady my nerves. Unable to stomach the sight of the hapless animals, I loaded them into a plastic garbage bag and deposited them in the trash can behind the house. Elmo stayed two steps behind me, for which I was grateful. Locating the bacterial soap in the kitchen sink, I scrubbed up to my elbows, certain Lady Macbeth never washed her hands as thoroughly.

So Spider Eye must have followed me home from the Cedars parking garage. Yet I remembered checking my rearview mirror, and there was no one following me. This was his way of saying I could end up like Barrett if I talked to the police. The fax and the dead rats were both designed just to scare me, because if he'd wanted to kill me, there's a good chance he could have gotten away with it. The hair stood up on the back of my neck.

❖

At four in the morning, I called Cedars one more time to check on Barrett. The nurse said she could only tell me that Ms. Silvers was "stabilized." *But "stabilized" in what form? Is she vegetable stabilized or back-to-normal-soon stabilized?* I said a prayer for her before packing the car behind my locked gates, in case someone was watching for an easy target. Target or not, I had to get to Tulsa for my parents' anniversary.

My attendance record at family gatherings was appalling, even by my own standards. I drove back to Tulsa often. It was just that none of my trips seemed to coincide with life's important moments. I'd managed to miss my brother's wedding because I was in production, my kid sister's graduation because the roads were impassible and the flights were all booked, and all of my parents' anniversaries because the timing was wrong. Like interstitial programming, I seemed to arrive between episodes. My sister would be out of town, unable to attend this particular soiree, so this trip was my concerted effort to be there when it counted, even if some guy tried to knock me off while I was loading the car.

CHAPTER THREE

Elmo and I hit the road, maneuvering the 210 while it was still dark. We drove across the Mohave and watched the sun come up over the desert with genuine joy in our hearts, glad to be leaving our troubles behind.

Several hours later, we crossed the border into Arizona, winding our way up the mountain to Flagstaff, then back down the other side, past the crater, where fifty thousand years ago, a meteor left a hole the length of twenty football fields just south of where I-40 leads to Winslow. Seeing vast stretches of sand, devoid of humanity, where lizards and prairie dogs eked out an existence in 120-degree heat amidst a formidable array of Spanish bayonets, scrub brush, and cacti, made my human struggles seem less serious. I turned up the radio and sang along to a love triangle about a heartbroken trucker who drove his eighteen-wheeler through a local motel room to kill his cheating wife, apparently loving her to death.

I noticed a dark blue Buick in the rearview mirror and slowed down to get a better look. The car slowed too, deciding not to pass me. I thought I'd seen the same car in Needles. I pulled off at the first Winslow exit into a gas station where a family with several small children was gassing up their car. Their mere presence made me feel safer. The blue sedan didn't exit. I felt relieved and unloaded Elmo, hoisting his short-legged body out of the Jeep to save his arthritic shoulders. The moment his paws touched the sand, he pulled up short and let out a mournful sob. I knelt and quickly removed several cockleburs from the pad of his foot and pulled him in for a hug. A little girl with Shirley Temple hair and wearing pink shorts walked over to ask what kind of dog he was and then trotted back to her car, telling her mother, "That lady has a basket hound."

"You are a basket hound." I patted Elmo, grateful for a little comic relief.

❖

We pulled into Tucumcari about midnight. I entered the faded turquoise lobby of the Holiday Inn, gave my name to the slight-of-frame desk clerk, and signed the register. Wearing a Raiders jacket, a young man with scraggly hair slouched in the lobby, watching the game on an old TV set. Other than that, all was quiet.

I yanked the luggage out of the Jeep and then backed the vehicle up until its tailgate almost touched the motel room door. New Mexico was a collection point for the theft of Jeep Cherokees. Stolen at night from tourists, they were collected in an area outside of town and trucked down to Mexico before sunrise. I was determined not to awaken and find myself on foot.

❖

Morning in New Mexico was breathtaking from my small motel window: a backdrop of lapis skies and white puffy clouds floating above the odd plateaus surrounding Tucumcari, beauty orchestrated to the sweet drumbeat of Elmo's tail against the dresser as he signaled the need for a walk.

I stepped outside and took in a deep, clean breath of fresh air before packing up our duffel bags and checking out. Elmo and I went straight to DeRoy's Restaurant across the street from a pasture where this morning a young boy and a middle-aged man were wrestling four nanny goats. I took a booth next to the window to watch the show. The biggest goat butted the skinny boy onto his behind as several leather-faced men in the restaurant chuckled and sipped their morning coffee at the gray Formica tables.

I looked up when I heard a familiar voice across the room taking a breakfast order. She was here: the tall waitress, French perhaps, with jet-black hair swept back from her face in the manner of a society matron, impeccably dressed as if she'd been beamed up while dining on caviar in Hyannis Port and accidentally beamed down in Tucumcari slinging hash, a *Town and Country* model set against a backdrop of counter stools and pie racks.

"Well, hello!" she said brightly, not knowing my name but recognizing the face. "How was your trip?" I told her my trip was just fine.

"Apple, cherry, homemade-this-morning banana cream, butterscotch cream, and lemon meringue."

"Butterscotch now, banana cream to go." I smiled.

"Wise choice." She smiled back before going to the pie case.

I wondered if she had a husband or a boyfriend who knew how attractive she was and that she was wasted on this prairie plateau like pâté in a lunchbox.

Outside the window, the goats were safely behind the barbed wire fence and the wind was rumpling the wheat-colored grass like a hand through a small boy's hair. I could see why people stayed on here.

The waitress came back with what looked like a quarter of a pie so thick I could lose my fork in it and gave me a beautiful smile. "I thought you might like a piece of chocolate French silk, on me." Her dark taffeta skirt and matching apron, bordered by white lace not unlike the white meringue on top of the pie, brushed my face. The breeze from the open window washed her perfume over me. The restaurant had cleared out, the farmers heading off for their early morning work. I walked behind the counter and she turned to face me as if she'd been expecting me.

I pulled her dark chocolate skirt up and slid my hand under the elastic of her white lace panties and into the delicate white meringue of her body, silencing her surprise with my mouth and going deep inside both warm, wet places with a slow, rhythmic intensity as she pushed against me with feverish strokes, seemingly as starved for the touch of a lover as I was. She was the soft, silky, chocolate French desert I had hungered for, right up until the moment that a large, hairy hand slammed a cup of coffee down in front of me. "You need more coffee?" the grubby cook in his stained white apron asked.

"Uh, no." I snapped back into my body.

"Your waitress is in back. You can pay me when you're ready. What kind of pie to go?"

"Banana cream...and chocolate French silk," I said sheepishly.

Fifteen minutes later, heading west again on I-40, Elmo and I shared the chocolate French silk pie at speeds in excess of seventy miles an hour.

"It's getting bad, Elmo. I'm starting to have these Ally McBeal fantasy moments. You have no idea what it's like to face forty-one alone."

"Ruff," Elmo barked for more pie.

"Thank you for acknowledging that. It *is* rough."

I tried to feed him with one hand and myself with the other, managing to sling the whipped topping onto the dashboard and across my shirtfront and coating the steering wheel. Elmo had banana cream on both ears. The front seat looked like the eating scene in *Tom Jones.*

"You, of course, can see a girl you like, go up behind her, jump on her, and hump her damned ass off. I, on the other hand, am expected to be a little more civilized. Being a guy is easier. It just is." Elmo put his face into the piece of pie I'd balanced on my leg. "That was mine, by the way. Help yourself," I said to him, attempting to clean us both up with a damp napkin. Elmo's ears elevated a half inch at the base of his head, an indication he was finally having a good time.

My cell phone rang, the unexpected shrill sound nearly causing me to drive off the road. I'd forgotten about the cellular company somewhere near the Texas panhandle that automatically dials travelers on the highway and connects them to annoying commercials. I grabbed the phone, preparing to disconnect the call, when a pleasant voice said my name.

"Who is this?" I asked.

"Mark Silvers in L.A., Barrett's brother. I'm calling because you're the last one who saw Barrett before she was attacked. Can you still hear me?"

"Not well."

"Our family is so worried about Barrett. She's still unconscious. Did she mention anything to you about what she's involved in? I mean, do you know why anyone would want to do this to her?"

"Nothing that made any sense," I said cautiously. "Maybe we can talk when I get back, Mark, I'm losing the connection. Give me your number," I requested, noting the caller ID read Unavailable.

"We've had enough crises. I don't want to cause a wreck. I'll be in touch. You have a safe trip."

"Oh, by the way"—I kept him from hanging up—"Barrett doesn't have a brother."

A pregnant silence ensued, then the caller hung up.

An involuntary shiver ran down my spine. *Who called me? And how* did *he get my cell phone number?* Someone wanted to know how much I knew. Was he driving alongside me right now and I didn't know it?

I glanced in my rearview mirror and my heart leapt into my throat. At eighty miles per hour, the dark blue sedan had its bumper inches from mine. Suddenly I felt the metal crunch, and I gripped the wheel, my body lurching forward into it. I stepped on the accelerator wanting to get off the open road to safety, but there was nowhere to go. The blue sedan pulled up along my left side, keeping pace with me, edging me farther off the shoulder. Two hundred yards up ahead, the shoulder merged into the abutment of a bridge. That's where he was forcing me at high speed. The options flashed through my head: pull off and stop, keep trying to outjockey him to get back on the road, or beat him to the bridge. I floorboarded the gas pedal. The cars ahead of us were panicked at being caught in a road race, and several of them scattered over both lanes. The shoulder was lumpy and precarious. The high speed rocked the Jeep, making me think I would teeter over the right side of the embankment, but I held my breath and kept my foot jammed to the floorboard. The distance between me and the abutment narrowed faster and faster as my heart raced. Two hundred yards, a hundred and fifty yards, a hundred, fifty, twenty-five, fifteen, five. I could see the pores in the concrete pilings!

At the last possible moment, I cleared the car ahead of me and skidded back onto the interstate, dodging the abutment, my heart nearly pounding out of my shirt. It only took him a second to catch up with me. I increased my speed to eighty-five, ninety, ninety-five, and broke into a sweat. If anything bigger than a grasshopper jumped into the road, we would both explode like pumpkins all over the freeway. Drivers catching sight of us bearing down on them moved to the right lane to let us fly by. We flew past the *Welcome to Texas* sign so fast that I couldn't read the gigantic lettering.

My mind raced. It was obvious this guy wanted to run me off the road and make it look like I'd lost control of the car. Well, he'd made two mistakes. He'd underestimated my driving skills, and he'd attempted it in broad daylight. A nice dark night in the rain would have given me problems, but now I was just getting mad. *Where the hell is the highway patrol when I need them?* I reached down between my seat and the door and felt for the short-handled fire ax I always carried for emergencies. The feel of the rubber-wrapped handle gave me comfort.

Elmo began to gag. An entire pie and a thrill ride down the highway had turned his stomach upside down. "I can't stop, buddy. You're going to have to take a deep breath and just think good thoughts." Elmo let out a loud belch and stretched out flat on the backseat.

The maniac tailing me edged up on my left rear bumper. I could hear the crunch of metal as he tried to force me to spin out. Elmo whined and panted. We whipped past Vega, Texas, a mere bump in the prairie, and flew by a sign reading: Amarillo 20 miles. I said a prayer and pushed the speedometer up to a hundred miles per hour. If in the next twenty miles I could keep from killing myself or someone else, this jackass would be history. I concentrated on the road and not overcorrecting for any road hazard. At this speed, the slightest turn of the wheel could put me in a tailspin.

"Holy shit!" I said out loud. Up ahead an eighteen-wheeler had decided to pass on a slight uphill grade and was now parallel and struggling next to a red Honda. I tried to slow down, but at a hundred miles an hour, I was closing on the trailer. I hit the ABS brakes and prepared for the ride of my life. The brakes grabbed. I kept my foot jammed to the floor even though the sound was terrifying, like metal ripping the bottom out of the car.

The brake pedal vibrated up and down, but I never let up, remembering two cops who were killed in squad cars with ABS brakes when they panicked over the sound and let up. I decelerated to forty miles an hour, ten feet before I was about to breed my Jeep with an orange-juice ad on the back of the truck doors. The Honda driver saw me coming in his rearview mirror and pulled off on the right shoulder. I floorboarded the gas pedal again and whipped between the truck and the Honda. I was about twenty feet out in front of the truck when the blue Buick, following my same route, cut in front of the truck and came up alongside me pointing a gun across the passenger seat at me.

I slid down in the seat trying to make myself less of a target and jammed the gas pedal down farther as the skyscape of Amarillo came into view. I was picking up traffic and intentionally zigzagged from lane to lane, making it harder for him to tail me. Just as we crested the ridge on I-40 in the middle of town, I slammed on the brakes and whipped my car to the side of the road. He went forward another hundred feet and the sirens blared, two big, beautiful, red flashing lights screaming after him. I had led him into the one speed trap in the whole United States I could count on, because I'd been ticketed there twice myself. In fact, another two hundred yards down the road there's a billboard asking anyone who feels he's been unfairly arrested for speeding to call the law firm on the billboard.

I pulled back on the road and drove slowly past the trap, breathing for what seemed like the first time in hours. Two squad cars and two officers with guns drawn had a white man with blond, scraggly hair, in his late twenties, spread-eagle against the hood of a blue Buick. I recognized the jacket as belonging to the man in the motel lobby. Someone was going to a lot of trouble to try to kill me, and I had no idea why. I could have told the Amarillo police, but having been a cop, I knew that when the whole interrogation was over, "Raider" would end up knowing more about me than I would about him.

CHAPTER FOUR

I drove into Tulsa around five thirty Sunday evening. For a town that annually endured bone-chilling winters, stifling summers, and the often-carried-out threat of tornadoes, Tulsa always managed to look as pristine as a Southern belle after a twelve-hour train ride, not a hair out of place. I had to admit, it was comforting coming home to a place where no one had ever heard of a three-step deal and where a "power breakfast" was prunes.

Maneuvering the Jeep past upscale malls and state-of-the-art medical facilities, I passed the sixty-foot bronze statue of praying hands, a humorous source of collegiate speculation about the size of the rest of the bronze man's anatomy, which remained mercifully underground.

I turned off Lewis into a neighborhood with neatly kept wood-frame houses and yards filled with ancient oaks. The branches overhanging the street rustled gently in greeting, creating a cool, sun-filtered canopy. I let out an audible sigh, releasing the tension I'd held inside for two days, and swung into the driveway of a house with a long front porch. I was home. Safe.

My parents popped out on the lawn as if spring-loaded. Mother, the size of a wiry sparrow, pulled us from the car and kissed us hello. Dad made one lap around the car's exterior and said, "What happened to your car? You should get those dents in the rear fixed."

"Is that all you can say to your daughter, Ben?" Mother chastised.

"Hi, sugar." He gave me a chipper kiss on the cheek.

"Elmo, precious, has your mommy endangered your life by driving all alone across the country?" Mother asked the exhausted hound, who looked as if he might go into a drool state from sheer fatigue. She towed Elmo up the steps. "Now, none of us wants to miss tonight's news about Frank Anthony! He was set on fire!" Mom nearly shouted.

"Is that a euphemism for 'found God'?" I smiled at her.

"He was torched!" Mother regurgitated the word being used by a reporter. "He was shot once in the head and once in the chest, then set on fire!"

"Once in the head and once in the chest usually means we'd prefer this little incident go un-discussed," my dad said with a dark humor I had grown to appreciate more and more with time.

"You should see if Mrs. Anthony will let you make a movie out of it. Frank Anthony was a wonderfully kind man," Mother continued.

"Studios don't want stories about wonderfully kind men. They want tits, ass, action, and murder," I replied.

"Well, maybe there's some of that too. Call Mrs. Anthony and talk to her," Mom instructed me.

Maybe she's right, I thought. *Focusing on someone else's murderer beats the hell out of focusing on the guy who tried to be mine.* "I'll check it out," I said.

Dad resumed his dinner, slamming down two hamburgers with four strips of bacon in under five minutes, confirming my suspicion that I was descended from a pack of wild dogs, and then he turned on the evening news. Deaf from a lifetime of oil derricks and high-powered rifles, he cranked the volume up to atom-splitting levels to hear the latest police bulletin. The police sergeant being interviewed was none other than my old buddy Wade Garner, who looked appropriately serious and competent as he told a reporter that the police now believed Frank Anthony was killed by professional assassins. Police were asking for the public's help in locating a dark green Lincoln Town Car with two men inside. The broadcaster then noted that Mr. Anthony was an international businessman with ties to many organizations, including Celluloid Partners, one of the principal investors in some of Hollywood's biggest motion picture studios.

"So Frank Anthony suffered from fits of glitz," I mused.

"I don't think he suffered from fits." Mother waved at Dad and mimed muting the TV. Dad turned the sound down, and the effect was akin to having the dentist take his drill out of my mouth. My body relaxed immediately. "Now, my friend Callie Rivers could tell you if he suffered from fits, and she can tell you whether you should pursue this Anthony story. She's a psychic astrologer."

"You go to a psychic?" I was slightly amused.

"I don't go to a psychic. I know a psychic astrologer."

"And I need to know her?" I said with just enough flippancy to set Mother off.

"Well, maybe you don't!" Mother had her back up faster than a hound. I recognized my error immediately and tried to calm her down, but Dad was grinning at me as if to say I was in for it now.

"Maybe you already know everyone you need to know, and maybe I don't know anyone who would be of interest to someone from Los Angeles, but then maybe I do!" She slapped her address book into my hand like forceps.

I escaped to the den to make the call, thoroughly ashamed at how quickly I could turn into a thirteen-year-old girl around my mother. I left my phone number on Callie Rivers's answering machine, saying only that I was Lu Richfield's daughter, and then I fell into line behind Elmo, who was already headed for the guestroom. In one graceful gallump, he hoisted his huge frame onto the bed and burrowed into the soft quilt. I was about to hoist him off when Mother appeared in the doorway. "Leave him alone! He can't hurt that quilt. It needs washing anyway." A graceful lie on her part. In minutes Elmo and I had buried our heads into the quilt's downy folds and were asleep. We'd both reached basset nirvana.

The phone rang at midnight, awakening me. A voice on the other end sounded so bright and chipper that I had to check the clock to make sure it wasn't morning. "Teague? Did I wake you? Sorry, I always assume everyone keeps my hours. This is Callie Rivers. Your mother's friend," she said, and there was something in her voice that made me feel as if a hand had gently swept the back of my neck, causing my hair to stand on end.

"Why don't you come over?" she asked.

"Now?"

"My days are pretty booked." She recited her address and hung up before I could object.

I stared at the phone and shook my head like Elmo when he's baffled or disturbed. "I can go back to bed, and toss and turn and analyze her call, or I can do as the lady asks and show up," I said to Elmo. "I've done crazier things. Maybe she'll tell me who tried to kill Barrett and me, or who killed Frank Anthony, or maybe she'll tell me when I'll meet my true love." Elmo yawned, letting me know he was particularly bored with the last topic.

I crawled out of bed and went into the bathroom to brush my teeth, still rationalizing my behavior to Elmo, who hated his nights interrupted. "I might as well go tonight, because God knows, I'd rather face killers in the front yard than have Mother ask me one more freaking time if I've called her friend Callie Rivers." I ran a brush through my hair. "How weird is this appointment time? But a lot of older people can't sleep at night. Maybe Callie Rivers is just an insomniac and she's making it pay off for her by scheduling late-night appointments. It's something about her voice. I feel like I know her from somewhere." I checked myself out in the mirror. "If she's wearing bones around her neck, I'll bring you one." I chucked Elmo under the chin and he groaned, indicating I should turn out the light.

I drove west toward the river, where a pair of high-rise condos punctured the heavens. I parked directly in front of the entrance, entered the ornate marble lobby, and waited for the gold-encrusted elevator doors to open and take me up to the twelfth floor. Once upstairs, the doors opened to face a beautiful gold and black bull's-eye mirror hanging over an antique marble table supporting a vase of fresh mauve tulips. *Not a bad place to live,* I thought, and rang the bell to apartment 1201.

The door swung open to reveal a drop-dead gorgeous blonde. Her hair swept back off her fabulous features as if some heavenly wind blew it in that direction as she sailed across the sky on angel wings. Her pale and perfect skin and ethereal blue eyes almost stopped my heart.

"You're Callie Rivers?" I asked breathlessly.

"And you're Teague." She hugged me, pressing her soft cheek against mine, and to my delight bumped me ever so lightly with her pelvis, the kind of bump that could have been accidental, or not.

"Come in, please." I followed her trail of orgasmic perfume, pretending to check out the floor-to-ceiling glass that provided a nice view of the river, and the beamed ceilings and white walls that gave the place the airiness of a chapel, but mostly I was checking out her fabulously small, tight ass and wondering how any one woman could have such a diminutive derriere and such voluptuous breasts both at the same time. What an amazing package! The sexual tension on my part was palpable. For the first time in my life, I understood how it felt to be a teenage boy. I didn't care if she were the biggest psychic airhead on the planet or if she could conjugate a verb, I just wanted to take her to bed right now and make love to her, or fuck her, or both. The room felt full of her, and that fullness danced around me like electricity.

"That's a very unusual ring." She took my right hand, and I hoped she'd never let go.

"It was a gift I bought myself after selling my first script," I said to impress her. It was a wide band of gold with diamonds of varying sizes set alongside ruby and aquamarine teardrops. She studied it for a moment, her mind somewhere in the past.

"Lu said you wanted to know about the Anthony murder. Should you pursue the story, right? What time is it?"

I told her it was 12:47 a.m. She moved to a bank of computers, punched in some data, along with the time, 12:47, and hit a button. A moment later a strange circular wheel covered in astrological symbols rolled off the printer.

"This is a horary chart. You like documentation. Read this page," she commanded, handing me a thick book on horary astrology.

I tried to read what was on the page. Something about ancient civilizations employing crude forms of horary astrology to answer questions of import, like who will win the battle at dawn, but I was too distracted by her to care about battles at dawn unless they involved Callie Rivers and took place on clean sheets.

"The king would call in his priests and ask the question. They would draw up a chart at the moment the question was asked, because that was the moment of greatest emotional intensity. The priests would interpret the chart and give the king his answer," Callie explained.

"So if they were right, they lived and prospered. If they were wrong, they were dead wrong. Hollywood should employ that practice during pilot season." I wanted her to think I was funny, but it didn't seem to be working.

She studied the astrology chart carefully, picked up a pen and drew a few foreign-looking symbols on it, then sank back onto a white leather couch. "This is huge! Frank Anthony had something on someone. Oh, look at this, Mars Combust the Sun."

I feigned interest in the chart so I could join her on the couch. "So, what does that mean exactly?"

"Murder by fire, maybe? Well, that's really not the question, is it? I would say you should drop the story if you're easily frightened." She leaned in to study it more closely. Only a moment before, she had appeared to be a golden flea, flitting across the room; now she took on an aura of light and strength.

"No, you can't avoid it. Mercury is retrograding toward Mars Combust the Sun. There will be something explosive about this story. The Fourth House Cusp represents the end of the matter. In this case, the Fourth House Cusp is ruled by Mars. The Moon, co-ruler of the Ascendant, representing you, the querent, is conjunct Mars. Moon, Mars, and Sun are all quincunx Pluto in Sagittarius in the Twelfth House. Sagittarius being a fire sign, Twelfth House being in secret. To me it signifies death by fire behind the scenes. Here's something interesting, Jupiter at zero degrees Gemini in the Fifth House of creativity means the story will be big." She paused and glanced heavenward. "You have something they want. I feel that psychically. Expertise maybe, although it feels like something tangible."

My head had started to hum and my body was tingling. I felt as if I'd been pleasantly drugged. I stared at her, not hearing a word she said, just wondering how anyone this gorgeous could be here with me. "Are you married?" I interrupted her.

She smiled at me. "Right now you need to know about the Anthony murder. Mercury is conjunct Venus. Conjunct, within a five-degree orb, let's say, for argument's sake. And in this instance, that conjunction would seem to indicate a beneficial relationship between you and a woman. Maybe you'll be protected by a woman, because that conjunction falls in your Seventh House of partnerships and/or open enemies. Nonetheless, it's all quincunx Pluto in your Twelfth House, which again could indicate hidden danger." She looked up and caught me staring hopelessly into her eyes.

"We'd work well together. Good energy." She smiled at me. "You're shy. People don't know that about you. And you live in your head a lot." She gave me a sly grin.

I felt the heat of embarrassment rising up around my collar, as if she could see every sexual fantasy that had ever gone through my head.

"You need to know that in relation to this Anthony murder, I see someone who has been very, very frightened…unable to sleep nights. This person phoned the dead man just before he died."

It was evident to her that I wasn't paying attention, and that no amount of schooling in the art of astrology was going to take place tonight. I was hopeless.

Callie sat back on the couch and took a deep breath, silent for a while, as if deciding whether or not to confide in me. "What am I going to do about you?" she said softly, looking at me with eyes that were on fire.

"Anything you want," I breathed.

"You were promised to me, Teague," she said quietly.

I felt my groin tighten with exquisite pain. "Promised to you?"

"Through my dreams. A partner is coming into my life. You're five foot seven, aren't you? And you wear only Italian shoes, you brush your hair up off your face, and you never take off that unusual ring." She was so spectacularly beautiful that I wondered if she was crazy, the wrong ratio of sexiness to synapses.

She must have read my mind. "You're really not ready for me. It will take time."

"I am absolutely ready for you." I pulled her in too quickly and put my mouth on hers too abruptly. She pushed me away as if to end it. Then suddenly, she gave in, sliding her tongue inside my mouth, where it belonged, wet and hot and wanting, sliding and coupling with my own, our pulse and our breathing intensifying with *Bolero*-like speed until our bodies were writhing in rhythm to the sub-lingual-cum-labial dance of our tongues, creating a heat flash that exploded across my body like an atomic blast.

My knees buckled. Callie Rivers could by-God kiss! In an instant she had set me on fire. I was personally and undeniably Combust the Sun. I was also wet in every orifice of the human anatomy that had any capacity to create moisture, as if my body were trying to save itself from the flames. Callie slowly slid out of my grasp and pushed me gently out the door. "Play that in your head," she said, and the door clicked shut in my face. I stood in the hallway, swaying like a drunk, my mind as unsteady as my body.

What in hell just happened? How did it happen so fast? I don't even know this woman, and I'm hooked on her. She said we were destined for each other. Richfield and Rivers. Perfect. The Psycho and the Psychic. But no amount of mental sarcasm could destroy the feeling

I was experiencing. I knew I'd been struck by an uncommon meteor, something one sees only once in a lifetime, someone who was destined to change my life.

The night sky suddenly seemed clearer, the stars more radiant, the moon much shinier, and life itself seemed to hold infinite possibilities.

As I approached my car, I was jolted back into my body by the sight of a dark blob on my windshield. I looked around to see if there was anyone else in the parking lot, but I was alone. I told myself to snap out of it and pay attention. I was in danger. I moved cautiously toward the car and then decided to open the rear door and grab a flashlight before approaching the blob. I flashed the light on the windshield and panned across it. The hair on my arms stood up in fear. Globs of barely coagulated blood spelled out, "Retern it."

I wanted to stand in the parking lot and shout for the little coward to come out, but suddenly the idea of being tracked by someone who couldn't spell two-syllable words was more frightening than dodging Hannibal Lecter. I jumped in my car and turned on the windshield wipers, heading down Riverside at seventy miles an hour, my head swiveling around like Linda Blair's in the *Exorcist* as the red liquid ran off my windshield in rivulets. I knew whoever was tailing me wasn't going to give up. *How did they know I was here tonight? No one knew that. No one except Callie Rivers.* My heart sank as I contemplated the fact that Callie Rivers could be involved in all this.

CHAPTER FIVE

I lay in bed awake—wide awake—rewinding the entire evening. Callie Rivers was the most phenomenal person I'd ever met. How could she have had anything to do with the message on my car window? She couldn't have. She was my mother's friend, for God's sake! Nonetheless, I assured myself that I would be sensible about the whole thing and do some more checking on her.

If need be, I'll ask her point-blank if she's involved. I want to see her again anyway.

The mere thought of seeing her again triggered all my fantasies. Callie had embedded her taste, her touch, her smell, into my senses, until I felt her presence all around me. I thought about her, holding my breath, closing my eyes and focusing on what kissing her had felt like. Nearly cramping with the erotic pain, I could almost visually recreate it, that orgasmic moment when mind and body separate on a viscous white wave of ecstasy. Callie was right. I played it in my head. I placed a pillow between my legs to stop the throbbing. I wished I were the self-gratification type, able in a few strokes to end my own longing, but if ever there were a service improved by outsourcing, lovemaking was it.

The light seeped in through the shutters and I was aware it was dawn. No sleep, and yet I leapt out of bed, happy and looking like I'd slept twelve hours. Standing on the scales, I realized I'd lost three pounds. "If we could bottle sexual ecstasy, Elmo, we would all look like supermodels."

I bounced into the kitchen and wished Mom and Dad a happy

forty-second anniversary, telling Mom I'd seen her friend Callie Rivers last night.

"Did you like her?"

"I did." I tried to sound nonchalant. "So what do you know about her?"

"She likes women," Dad interjected without looking up from the paper.

"What does that mean?" I asked absently.

"It's not even a compound sentence, Teague. Figure it out." Dad looked at me over the top of his glasses.

"She likes everyone." Mother covered for anyone Dad attacked. "Just when you think you know her, though, she surprises you."

I buried my face in a section of the morning paper, not wanting to seem overly interested in Callie Rivers. My eyes came to rest on the newspaper accounts of Frank Anthony's death. The first article speculated that he was killed because his company was involved in a greenmail takeover of a publishing house back East. A second report said it was a case of mistaken identity, since Frank had put his shoes in locker 34, a locker that didn't belong to him. The third report said they had not ruled out suicide. The police never ruled out suicide in Oklahoma. Even when a guy had to shoot himself in the stomach, then in the head, and then set himself on fire afterward.

I thought about giving Detective Curtis a call to report the road race with Raider and last night's message on my windshield, but so far Curtis had been useless as tits on a boar and he had no jurisdiction in Oklahoma, so I called Wade Garner instead. Wade was a big, handsome, square-jawed police sergeant of infinite good sense who'd befriended me when I did my short stint as a member of the local police department. I got him on the phone, and after a few quick pleasantries, told him about the guy who'd attacked Barrett at Orca's, then me in the parking garage, and then I told him about the incident on the highway in Texas.

"Same guy?" he asked.

"No, guy in L.A. was Latin with a spider tattoo at his left eye. The guy on the highway was some blond kid."

"What the hell ya doin' makin' guys mad at ya coast to coast?"

"It's a knack," I said, and I could hear him grinning. He took down the license plate number and ran a check while I waited.

"Vehicle's been junked. Somebody probably stole the plates and put 'em on your road-rager's car. I'll turn the report over to auto theft and see what they find."

"Last night after one a.m., I go out to my car and there's blood on the windshield…"

"Does this story ever end? Where were you?"

"Riverside Drive," I said and gave him the exact address.

"Doin' what?"

I hesitated, not wanting to say it. "Seeing a psychic, a friend of my mother's." Wade held his mouth away from the phone and belly-laughed. "So how come you didn't know there was blood bein' put on your car while you were talking to the psychic?"

"And…" I interrupted him loudly, "the blood spelled out 'Retern It.'"

"Return what? Hey, ask the psychic!" He burst out laughing again. "Man, you need a keeper. Let me see if the security cameras caught anything. Am I gonna see ya this trip?"

"Yeah, if you get your glasses fixed," I said, and he snorted.

❖

From the newspaper accounts, it appeared that Frank Anthony's demise would make a good movie. It had wealth, power, Hollywood ties, and murder, for starters. I decided just to show up at the Anthony mansion and see what I could learn. As I selected an appropriately somber blazer for the occasion, I stepped over Elmo twice. The danger of my tripping and falling on him was not enough for him to give up his comfortable spot on the floor. "I know, Elmo, since I'm your only meal ticket, that you're worried about how I'm going to get into the Anthony mansion without being arrested." Elmo kept his eyes fixed on me. "I simply create a fabulous lie and then convince myself it's the truth, since there's truth in all things. And because I believe it's the truth, others will believe it as well. Just as I believe that you are truly not a dog, but a person in a dog suit." Elmo rolled his eyes and began to lick a decidedly private part of his anatomy. "Stop that, or your lips will never touch mine!" Elmo ceased licking. "Thank you," I said, and patted him good-bye on his big soft head.

❖

There were a half dozen Jags and Ferraris parked out in front of the Anthony mansion. When I rang the bell, a uniformed servant answered, looking appropriately solemn. I said I was a friend of the family's. He indicated a room to the left of the massive entry hall and said, in a tone reminiscent of Max's in *Sunset Boulevard*, "*Madam* is receiving in the parlor."

The parlor had twenty-foot ceilings, with baroque crown molding that depicted entire battle scenes, looming high above the gold-flecked marble floor. Definitely not the kind of living room where I imagined a guy ever wandered around in his Jockey shorts in search of his cigarettes.

A dozen or more guests munched canapés and spoke in subdued tones beneath the domed ceiling, consoling a woman wearing a gray designer suit trimmed in black. She tilted her head up to engage me with her soft gray eyes and extended her long, tapered hand. "Isabel Anthony." A blinding flash of gold and diamonds radiated off her wrist and fingers. I told her I was sorry to hear about Frank. Then, lying, I said I'd worked with him on a studio project in L.A. and I was shocked to learn of his death. She thanked me and turned her attention to the host of people gathered round her. Wakes were easier to crash than I'd imagined.

Across the sea of well-coifed heads, I caught sight of a tall, handsome woman in her early sixties with the angular features of an ex-model. I recognized her from news accounts as Ramona Mathers, one of Frank's many attorneys, although her picture in the paper had been decidedly younger. The tiny broken veins around her nose were an indication that alcohol figured prominently in all her activities, maybe enough so that she might talk to me openly about the Anthonys. I introduced myself and told the same lie about being Frank's friend.

"What a way to go," she said, finishing off her highball. "Makes you rethink your life. Shot in your gym shorts at the club, for God's sake! If Frank were here, he'd say, 'Had I known those were my last ten minutes on earth, I wouldn't have done those last twenty reps.' That's why I don't exercise. I'm afraid I'll get in shape just in time to find out I'm dead. Ramona Mathers." She extended her hand, showing a smattering of liver spots, and gave me a penetrating, questioning look that told me she'd slept with a good many people in her time and was still open for business.

"Lot of servants," I remarked.

"Frank's board members sent extra staff to help Isabel get through this."

"What board would that be?" I asked.

"Celluloid Partners, I imagine."

"Have the police found out anything about the murder?"

"Hank Caruthers, who was in the gym at the time, told me that Frank was found lying on the floor next to his towel, apparently trying to get his .38 out of his gym bag. Reaching for a revolver and you come up with a rock, now that's fate, isn't it?"

"A rock? What kind of rock?"

Ramona Mathers made a Vanna White gesture toward the study and took a short stagger-step in that direction. I followed her into a teak-paneled room, replete with leather-bound first editions and glass-enclosed displays of strange Egyptian antiquities. A long, gold scepter sparkling with jewels, a headdress trimmed in gold and black snakes, a large stone tablet covered with hieroglyphs, and case after case of little cups, jewelry, and broken pots.

"What was this used for?" I pointed to a miniature sarcophagus locked in a glass case.

"I'm not the docent. Tiny, tiny Egyptians?" She raised an eyebrow in an obvious appreciation for the outrageous.

"And this?"

"A petroglyph tracing of a rock called a death stone, ironically enough, used on the eyes of Egyptian corpses to hold the lids down immediately after death."

My God, it's just like the stone that was delivered to Barrett at Orca's, my mind raced, as I tried to remain calm. *What is a drawing of the stone left with Barrett doing in a display case fourteen hundred miles away? Are these stones common and everyone knows about them but me?*

"Replicas were very popular in Italy at the turn of the century. Unsavory characters used them as markers. A thug wearing the insignia of his mafia don would appear, demanding money from a man or perhaps merely demanding his silence in a matter. If the man refused, then very shortly thereafter a death stone would appear on or near him as a sign that he'd been marked for death. That way, the man knew by whom, and for what, he was being killed. A good thing to know, don't you think?" She took a long sip of her drink as I remained transfixed by the stone tracing. She bent her head toward me in an exaggerated style as if to inquire if I were still in my body.

"You're very knowledgeable." I laughed at being caught in my head. She locked eyes with me, letting me know there was something about my face lighting up that she found attractive. "I'm trying to impress you," she said softly.

I was charmed by her sense of humor and liked her svelte appearance. She had a thick head of silver-gray hair, Dresden china eyes, and an infectious smile. It was as if she knew a very funny secret about life but was trying not to tell me. Her small talk was peppered with clever turns of phrase and melodramatic gestures. She asked me if I'd like to join her for dinner tonight. I briefly contemplated an evening across the table from a delightfully witty woman. *No dating drunks,* the little voice in my head commanded. I gave her a polite excuse about having other plans, and in fact, I hoped I did. I intended to call Callie Rivers.

"Vandalism," Ramona remarked as we passed a case full of broken artifacts on our way out of the room. "Someone came in here just after Frank died and broke a good many of the finest pieces. Have no idea what it was all about, but it's made Isabel even more nervous. I hope I'll see you again soon." She handed me her business card, and I felt her eyes bore through me as I turned and walked away.

❖

Outside, I took a deep gulp of fresh air. The atmosphere in the Anthony mansion was stifling. I couldn't chalk up the appearance of death stones in both Frank Anthony's and Barrett Silvers's hands as being sheer coincidence. Up until a few days ago, I'd never even heard of a death stone, and now I knew two people who'd been marked by them.

Following up on Ramona's remarks about Frank's murder, I decided to drive down to the crime scene. The Tulsa Health Club, on the fifth floor of one of Tulsa's famous old art deco buildings, had been a bastion of male dominance for half a century. On the glass of the big double entrance doors, the club had etched a large revolver and the inscribed warning: Keep Guns Holstered while in the Gym. *No wonder guys in this town are so polite,* I thought, *each of them knows the other one's carrying a gun!*

A buxom young woman obviously hired for ornamentation swung her 38Ds into my face and asked what she could do for me. She had olive eyes, auburn hair, and a great smile, and for a moment, my mind drifted past the present into a future where Ms. 38D was giving me a head-to-foot rub: long, sensual, full-body strokes down my leg that somehow missed the mark and managed to glide across the center line, leaving me weak with anticipation as her large breasts rhythmically brushed my face until I captured them in my lips. Then, above me, I saw Callie's face, her eyes as crystal clear as a Canadian lake, looking into my soul, and I suddenly felt unfaithful. My fantasy went limp. *How can I be running around on Callie when I'm not even with Callie?* I thought, aggravated that Callie's image was censoring my fantasies.

"Could I help you?" The young woman leaned her 38Ds into me and raised her voice in volume as if I were hard of hearing. Being twenty years my junior, she probably thought I was hard of hearing, a fantasy buster in and of itself. I asked if Mr. Caruthers was in the gym. She said he wasn't. Just then, a man in his mid-fifties with thick arms, a rich, black head of hair, and a proud barrel chest that preceded him like the prow of a ship strode into the club.

"Hello, Mr. Caruthers," the woman behind the desk beamed. "Johnny will be ready for you in five minutes."

"No problem. How you doin,' Maggie? Your husband treatin' you right? Cuz if he's not, I'll come over there and give him a run for his money." Mr. Caruthers's words ricocheted off the walls as if he thought he owned all the airspace on the planet.

When I spoke his name, he turned, allowing me to introduce myself as a friend of Frank's. By now I'd said it so many times I was beginning to believe I was a friend of Frank's.

"Damn sad about Frank," he said.

I told him I was a writer from L.A. working on an article about Frank's life. Mr. Caruthers seemed to relish the fact that he would be in print.

"Well, if you do, say that we're going to find out who the slimy little coward is who killed Frank and give him a little Oklahoma justice."

I asked him if he knew where Frank had been before he came to the gym that day. Caruthers shrugged, saying he had no idea, and when I repeated that Ramona Mathers told me Frank was clutching a rock in his gym bag when he died, Caruthers laughed.

"Never heard that. Sure she didn't say *cock*? I'm sorry. Excuse me, ladies, but Ramona Mathers always liked her hooch, ya know? She and Frank got it on a couple of times, but don't go printin' that, now!" He laughed appreciatively. "You girls are gonna get me in trouble!"

A man, naked to the waist, appeared in the doorway announcing he was ready to give Mr. Caruthers his massage. The man's upper body was so buffed out that his head looked like a tiny pea resting in a sea of mahogany-hard triceps and biceps.

"Be right there, Johnny," Mr. Caruthers boomed. He waved goodbye to us, pushed open the big double doors to the sauna, and swaggered off into a cloud of steam. Hank Caruthers was a typical oilman. Slick.

I headed for my car. Jamming my hand into my pocket looking for my keys. I came up with Callie's phone number.

"If I were Callie, I'd say it must be a sign," I said out loud to no one.

Callie didn't seem at all surprised to hear from me, saying she'd been sending me "brain waves" to phone her and let her know what was happening. I drove straight to her high-rise.

CHAPTER SIX

Callie was waiting in the doorway of her apartment wearing a white silk jumpsuit and looking like a Lancôme ad. "Don't you look smashing?" She smiled.

"Thanks. You know, with the blond hair, and the white jumpsuit, and the white carpet, and the white leather furniture, I have the feeling when I get here that I've died and gone to heaven." I pulled her into me.

"Teague, I'm not sleeping with you," she said, establishing the ground rules.

"I don't recall asking you to." I grinned, getting my bearings on her style. I wasn't going to let Callie Rivers bowl me over like she had last night.

"But just out of curiosity—" I interrupted the thought by kissing her with a slow, sensual warmth. "Why *aren't* we sleeping together?"

"Because"—she began, and then had to pause to catch her breath, I noted with satisfaction—"you need to focus on staying alive, Teague. You're behaving as if what's happening around you isn't life threatening."

I thought about telling Callie how I'd grown up in a family so combative that breakfast could be considered life threatening, that by the age of eight I'd mastered Zen and the art of flying flatware, and that I did have fear, but most of it was inherited. Instead, I kissed her again and assured her that I was focused on both of us staying alive. I sagged into a chair and kicked off my shoes, working on feeling at home, in a platonic kind of way.

"I just crashed Frank Anthony's wake and met one of his attorneys,

Ramona Mathers. She told me that, according to Hank Caruthers, Frank Anthony died clutching a rock in his hand, and when she showed me the petroglyph tracing, it was almost identical to the rock Barrett had been given by the Latin guy who tried to kill her. Hank Caruthers, whom I met at the gym today and who was in the gym when Frank died, told me there was no rock. The rocks are called death stones, by the way," I said.

"So your friend in L.A. was marked by whoever owned the death stones."

"Marked by a dead man. The owner of the rock was Frank Anthony, and he was killed before the stone ever got to Barrett Silvers," I said.

"So whoever killed Frank Anthony pried the stone loose from his hand and delivered it to your friend in L.A?"

"Could be, but why go to all that trouble?" I asked.

"You said she was terrified when she saw it, so obviously she knew what it meant. Perhaps she knew it belonged to Frank Anthony, and its arrival without Frank meant he was dead, and she was next."

"That means she had to have known Frank Anthony, but how?"

"Your friend in L.A. knows more than she's telling you. Start with her," Callie replied.

"Maybe all my friends know more than they're telling me. Last night when I left here, there was blood on my windshield and the words 'Retern it.' No one knew I was here—except you." I blurted it out, wanting to clear up the matter once and for all.

"You believe I would tell someone who might harm you that you were here?" Callie's hurt expression shifted immediately to anger.

"I just don't know you—"

"But you know me well enough to try to sleep with me?"

"I'm sorry. Forget it."

"How can I forget it? Do you think I want you here if you don't completely trust me?"

"I trust you."

"Then why would you accuse me of something like that?"

"I didn't. I don't know. I'm confused. I've been chased by weird guys doing weird things and suddenly I'm here, and he's in the parking lot..."

"Oh, Teague..." Her voice trailed off in disappointment.

"I'd better go." And I found myself outside her closed door again.

❖

Damn! What in the hell is wrong with me! Things were going great—great—and now they suck! I had a habit of doing that. Being too abrupt. *It's simply that life is short. Why not get to the point?* I tried to defend myself to myself, but even I wasn't buying it. I took the elevator downstairs and headed toward 21st and Utica.

I should buy her something to apologize, I thought. *So how can I, an army green, navy blue person, buy her, an electric orange, hot pink person, the right gift? And what is the definition of right: looks right on her? Or gets her right into bed with me?*

I had always made it a point never even to glance at the kinds of items Callie Rivers undoubtedly wore: shoes with feathers, shorts with bows on the sides, and any cosmetic item where they offered a free gift with purchase. I strolled inside one of the more chic shops in Utica Square and went right to the lizard handbags in an array of colors no self-respecting lizard had ever worn. There was a small, orange-ish bag with a beautiful gold clasp. I bought it without even opening it, happy that it cost hundreds of dollars, thinking of it as a Medieval Indulgence that might buy my way to heaven.

Imagine, me feeling happy leaving a store, clutching a new purse. My God, it's a first! I thought grinning, and crossed the parking lot with a snap in my step. To my right was the damned blue Buick parked a hundred yards away, obviously trying to stay back, but not to the point that any fool with an IQ of six couldn't have figured it out.

I got in my car and drove slowly out of the Utica Square parking lot, made a tight U-turn, and pulled up to the east entrance of the store. I dumped the purse out of the shopping bag and replaced it with my twelve-inch fire ax. Then I hopped out of the car and dashed inside as if I'd forgotten something. I exited out the south entrance while the driver stayed focused on the store's east doors. I came around on the driver's side with a shout, bringing the fire ax down so hard that it nearly amputated his door handle. I reached inside and grabbed the man by his black leather jacket and pulled his head, suddenly and violently, through the open window, delivering a palm strike to his face.

"You tell whoever you work for to get off my ass, or so help me, I'll amputate your arm and every other damned part of your anatomy!" I shouted.

His car squealed out of the parking lot, leaving me standing in the middle of the concrete, clutching a fire ax in my trembling hand as shoppers cut a wide swath around me.

❖

I phoned Wade and told him what had happened and gave him a description of the guy, saying I would bet a hundred dollar bill he was my Texas rager. Then I went home and put an ice pack on my hand. Only in the movies did people beat one another up without any physical ill effects. My palm strike had rearranged Raider's jaw, but it had also bruised my hand. Mother was alarmed at how swollen it was and asked me how it happened.

"Looks like she punched somebody out." Dad leaned over to examine my hand, looking debonair in his shiny black tux and tartan cummerbund while speaking of me in the third person. "Looks like the kind of bruise you get when you whack the bejesus out of someone," Dad repeated, giving me one more chance to 'fess up.

"For heaven's sake, Ben, she doesn't hit people!" Mother said, rustling her taffeta.

"Don't you both look fabulous!" I swooned, pulling my hand away.

"We clean up real nice, don't we?" Dad grinned. "And you've got ten minutes to do the same." I jumped into the shower, delighted to have a reason to end the inquisition.

In thirty minutes I was wearing a designer tux-suit and an excruciatingly painful pair of spike heels, obviously created by an Italian gay guy who could have found comfort in a straitjacket.

"So how do I look, Elmo?" He let out a long appreciative sigh and flopped onto the floor. "Well, thanks, but then you're prejudiced." I stroked his soft head.

It was only a five-minute ride to the club where a huge banner hung over the entrance announcing LU AND BEN, LOVERS FOR 42 YEARS! Mother whispered, "Couldn't they have just said married for forty-two years? That's bad enough."

Inside, beyond the cavernous entry hall and south to the ballroom, Aunt Jen, the tallest person in our family, billowed toward me in a bright pink flowered dress made of so much fabric, Christo could have used it to wrap an island. "Happy anniversary, Ben and Lu," she gushed.

"Teeeeeeeeee!" She grabbed me with her beefy arms and yanked my head into her gargantuan pink bosom, burying me in a veritable sea of bad perfume. Her breasts chafed my cheeks as I struggled to free myself, and the giant pink helium balloons overhead squeaked up against one another in accompaniment. *Aunt Jen is simply too large to be straight*, I thought.

❖

Straight ahead was the buffet line the length of a landing field that was nearly collapsing under the weight of roast beef and fresh shrimp.

"A live band!" I exclaimed.

"Semi-live," Aunt Jen quipped. "Most of them can barely move, much less play." A gray tidal wave, arms outstretched, rolled toward Mom and Dad to hug them and then tottered out onto the parquet dance floor, taking advantage of their arm position and their own forward motion.

I stood back to avoid being squashed and to savor this moment, looking at my parents. They'd made it through the death of my brother, through my dad's drinking, through Mom's brief flirtation with another man, through a five-hundred-year flood, a bankruptcy, my dad's heart attacks, and damned near everything else that could happen to two people in forty-two years, and they were still here, their arms around one another.

A hand touched my arm and I turned to find Callie standing beside me. *Of course, she'd be invited to the party,* I thought.

"Very sweet, aren't they?" she said, and I loved the tenderness in her voice.

She looked exquisite in her cream silk pants and high heels and the little jeweled Eisenhower jacket, her hair gorgeous, her makeup perfect, and that air of purity and kindness that emanated from her. Suddenly, I wanted to spend the next forty-two years with her.

As my mind registered that thought, I felt an electrical charge go through me as if I were trying to shock myself into reality.

What in hell am I thinking! Well, it's obvious. I'm vulnerable because I haven't been in a relationship for a while, and now I'm watching my parents grow old, and I'm thinking I should settle down, and that's exactly how people end up with the wrong mate. By acting like chimps in heat!

"I'm sorry about this afternoon," I said.

"What happened to your hand?" She reached for my bruised palm and I felt my knees buckling from the pure pleasure of her touch and my body turning into a chimp.

"I hit the guy who was following me. You know, I could use some help with the desserts," I lied and signaled her to follow me through the banquet hall, into the bar, and deeper into the wine cellar, where I shut the door and pulled her gently into me and kissed her.

"What are you doing?" she asked nervously.

I wasn't the kind of woman who would ever risk being caught in a wine closet at her parents' anniversary bash, but I was so physically obsessed with Callie that I had lost all sense of propriety and certainly any fear of being caught.

"Let me do it again and see if you can figure it out." I kissed her again. The electrical current between us could have served as the backup generator for New York City.

"So you no longer think I'm trying to kill you?"

"Being without you is killing me." I slid her loose knit top down over her small, white shoulders and slid my hands up under it, kissing her shoulders and holding her soft breasts—breasts so soft they were almost sedating. The world slowed. I floated in some ether state, adrift in a wet sea of my own imagining.

The door rattled. I jumped back, and Callie snapped her shirt up over her shoulders as the bartender entered. "Hello," he said, amused.

"My parents' anniversary, and we were looking for something really special…"

"Looks to me like you found it," he said, eyeing Callie.

"Maybe an Ice wine, 1997 Reserve, by any chance?" I tried to maintain a shred of decency.

"No," he said as we exited.

Giggling like two teenagers, we made our way back to the ballroom, where across the sea of revelers, Ely Mason, a silver-haired oilman who had to be at least eighty-five, was tapping the microphone and preparing a toast. "Is this thing on?"

"I think I should drive back to L.A. with you." Callie leaned into me and spoke softly. "Looking at your progressed chart and your transits, it would be a good idea to have a traveling companion if you're going cross-country during this planetary phase. Your mother agrees with me."

Drive back to L.A. with me. What does that mean? She would drive back with me and then fly home? Or drive back with me and be a houseguest? Or drive back with me and live with me? I got more nervous as I thought about the old joke: What do lesbians take on a second date? A U-haul!

"What do you think?" Callie interrupted my thinking.

"I think I'll be safer…if I don't have to worry about your safety and I can just take care of myself," I said. "And why are you consulting my mother about me?"

"She's my friend, and we both care about you."

Ely's voice blared across the room. Tap, tap,tap. He slapped the mike as if he'd just delivered it and he was trying to get it to breathe. "Can you hear me?" Suddenly the mike let out a long, high-pitched electronic squeal.

Callie took my hand, without regard to who might see us, and for the first time in my life, I didn't mind if someone saw me holding hands with a woman.

"I think you need me," she said.

"I definitely need you," I replied.

"As a traveling companion." Her voice held a smile.

"Callie, I'm being tracked by very dangerous people. You are a huge distraction, and lack of focus could get us both killed. I won't risk your life. When this is over, I would love to—"

"Have a safe trip." She pivoted and walked away. Her leaving left the room dark, as if someone had turned off all the klieg lights. For me, the party was over. I remembered my dad saying something once about little women being dynamite in small packages. *Note to self: Callie Rivers has a very short fuse. No wonder she lives alone. This is one difficult woman.*

❖

Before going to bed, I rang Cedars to inquire about Barrett. The nurse on duty said she was improving, so I went to sleep feeling better on at least one front.

Several hours later, I was dreaming that I was about to be shot when the phone rang beside my bed, frightening me and leaving me gasping for air. I picked up the receiver, still panting. The phone went dead. I looked at the clock. It was three in the morning. Callie was the only person I knew who kept late hours, so I dialed her number, asking if she'd just phoned me.

"I thought we'd said our good-byes." Her voice was seductive. "No, I didn't phone you," she said, and hung up in that abrupt way she had of ending conversations.

I rang Callie back, exasperated over my own lack of resolve when it came to this woman. "We leave for L.A. Friday at eight a.m. There's room for one suitcase. I am not real cheery in the mornings, and I hope you like a steady diet of swirling dog hair."

"I'm already packed. Good night." She hung up on me. I was going to have to talk to her about that. People should mutually agree the conversation is over. I flopped back on the bed, jostling Elmo, who was resting on the foot of it.

"I know I should have checked with you first, Elmo. I don't know what got into me," I admitted apologetically. "Something about her gets me. She's sort of unpredictable and wild, and she looks fabulous and she smells great. Same reasons you pick a girl." Elmo let out a loud sigh of annoyance, and we both settled down to try to get some sleep.

If I were to mark an event that changed my life, I would have to highlight this one in Day-Glo yellow. I had just agreed to drive fourteen hundred miles with a cranky basset, a crazy psychic, and several guys who were trying to kill me.

CHAPTER SEVEN

I busied myself with the Jeep, masking my sadness over leaving by feigning concern over tire pressure and battery fluid levels, only giving my parents a quick kiss at the last moment as I hurriedly backed out of the driveway. Mom smiled broadly and waved energetically as if to assure me she'd always be standing on that porch for me. Dad seemed less certain.

In the rearview mirror, I could see Mom walking back inside the house, but my dad's lone figure stood in the front yard, waiting until I was completely out of sight. Tears flowed freely down my cheeks.

I reached Riverside Drive and Callie's condo, where she was patiently waiting out in front of the gleaming twenty-story building wearing white Reeboks, a white T-shirt, a tiny pair of blue jeans, and a big smile. The radio was playing and a country singer was admitting that she knows what crazy means—seeing her guy in a pair of jeans. I could relate. I was blown away and insane over the way Callie Rivers looked in her jeans. I was just short of howling like Elmo. I was going to be in a car for two days with this woman, and it made my heart race like a NASCAR engine. *I may be in danger of some sort of sexual blowout,* I thought.

She glanced down at my tennis shoes, so beaten up that the brand name was indiscernible, and said, "I want to buy you some cute tennis shoes, Teague," and I knew that all my casual clothes were in danger of debuting at Goodwill.

I caught sight of her three metallic silver suitcases lined up on the curb. I reminded her that we'd agreed on one suitcase.

"We didn't agree. You informed me that one was all I was allowed. I'm very high maintenance, Teague."

"You're right." I shrugged. "How could anyone possibly look like you look, out of one suitcase?" I began shifting everything around inside the Jeep, scrunching Elmo up to steal a few more feet. The third suitcase had to be bungee-corded to the roof rack. I was panting when it was all over. Callie took this time to introduce herself to Elmo.

"He's huge and he's so beautiful!" she said, stroking his long white frame with its big black and tan spots. Elmo happily banged his tail against the back door. Callie disappeared around the car to locate her makeup mirror, giving me time to talk to Elmo, who was making tight circles and fretting over his loss of personal space.

"Be nice to her, she's from another planet," I told him.

Callie returned with a box of chocolate doughnuts and a thermos of coffee, climbed into the passenger seat, and said she thought this might cheer me up.

"They're homemade," she said. "I made them last night."

I was happily amazed. I didn't know anyone who knew how to make doughnuts, much less chocolate doughnuts, which happened to be my favorites. I bit into one. It was without a doubt the best doughnut I'd ever eaten. The coffee she poured me was black and strong, just like I liked it. I was beginning to relax and told her that taking her on as a traveling companion was proving to be an excellent decision on my part. I was glad I'd thought of it.

"You're a woman of great insight," she said sweetly. I checked her eyes for sarcasm. Callie Rivers had apparently had a sarcasm bypass. How could that be? No one could live on this planet and not use sarcasm to defuse life's basic asininities. *How will we ever communicate?* As if in response, she handed me a second doughnut, and I ate it immediately, giving Elmo the last bite.

"Chocolate's bad for dogs," Callie said.

"It's okay. Elmo's not a dog." I grinned, and Elmo nodded on cue, making Callie laugh.

"Sorry, Elmo." Callie patted him. "Case of mistaken identity."

"So do you have clients who'll miss you while you're gone?" I asked.

"A few," she replied enigmatically.

"And you live entirely alone…no pets, no lover?"

"I'm able to live with my choices. I just remind myself that we experience greater growth through wrong choices than through right ones, and if the wrong choices help us grow, then how can they really be wrong?"

"Speaking of choices," I switched gears, grateful for a segue out of her tie-dye philosophy, "reach behind you on the floor. There's a shopping bag with something in it."

Callie rooted around in the backseat and came up with the bag. "What do you want me to do with it?"

"Open it. I bought you something."

Callie carefully extracted the lizard handbag and gasped so loudly that Elmo rose to a standing position and pricked his ears.

"Oh, Tee, it's gorgeous! I love it! How did you know what to buy me?"

"I just went for something expensive that, personally, I would never own…"

"Well!" She feigned being offended.

"…but would look smashing on someone as lovely as you."

She unbuckled her seat belt and leaned way over and gave me a long, warm kiss on my neck just below my ear. I went red with pleasure.

"Thank you so much," she whispered sincerely.

"You're welcome."

Callie rocked her seat back, clutching her purse like a teddy bear, closed her eyes, and wrapped her small, perfectly manicured fingers over the top of the waistband on my faded jeans, the bouncing Jeep allowing the tips of her fingers to brush my naked skin. I gave out a large bassetlike sigh as Callie fell asleep. I wanted to buy her a gift every day just to see her sweet, childlike joy. *How could anyone live to be our age and still have so much joy for the small things?*

I glanced over at her gorgeous face. She had a sharply chiseled profile, her nose straight and elegant. She was really stunning looking. Why did she spend all of her time talking like an alien philosopher trying to put the planet in perspective? *What in the world do we have in common other than my intense desire for her? Maybe that's why God gives us desire, to keep us sexually hooked on one another until we have time to figure out we have other things in common.* Whatever drew me to her, I knew that I couldn't remember ever feeling this much at peace in all my forty-one years. Callie Rivers touching me as she slept seemed to calm every nerve in my body.

❖

We moved through the Texas panhandle while it was still daylight. The land on the north side of I-40 was so flat that if a prairie dog raised its head in Canada, I was certain we would spot him. Callie talked about her family and how her brother died of a drug overdose when he was just twenty-two. How her mother was psychic and her father's mother had predicted the moment of her own death, based on a dream she had, and how Callie herself felt she was directed by her dreams.

"In my dream there were three flashing neon signs with showgirls all kicking their legs in the air. I threw a ball to them, and it dropped down between the girls into this slot and one of the showgirls kicked it and the ball exploded into the number fifty with three more zeros on the end of it. So I knew I was supposed to go to Las Vegas, play the slots, and win $50,000. So I did and I did!"

"You won $50,000 on the slots based on a dream? If I'd had that dream, I would have gone to Radio City Music Hall, dropped my token in the subway *slot*, and ridden the damned train along with 50,000 other people wondering what in the hell the dream meant!"

"It's not interpreting the dream correctly that makes you win. It's believing in the dream." She smiled at me, and I smiled back.

❖

By ten p.m. we were just east of Albuquerque, under a dark blue sky dotted with stars, singing along to a country song about some woman's anatomical boogie woogie and where she was putting it, which included places like the ceiling. It dawned on me that if we ever stopped to analyze half of what we sing, we'd be highly perplexed. There wasn't a lot of traffic on the road except for truckers. In the rearview mirror I spotted a beat-up pickup weaving across the double line. I asked Callie if she was belted in. New Mexico at night was notorious for drunk drivers. Suddenly the pickup moved up quickly behind us, then swung around to pass us. Callie's voice was shrill and insistent.

"Swerve off the road. Get off the road!" I pulled to the right a little, but at seventy miles an hour, no right-minded person "swerves" off the road. That's when I heard the first blast. Callie was screaming now, covering her face with her right hand and pulling herself toward me with her left. Out of the corner of my eye I saw the blasts coming from the truck window, and I took the Jeep over the side of the embankment at about sixty-five miles per hour.

My seat belt snapped tight and luggage flew around our heads as the car rolled over and Elmo wailed. My mind seemed to leave my body. I was steering, but I wasn't in the car. I was editing our crash. Little four-frame, butt cuts flashing before my eyes: the latch on my luggage by my right eye, Elmo pinned against the door, then not pinned, my mom and dad waving good-bye from the porch, us bleeding at the bottom of the embankment, although we weren't there yet, telling someone I wanted a vet for my dog, seeing my hand twist and go numb, Callie's face contorted in pain, sand flying up around the windows. Ten seconds and sixty edits later, it was over. We were silent except for Elmo's low sobs. We were not on fire. We were down below the road.

My insides were frantic as I felt for Elmo and asked Callie if she was badly injured. But Callie didn't answer. She was staring back up at the highway. She gripped my hand and told me to lay my head back and look dead. A moment later, a large light shone down on us from the road. We lay still, slumped in our seats. My heart was slamming against my chest so hard that my inner ears pulsed to the rhythm. We couldn't just lie here like sitting ducks and let them come finish us off. Moving nothing but my lips, I told Callie I had to get to the gun.

"Don't move or they'll kill us."

"With the gun we have a chance," I said.

"Lie still and picture a white light all around us. A white protective light. They are being pushed back, they are being pushed back," she chanted a wishful mantra.

Remaining stone-still was the biggest gamble I would ever take in my life. Callie's calm, sure voice made me override my own instincts, and I obeyed the hypnotic instructions that were whispered beneath the muttering of angry male voices up above. They were deciding whether to crawl down the hill and check on us. If they came down, we were dead. I spoke quietly to Elmo, who was sobbing and struggling to free himself from the topsy-turvy luggage, telling him to be quiet, everything was okay. The thickly accented voices above us seemed to argue forever, although in real time it probably lasted thirty seconds. After a moment, one of the men swore at the other two and they moved out of our line of sight. Apparently no one wanted the honor of descending the hill to examine bloody bodies. There was too much road traffic.

I dug hurriedly through the Jeep debris and located my cell phone. No cell tower signal. That was the last straw!

"What is the fucking purpose of having a phone to save me, when there's no signal? Do I need to be saved in a populated area? No! I need to be saved when I'm in the middle of butt-fuck nowhere, shot at by a bunch of cowardly little assholes…"

"You're bleeding. I think it's coming from your mouth, along with a few other terrible things, like your language."

"My language? You don't think this is a situation that might call for a little language?" I shouted at her, glancing over my shoulder up the hill to make certain we weren't on the second wave of a death charge.

Even though Elmo was crying out in pain, I steeled myself and crawled over him to the luggage to retrieve my .357 and shells, shaking so badly I could barely load the gun.

Suddenly the men were back, descending the hill, sliding down the sand toward us, two of them. They must have been waiting for the traffic to clear before coming after us.

Callie whispered, "Oh my God!" and clutched Elmo to her.

I was shaking horribly now, the barrel of the gun moving back and forth like a psychotic metronome. *Six bullets, two men. Maybe. They obviously have guns, but they might not realize we do too.* I slithered down in the seat to rest the gun barrel on the window ledge to steady my shaking hand and got my head down as close to the gun as possible, telling Callie to lie still. I wanted them to get very close. Close was my only hope.

The two men loped toward the car abreast of one another. Barrel-chested, linebacker-looking men. They were no more than twenty strides from us. I knew I had to pull the trigger. Suddenly, from up above, a shrill whistle pierced the air. The men stopped in their tracks. A man on the hilltop frantically waved his arms in the air as if directing a jetliner into its berth. The men below turned and, without a sound, scrambled back up the hillside. Three car doors slammed. Tires squealed onto the highway. Thirty seconds later a highway patrol car, its red light on, whizzed past us up above, having apparently scared them into moving on. I yelled up to the patrol car and hit my car horn, which made no sound.

"Omigod, this is a nightmare! I told you it was a bad idea for you to come on this trip, and now I've almost gotten you killed!"

"It's okay, Teague. It was just a very close call, but we pushed them back with our energy and the white light," Callie said.

"The guy whistled. That's why they went back," I said sarcastically.

"We put the protective energy out there, and it merely manifested itself as the guy whistling them back," Callie said. I couldn't respond because she had hold of my jaw. "I think you bit your tongue," she said, crawling into the backseat and opening an ice chest, taking out a few cubes and wrapping them in a handkerchief. "Hold this against your tongue." As she tried to help me, she could barely use her arm and I worried out loud that it was broken. She insisted it wasn't but said I could take a look at it for her when we got to the motel room. I didn't want to tell her that I wasn't sure if that would be tonight or two days from now. We were out of sight of the highway. It was pitch dark, I had no idea if the tires were flat or the gas tank leaking, or if the car would even run. Callie pulled herself slowly out of the car, circled it, looked under it, and reported that she thought we just needed to find a trail that would get us back up on the road.

"The top of this car is completely bashed in. My cosmetic mirror *would* be in the suitcase on top of the car. I hope it's not broken," she said seriously.

"Oh, me too," I smirked.

I found Elmo's "Bute" painkiller before cranking over the engine and forced a pill down him. My legs were Jell-O like from fear, and my body felt like I'd been pummeled with a large meat-tenderizing mallet. Callie pulled on Elmo's shoulder only slightly and then rested her hands on him. Her touch made him release a huge sigh, and he stopped sobbing.

We drove slowly over the sand and sagebrush, not having any idea whether we were about to run into barbed wire or Black Angus. Fifteen minutes later, it appeared that the distance between the highway above us and our battered Jeep had narrowed. It was now or never. I prayed the men weren't waiting for us up above and told Callie this was the point in time where we'd find out if the TV commercials lied. The

Jeep's wheels spun, then locked onto the earth and slowly pulled us to the top. When the front tires hit asphalt, Callie and I executed a pitiful and painful high-five!

Why in the goddamned hell are we being chased by these guys? I wondered.

As if Callie could read my mind, she said, "You have something they want, Teague. Think. What could it be?"

CHAPTER EIGHT

I drove, Elmo whimpered, and Callie dug through the first aid kit, putting Neosporin on all three of us. She had scraped legs and a cut across her arm. I had a deep gouge in my leg by the knee. Elmo had a sprained shoulder. All in all, we were very lucky.

"Who do you think they were?" I asked Callie through the darkness.

"I don't know, but there's definitely a connection between what happened to your friend Barrett and what happened to Frank Anthony," Callie replied. "Tell me everything from the beginning."

I began with the phone call from Barrett inviting me to lunch, explaining that I went hoping for a writing assignment from Marathon. Callie looked interested when I mentioned the studio. I told her Barrett had begun discussing a barter system at the studio that involved everything from drugs to prostitution and she was experiencing fear, and maybe a little guilt, about her part in it. Before we could finish the conversation, the Latin man had kissed her and Barrett had collapsed.

"Who did Barrett feel was behind it?"

"She said she didn't know and that for me to know would be dangerous. Maybe it goes right up the chain of command. She answers to Robert Isaacs, who reports to Lee Talbot, who's accountable to the Marathon board of directors."

Callie stiffened at the mention of their names and looked ashen.

"What's wrong?"

"Quick karma, that's all."

"Well, I can't think of any deeds I've done in this lifetime that would warrant my being stalked and murdered."

We drove directly to the Albuquerque police station and reported the incident. An officer filled out a vehicle damage report, interviewed us, asked for a description of our pursuers, and said they'd be in touch. *Not,* I thought.

I left the LAPD number and asked the New Mexico police officer on duty to let Detective Curtis know about the incident. Since we were headed back to L.A., Curtis was once again my cop du jour.

❖

We checked into a room at the Holiday Inn, after quickly walking Elmo together. Callie disappeared into the bathroom for half an hour. Her small jeans were tossed across the bed. I could just make out the tag: size 2.

Size 2! At birth, I had nothing that was a 2. I stared at the label. *How can I, the person who finds comfort in women well over 5'9", ever be insatiably attracted to a 5'4" size 2!*

Callie returned wearing a long white cotton T-shirt with a plunging neckline and a RL logo on it. I thought it was the sexiest outfit I'd ever seen anyone wear. In fact, I loved it so much I wanted to take it right off her. She crawled into the double bed across from mine.

"Where are you going?" I asked. "I thought you wanted me to work on your arm."

"You don't need to," she said, "I know you're in pain."

"I want to, but it requires that you come over here because I am totally busted." I grimaced as I tried to raise up on one elbow. "Besides, you're in Elmo's bed. He likes pillows." On cue, Elmo left his water bowl, bounded up on the bed, and flopped his loose, damp jowls down on Callie's pillow.

She bailed out seconds later as I gave Elmo an appreciative wink and made a mental note to buy that dog more cookies. She clambered into bed beside me and slid her hurt arm across my chest. I gently massaged it and her shoulder as she winced in pain. "So you are in pain, but you deny it."

"If you talk about it, you give it more negative energy. I just see it completely healed," she said.

I continued to rub her arm and shoulder and down her back, so soft and cool to the touch. *She must take cool showers,* I thought, *or she would be warmer.* I lifted the sheet slightly to see the light blond hairs that were barely perceptible on her body. I tried not to think about what else I'd like to massage. She took a small, short breath, sighing like a baby. Callie Rivers was fast asleep across my chest.

I lay awake all night, the electrical circuitry of our bodies closing in a tight loop that pulsed through me, an erotic charge keeping every nerve ending in my body erect. I cupped my hand over her small buttock. It was breathtakingly soft. I closed my eyes, envisioning my mouth caressing those very cheeks. When I opened my eyes, Elmo was staring at me. He licked his lips as if to say, "Do it and your lips will never touch mine." I chuckled softly.

❖

At dawn, I groaned in agony as I tried to roll over. Lying still all night had caused all my battered and bruised joints to gel and stiffen. I winced before opening my eyes. Callie's beautiful face was smiling down at me. I smiled broadly in return.

"Good morning," she said sweetly and kissed me on the forehead as one would an irritable child and then handed me a hot cup of coffee.

"We were protected yesterday and we will be again," Callie said with eternal optimism.

"I don't call rolling off a highway down a thirty-foot ravine 'being protected' even if I did live to bitch about it. I call that *non*-protected. Protected would be if their guns had misfired and blown up in their hands, killing them instantly. Now that's being protected."

"That's revenge."

"I like revenge," I said mildly.

"You know that's not true," she scolded.

"It's true for me. My truth may be different than your truth, but thank you so much for the coffee. And that's the truth."

Callie placed her hand on my forehead, breathed deeply, and then pulled some invisible something out of my head and threw it into the air, as if removing a restless spirit from me. In the blink of an eye, I felt better, even optimistic.

"What did you just do?" I asked.

"Just cleansing your third eye."

"Had I known I had a spare, I would have rested one of my other ones."

"Ah-ah, don't make fun," she warned, determined not to let me denigrate her belief system and clearly bent on enlightening me.

❖

We merged onto I-40 looking over our shoulders, afraid someone would shoot us, run us off the road, or even talk to us, for that matter, but no one bothered. Elmo's shoulder was better. He hung his head in between the split front seats and rested his large jowls on the storage console separating Callie's seat from mine, so he could press his nose up against her arm. She continually massaged the big white milk-bone design on the top of his caramel-colored head. Victims of a near disaster, they had apparently bonded with one another.

"I brought your birth chart. Pisces, Virgo rising. So that's why you're so grounded, but yet creative."

"I know all about Pisces, Virgo rising." And off her shocked look, I said, "There's a song about Pisces, Virgo rising, being a good sign, and if the song's accurate, then I am, in addition, strong and kind."

"Do you know that you have Mercury in Aries?"

"Hum a few bars and I'll tell you," I replied.

"It means you're verbally quick, sometimes maybe too quick, perhaps even cutting," she said without judgment.

"Never heard that," I lied.

❖

We drove into the San Fernando Valley about eight p.m., down the 5 and onto the 134 exiting in Studio City. Down a pretty side street, I punched the automatic gate opener above the visor and the iron gates in my driveway swung open, allowing us to drive safely in before clanging shut behind us. I was happy to come home to a fortress.

When I put my key in the lock, I stood stock still, every nerve ending on edge.

"What's the matter?" Callie leaned in near me.

"Dead bolt's off." I signaled her to back away from the house and get into the car. I followed her and retrieved the gun that I now kept lodged between my front seat and the storage compartment. Once I had it in my hand, I felt more secure and a great surge of anger welled up inside me.

"You stay in the car with Elmo," I whispered.

"No, we both need to drive away and call the police." Her voice was urgent.

"In L.A. we'd be on a walker before they show up. Just stay here."

I went back to the rear door of the house, leaned up against the wall to get my breath, then kicked the door open and flicked the lights on to my right, sweeping the gun from left to right.

"Hands above your head!" I shouted at no one. I glanced at the floor strewn with dishes and silverware, a wall with pictures askew, and a closet erupting its contents onto the floor. I moved into the living room, where DVDs and books were randomly scattered, and then into the office, where every file I owned was on the floor.

"They're looking for something," the voice said behind me.

I whirled and pointed the gun at Callie, then quickly pointed it away.

"That's a damned good way to get yourself killed! I told you to stay outside."

"Stop giving orders. Let's see what they were after," Callie said practically.

I dialed Detective Curtis's direct line. "Did the New Mexico police call you?" I asked. He said they hadn't, so I told him about the men who ran us off the highway.

"I think it's all the same guys harassing you," Curtis said. "We've got a break in the case. An informant in a gang here in L.A. who seems to know your guy with the spider tattoo. The gang mostly deals in drugs. Don't know why they targeted you or your friend, but we intend to make an arrest. When we do, I'll want you down at the station to ID him."

I told him I would be delighted, but in the meantime, I'd been burglarized, and I described the condition of my home. Curtis had the attention span of a gnat when it came to burglaries in which household items were rearranged but not stolen. He asked me to get some digital shots, take an inventory, and call the LAPD's main number. They'd send an officer who'd make a report for my insurance company. *All of which will be put in my file and presumably read by an interested human only in the event of my death,* I thought.

"LAPD," I snorted. "If this were the TPD they'd be here already!"

A short ring and then a fax glided off the machine. Its anonymous and cryptic message said, "Welcome Home."

Callie stared at it. "This was sent by whomever the Latins work for."

"And who's that?"

"A white man, not a very powerful man, really, but a man who wants to be powerful. He disguises himself."

"Literally disguises himself?"

"No. You would never know the power connections he has by looking at him. That kind of disguise."

"Be more specific."

"Sorry, I can't, but right now I'm feeling you should call Barrett."

I dialed Barrett's home number, hoping she'd been released from the hospital. When Barrett answered, I admit I was happy to hear her voice and to know that she was up and around. I told her I'd just returned from Oklahoma and had been thinking about her ever since our lunch at Orca's. In fact, I'd called the hospital long distance to ask how she was. Barrett interrupted me to say she was fine and very busy. I tried to book a lunch with her.

"Unavailable, Teague. In fact, I'm booked all week. Got several screenings to attend," Barrett said. When I suggested the following week, she added, "Sorry, still maxed. I'll be in New York."

By the time I hung up, it was clear to me that someone had gotten to Barrett and given her the choice of getting back on the team or getting buried. She'd obviously chosen the former.

"She's involved in the Anthony murder," Callie said flatly.

"That would be a big coincidence," I remarked.

"Coincidence is a word people use to keep themselves from being frightened by the truth." Callie stared at me with those ethereal blue eyes, and I knew she was a woman who knew the truth.

Late that night, I checked myself out in the mirror and then plopped down in a chair. I'd lost ten pounds, and I had circles under my eyes that made me look like a raccoon. I was still nervous about the ransacking of my house. Elmo inexplicably paced and moaned and fretted as I pulled all the blinds shut, put the alarm on, and called the LAPD to ask for the occasional drive-by patrol car, just to keep an eye on things. But that wasn't all that was worrying me. Being with Callie, and not being able to have Callie, was taking its toll. *I don't want her getting the idea that we're just roommates. The mere thought is making me gaunt and thin! By the time she gives in, if she gives in, I'll undoubtedly be too weak to take advantage of my good fortune,* I thought, only half in jest. Callie must have read my mind.

"What's the matter?" She came up behind me and put her delightfully small hand on the back of my neck. "You feel hot."

"Aside from the usual things—mayhem and murder—I'm attracted to someone who isn't showing any interest in me at all," I said.

Callie spun my swivel chair around to face her and straddled me with her legs spread wide across mine, her face inches from my own. "This is a very sad story," she said feigning sympathy.

"Don't tease me," I said, "I'm not kidding."

"Okay." She looked at me closely to make sure I was serious.

"So the truth is…" I began, but she silenced me with her fingers over my lips. I immediately took her fingers into my mouth. They smelled of her perfume.

"The truth is, I want you as much as you want me." And with that Callie Rivers gave me the most deliciously erotic kiss and allowed me to slip my hand inside the leg of her loose shorts, where to my delight, she was wearing nothing but the moist heat created by our kissing. She rocked slowly forward on me only once, and I moaned at how good she felt. She pushed against me, snuggling into my neck, when suddenly our chair moved side to side at a ninety degree angle. Moments later, the chair took three forward bounces, and both of us were thrust back into reality. I looked up and the furniture was moving. I pulled Callie under the Parsons table that rested against the wall as the interior doors slammed open and shut and dishes broke and alarms went off.

"It's an earthquake," I whispered, panting from a mix of too many adrenaline-rush activities. "Elmo! Stay!" I could see him hunkered down next to the couch. He wasn't moving, protected by the large rolled arms above him.

"We should have read the signs. Elmo has been nervous and pacing," Callie said.

I reached above my head for the small portable radio resting on the table and punched the On button. An announcer interrupted programming. *"If you're listening in the Valley, we have reports coming in of an earthquake in that area. Magnitude not official yet, but we're hearing from listeners that they believe it to be in the range of a 5.9 to 6.2."*

Callie tried to crawl out of our hiding place, but I pulled her back. "Let's hang out here a minute. There could be aftershocks, or worst case, this could be the foreshock to a bigger one." I could feel her tense up, and I pulled her body toward mine. "I can now say that when we even begin to make love, the earth moves," I grinned.

"You're moving. You can't live in a place where your furniture gets rearranged by Mother Nature!"

I didn't reply. At forty-one, my life was semisolid. Where I lived, what I did for a living. Her remark about my moving was a reminder that a relationship for anyone over twenty came with a lot of baggage, like who would give up what in order to be together.

Be together, my mind quickly edited my own remarks, *the woman hasn't even slept with you yet, much less determined we should be together. Besides, what would living with Callie Rivers be like?*

"We're getting up," she said, "I'm not spending my life under a table."

It would be like that, I thought. *It would be total loss of control. It would be turning my every decision over for a second opinion. It would be constant discussions about dog jowls on pillowcases, and the trashing of comfortable clothes, and reminders not to drive recklessly or swear. Living with Callie Rivers would be bringing an earthquake into my life. I just need to enjoy the moment, the sensuality, and the companionship and not go down the forever-after road.*

A second tremor hit and Callie scurried back under the table with me, burying her head in my chest.

But she feels so damned good, I thought.

CHAPTER NINE

We drove the Jeep over to Van Nuys Auto Repair, where Marty, a weather-beaten guy in his sixties, strolled silently around the bashed-in sides and top and looked up at me with a grin. "Run her in a demolition derby?"

"Something like that," I replied.

"Insurance payin'?"

When I told him that it was, he went off to find me a serviceable rental while I took a call from Mom and Dad, who were wanting to make sure that the three of us were okay. They'd just heard about the earthquake.

"Earthquakes kill people!" Mother announced as if we hadn't figured that out. "So you three should think about moving back here." I refrained from saying that we were in more danger from human beings than earthquakes, but instead sent her our love.

❖

I just wanted to sit across from Callie and look into her eyes and forget what was going on around us for an hour, so I suggested lunch in Beverly Hills. On the drive over, I asked her point-blank, "So, you're psychic. How come you didn't know the earthquake was coming?"

"I knew it was highly probable in this lunar cycle, but I didn't pay attention. I wasn't focused on it. Being psychic plays out in different ways for different people. For me, the 'knowing' is random, unless I focus on the issue or unless someone out there causes me to focus on it."

"Out there would be…?"

"Out there." Callie casually extended her arms to take in the entire universe.

"Got it." I nodded.

"Now, don't make fun." She grinned at me, but her voice was warning.

"I'm not. It's just pretty far out…" Seeing her raised eyebrow, I added, "there."

❖

I parked our rented white Ford Taurus at the curb next to Il Faccio, one of my favorite lunch spots. As we pulled up, there was Barrett Silvers, as combed and curried as a show pony, bidding a studious-looking woman good-bye on the sidewalk.

"What are you doing here?" Her voice cracked when she saw me.

"Having lunch and trying to find out why, ever since I last saw you, someone's been hanging dead rats on my door, running me off a road in Texas, ransacking my house, and trying to kill me. And in my spare time, I've been trying to find out who tried to kill you."

"Writers!" She smirked. "No one tried to kill me. I mixed my medication. I'd taken a muscle relaxant for stress, and I didn't know it would react with the other medication I'd taken. Just a mix-up, but a serious one. I was lucky."

I had to admit she delivered this explanation in a very convincing manner.

"Introduce me to the beautiful woman in front of whom we've been airing our dirty laundry," she requested, and I introduced Callie. Barrett virtually undressed Callie with her eyes, lingering on her breasts and occasionally moving up to her hair.

"Are you a writer?" Barrett asked.

"A psychic, which means she knows better than to pitch to you." I casually blocked Callie from Barrett's view. "And the Judas kiss?"

Barrett looked a little too puzzled before she finally answered my question. "Oh, the Latin guy? He was just a messenger returning a stone artifact a friend had borrowed for an art show." Turning to Callie, she said, "You're gorgeous."

"My messenger service never kisses me when they deliver." I interrupted Barrett's stare, not liking her coming on to Callie. "So where's the stone now?"

"That's what my insurance adjuster wants to know. Apparently I had it in my hand when I had the attack, and somewhere between Orca's and the ER, it disappeared. Personally I think a waiter or med tech took it. It's not outrageously expensive, but worth some cash."

"Bzzzzz!" I made a game-show buzzer sound and simultaneously yanked her car keys out of her hand, dangling them in the air as if to say we'd both be receiving our mail here unless she told me what was going on.

She sagged against the car, resigned to satisfying my demand. "Okay. Talbot wanted us to sign Eddie Smith. Nobody signs Eddie for under a squillion dollars, so it ends up we have to settle for Benny Kaye. Only Benny knows we've already approached Eddie first, so there's an ego thing." Barrett lowered her voice, "Isaacs scouts around to find out what Benny's into, so we can send him a little ice breaker before Talbot has to call to talk a deal. Turns out, Benny's into snuff films."

"That's a bit more disconcerting than delivering hookers, isn't it?" I said.

Callie interrupted to ask what a snuff film was, and when I told her it was a film where people agree to be killed while having sex, her face went ashen.

"Anyway, Isaacs insisted I get these films off the black market. I just freaked and said I couldn't do it. When I talked to you at Orca's, I didn't know Isaacs had called it off, so I was still crazed. That's all."

"You see? Confession is good for the soul." I kissed her on the cheek and she snapped her head back reflexively. Barrett knew that Spider Eye's kiss had something to do with her collapse at Orca's. She was just too terrified and in too deep to admit it to me or the cops.

"We'll do lunch!" She waved to us as she hurried off to her car. "And bring your friend." She winked at Callie.

"She's lying," Callie said as Barrett drove away. "She's lying to cover for Isaacs."

We got back in the car, not really in the mood for lunch anymore. "Why did you kiss her?" Callie asked.

"Who?"

"Barrett. You kissed her good-bye."

"It was a Hollywood kiss. Did you see the way she was looking at you? If I hadn't been trying to get information from her, I would have broken her kneecaps."

"Don't be so violent," Callie said, and I could see she was still troubled by my kissing Barrett.

"Look, I have no feelings for Barrett, and I don't sleep around. In fact, in my entire life I've slept with very few people. Although I'm unclear why you're interested since we're never going to sleep together."

"I didn't ask you who you'd slept with."

"Sorry, sharing violation," I mocked.

"I just thought the kissing was unnecessary. That's all. From a hygienic perspective. There's a lot of disease out there."

Her clinical approach made me grin. "That wasn't kissing. This is kissing." I leaned across the front seat and kissed her on her bare shoulder, then on her neck and up around her ear, and finally on her mouth. She snuggled into me, enjoying it, before realizing we were still parked in front of Il Faccio's.

She pulled back, slightly undone. "There are people watching us."

I glanced up to see a couple, frozen in mid-bite, staring at us through the restaurant windows.

"Let's go," Callie said.

"They're just jealous that we're having a better lunch hour than they are."

❖

That afternoon, I sat in my office and mentally rewound Barrett's story about Hollywood's second-hottest comedian Benny Kaye as Callie studied astrology charts on her laptop. I wondered what had happened with Hollywood's number-one comic, Eddie Smith. If Marathon needed Benny Kaye right away, they must have screwed up their deal with Eddie. *What did Eddie want that the studio couldn't deliver? Someone on the studio lot has to know.*

I dialed the studio and asked for the public relations office, telling the young woman who answered that I was from the *LA Times* and we were getting a list of all of the upcoming studio events for a possible series in the business section. Could she tell me what was in the offing? She rattled off a list of events that included a soundstage ground-breaking, a premiere for the new motion picture *Action World,* and a stockholders' meeting. I asked where and when the stockholders' meeting was taking place. She said this Friday on the main lot. All shareholders were invited.

I hung up and called my broker, saying I needed to buy a few shares of Marathon and I needed him to fax me proof of the transaction. Callie brightened, saying this was going to be an exciting Friday. I told her I hoped so in light of the fact that this lunch had cost me five hundred dollars.

"We'll eat on Friday, sell the stock on Monday, and it'll be a free lunch," she said.

"No such thing as a free lunch," we said in unison and laughed.

For a brief moment, I was beyond the mere sexual wanting of her, basking in the comfort of her company, of her quick mind, and of our shared sense of humor. A gnawing little piece of me dreaded that moment when she might say she had to go back home. For me, she was starting to feel like home.

❖

Friday at eleven a.m., we were at the Marathon gates, an imposing stone archway with Olympic runners passing the torch overhead. The security guard located our name on the shareholders' list and cleared us to drive on. The lot was crowded, and we were forced to park a football field away from the soundstage where the stockholders' meeting would take place. My next-to-the-little toe was getting that weird cramp that makes me limp and curse the Ferragamo family who, for hundreds of dollars a pair, still couldn't see their way clear to put padding in my shoes!

We entered the soundstage, which had been converted into a giant press release, with twenty-foot movie posters hanging from wires all around the room, touting successes past and present, alongside equally large slabs of dangling cardboard that chronicled each movie's title, year, stars, awards, and box office gross. A sea of circular tables dotted the soundstage that boasted a seating capacity of two thousand. People milled along the buffet line picking up coffee and danish and staring at the gigantic ice sculpting of a man frozen in mid-run, ice droplets collected on his huge brow. The perfect symbol for the harried, frightened studio executive.

Around the room, corporate executives mingled with Brentwood yuppies and the occasional elderly couple from Des Moines who made the trip to check on the health of their ten shares. Studio shareholders' meetings were notoriously a time for hype and hoopla, and the Marathon meeting was no exception. Big gold-foil-wrapped M-shaped chocolates acted as paperweights, securing the Marathon annual report to the tables in front of each chair.

I picked up an annual report and thumbed through it, noting page after page of glossy 8x10 photos of CEO Talbot cutting ribbons, attending premieres, and shaking hands with stars. I flipped to the financial data. The bottom line message was clearly, "We've gone from red to black," and the adjusted gross of 784.6 million dollars verified that. Talbot, or Isaacs, or somebody was a miracle worker.

Isaacs banged his gavel on the tabletop podium, and in a tone just this side of saccharine, asked everyone to find a seat. The show was about to begin. Callie seemed fixated on Isaacs as he launched into a tribute to Talbot, calling him a Hollywood giant and a man of character, strength, and virtue. After fifteen minutes, he turned the microphone over to Talbot, who thanked Isaacs profusely, crediting him for much of the year's success.

The mutual back-patting went on far too long, if one could judge from the sound of crinkling foil. People were tearing into the gold foil wrappers, flopping the big chocolate Ms around and gnawing on the six-inch legs like bored terriers. Even Talbot recognized he was losing them as he elevated his voice to the tenor of a Baptist preacher and boomed, "Well, let's get on with the *big* news! Marathon Studios has once again crossed the finish line ahead of the pack. We have just signed"—he gave a long dramatic pause—"Eddie Smith for a three-picture deal!"

Talbot held out his arm pointing stage right, and Eddie Smith came bounding out right on cue.

"I'm all yours, baby!" He bellowed his trademark laugh line at Talbot.

"And I'm delighted!" Talbot roared in reply.

Giving Talbot a big bear hug, Eddie turned to the audience with perfect comedic timing and growled, "Whatsa mattuh? This the first time you ever seen two gay guys express their affection for each other?" The audience roared with laughter and applauded wildly. It was definitely something to tell the folks back home in Sioux City.

Callie and I exchanged looks. Benny Kaye was apparently out, because they had landed the prize of prizes, Eddie Smith.

"Eddie Smith's been offered a gazillion dollars to make a movie anywhere in town, and he's refused for five years," I said.

"Must mean someone got him what he wanted," Callie replied.

An hour later the show had been turned over to several corporate VPs armed with charts and graphs, who took us through the financial ups and downs of Marathon with rationales for every decision Marathon had made all year. The questions from the audience were respectful and good-humored, as opposed to last year, where it was reported a stockholder threw a chair at the stage. Having Eddie Smith warm up the crowd had done its job. I slid out of my chair and inched my way to the back of the room for more coffee, towing Callie in my wake. At the ever-present danish tray, I bumped into Marsha Brown wearing a large Marathon name tag. I'd met Marsha right after she'd left MGM to work for a small independent film company. I'd once pitched her a theatrical at the precise moment L.A. was struck by a magnitude 5.7 earthquake.

Marsha was the thin, nail-biting type to begin with, but when her large steel desk bounced three feet nearer the seventeenth-floor windows and the building did a few concrete hulas, I could have been a one-armed troglodyte and Marsha still would have clung to me. After the second shake, we extended our stay under her desk for another ten minutes. It had a bonding effect.

"So what did they barter Eddie?" I asked.

Marsha shot me a piercing look. "Bet it's nothing you can bank. Love to have you over tonight." She stepped in very close to me and slid her hand swiftly between my legs, a reminder that we'd once shared an evening together.

"Can you come?" she asked with a twinkle in her eye, and I jumped reflexively.

"No, I can't. Sorry," I said, and Callie shot me a look that indicated *sorry* was most likely not the appropriate word.

Marsha headed for the buffet table, and Callie put her arm around me in a proprietary way and whispered softly, "Have you slept with everyone in L.A.?"

"I never had sex with that woman," I said, imitating Bill Clinton. Callie was not amused.

❖

The financial presentation wrapped up and Eddie popped out from backstage and began working the room, shaking hands with the shareholders as if this were the room he'd waited a lifetime to play. He put his arm around a short, chunky, middle-aged woman with bright orange hair who looked very smart and colorful in a matching orange suit.

Marsha reappeared with a fresh cup of coffee and informed us that the woman in orange was Rita, Eddie's wife of twenty-seven years. "He's notorious for sleeping with anything in a skirt. She's threatened to leave him over the last one, who happened to be a call girl and gave her the disease of the week by proxy."

"That guy's got an aura darker than the Black Hole," Callie chimed in.

"Ever seen how they rear-screen fifty projectors?" I asked, dragging Callie backstage before she could make any other damaging remarks about Marathon's extended family.

We rounded a row of screens creating a backstage for the equipment. Off to the right at a thirty-degree angle were two more partitions to conceal equipment cases. I showed Callie the computer into which the fifty projectors were programmed.

"If anything goes wrong, you're out of sync for the rest of the show, but when it works it's impressive," I said.

A man's muffled voice spoke gruffly from behind the angled partition. "You've had two fiascoes and I don't want another! And I want the fuckin' list, or the only list you're gonna be on is in the obits. Eddie's deal is contingent. I had to kiss the little snake's butt to get him here today because you didn't deliver!" This voice was vaguely familiar.

"It's Isaacs," Callie said flatly.

"Okay, okay, we're doin' her tomorrow," the second voice said.

Isaacs burst forth from behind the partition, proving Callie right, and headed back out onto the floor.

"It is Isaacs. I believe you are psychic," I said.

She ignored me, her eyes following Isaacs. His demeanor

changed from irate to jovial the moment he came within view of the stockholders.

"So who was he talking to?" I whispered.

"That guy over there." Callie pointed to an older man in green coveralls who, from a distance, looked like a stage hand.

Suddenly Callie yanked the back of my suit jacket so hard I did an involuntary genuflect.

"Damn, I'm already so sore I need horse liniment. Do you have to yank me around?" I said irritably.

"Barrett Silvers."

I looked where she was pointing, and sure enough, Barrett had been within earshot of Isaacs's conversation. She seemed upset, and after looking around to make sure no one had spotted her, she disappeared.

"I thought she was an executive vice president. She has to resort to getting information from her boss the same way we do, by listening through walls?" Callie asked.

"And what do you suppose 'we're doin' her tomorrow' meant?" I asked.

Callie froze. "That's how they got Eddie. Yes, I'm getting an affirmation…"

"From whom?"

"The cosmos. I'm telling you," Callie said to quiet my disbelief. "They're killing a woman to get Eddie Smith. That's the trade they're making."

"I don't know about that," I said, not wanting to know about that. My nerves were getting the better of me. "And what list are they talking about?"

Marathon Studios was obviously in the middle of something that would give the mafia the jitters.

CHAPTER TEN

The phone rang late that afternoon, and I dodged the dancing Elmo to get to it. The voice on the other end of the line belonged to Wade Garner.

"Got intel on the Anthony murder. Last call Frank Anthony received before he died was from a gal in L.A. named Barrett Silvers. Ever hear of her?" Wade asked.

"She's a friend of mine!" I said, startled.

"Well your gal pal's gonna be getting a visit from the FBI," Wade said.

I thanked him, grabbed my jacket, and told Callie what Wade had just reported. "We need to corner Barrett and get the whole story," I added.

"The first night I met you, I told you someone who couldn't sleep nights called Frank Anthony just before he died. So it was your friend Barrett!" Callie said, seemingly amazed.

"Does it surprise you that you're right in your predictions?"

"Yes, because I just say what I see, or what I feel, at that moment. When it turns out to be true, it sort of validates…everything."

"Validation is good," I said, trying to be supportive.

❖

I told the guard at the Marathon gate that we'd left something behind during the stockholders' meeting and needed to go back for it. He said the soundstage was locked up.

"Aaaaarnold!" The guard yelled over the top of the car, nearly deafening us. An older man wearing one-piece zip-up coveralls stopped welding a metal sign at the entrance gate that said Drive Slow and ambled over to us.

The gate guard gave Callie a seductive wink. "Arnold's got friends in high places. He can get you into every nook and cranny of the place. He'll be glad to unlock the soundstage for you."

Arnold's scowling face didn't seem to bear that out. He wiped away a tiny trickle of blood running down the crease next to his mouth, as if his skin were so thin it couldn't hold the blood inside his face.

"The soundstage is open!" Callie leaned across me, waving her cell phone at the guard, as if someone on the line had just told her that.

The guard waved Arnold off, and us through, as I stared at Callie in amazement.

"Being blond works. It just does." She shrugged.

❖

We parked out of sight of the guard shack and walked directly to Barrett Silvers's office. She was meeting with someone, her door was closed, and her male secretary was seated next to a new guy who was obviously her bodyguard, judging from the fact that his forearms were the size of my thighs. Barrett's secretary asked if we had an appointment. I said we didn't, but we'd wait to see her. He assured me that wasn't possible. I suggested he tell Barrett we were outside. He disappeared into her office and was gone about thirty seconds, then returned striking a friendly but defiant pose. "She said she would just love to see you, but she just can't today."

"Hollywood friendships," I said to Callie and picked up a note pad and scribbled, "The FBI is looking for you." I folded the note in half, handed it to the annoyed secretary, and asked him to deliver it to Barrett while we waited. He disappeared back inside Barrett's office. In thirty seconds Barrett's "meeting" was ejected from her office like spent shell cartridges, and we were ushered in. She asked that we close the door behind us.

I was in no mood to be pleasant. "The FBI says the last phone call made to Frank Anthony's cell phone before he was murdered was from Barrett Silvers." I waited. I could see the wheels in Barrett's head grinding together like the innards of a three-dollar watch.

"So what?" she finally said.

I burst out laughing. "I'm glad you got to audition that ridiculous response on us instead of the feds. How the hell do you know Frank Anthony, Bare?" I asked.

"Look, after the incident with the snuff films, where I freaked on Isaacs, I called Frank because he was on the Marathon board and I'd met him before."

So, Frank was on the Marathon board. That's a connection between the stone at Orca's and the stone etching in Tulsa, I thought.

"I told him what had happened," Barrett continued. "I was just trying to put a stop to the craziness before I ended up in jail. I didn't want to phone the LAPD and get some cop who was going to sell my story to *Hard Copy*. That's it. Frank said he'd call a buddy of his at the FBI."

"Except Frank Anthony is dead," Callie reminded her.

"Somebody backstage at the shareholders' meeting was being threatened by Isaacs." I raised my voice, "And that somebody said, 'We're doin' her tomorrow.' Now, call me selfish, but I'd like to know who her is. Just to make sure it's not me!"

Barrett paused while her blood seemed to roll down into her shoes. "I have no idea what you're talking about."

"I'm not a detective. I'm just a writer, but you're acting real strange, Barrett, and pretty soon, you're going to have to tell someone what you know."

I locked eyes with her for just an instant before she turned her head away, saying, "Teague, go get a life, will you? You're acting like a bad Angela Lansbury!"

"Go fuck yourself!" I said, and on that note, we left.

Outside on the flower-trimmed walkway, Callie said we might not see Barrett again. When I asked her to elaborate, she got a vague look in her eyes and said something about color shifts around her.

"I just see her in an altered state," Callie said.

I didn't pursue the "color shifts," because I had all I could deal with in the real world. Barrett Silvers had turned on me.

"What's with you and tall, rude women? I'm getting a sense that you have some karmic tie that you might want to think about breaking,"

Callie offered. I wasn't about to tell her that all the women I'd dated had been tall, and arguably rude, and that the joke among my lesbian friends was whether it's fish or women, throw the small ones back.

❖

At home that night, I took every precaution: floodlights on, alarm set, blinds shut. My body now protected, it was my soul that ached. I found myself staring at Callie Rivers. I was so close to her all day that I could smell the way her perfume changed with the heat of her skin—from sweet, to potent, to sensually musky—as the day wore on. I knew now what that poor teaser horse at my grandmother's farm felt like every time they brought her in to get the stallion excited and then yanked her out to put the expensive brood mare under him. I was excited out of my skin with no outlet. Callie was loving and sweet and cuddling, but she had stuck to her word about not sleeping with me, the earthquake incident seeming to remind her that we'd ventured too close.

I propped myself up on the bed and picked up a book about 1930s Hollywood and the stars of that bygone era, determined to immerse myself in other people's lives and forget my own. However, reading that Marlene Dietrich loved women all her life and Tallulah Bankhead once announced that she'd always wanted to get into Marlene's pants didn't exactly chill me out.

Callie wandered through the room asking me what I was reading.

"Did you know that all the female megastars in Tinsel Town of old were fucking each other?"

"You mean loving each other," she corrected.

"Come look." I held up a photo and, when she walked over, I pulled her down playfully onto the bed. "Let me demonstrate." I kissed her seriously this time, with a convincing fervor that admitted I knew this was our moment.

She pulled back as she had in her apartment, but then, just as swiftly, gave in and her kisses were strong, and deep and probing. I kept my mouth on hers while I unbuttoned her shirt and pulled it away from her, unsnapping the bra she wore and releasing her huge, firm breasts. I slid her pants down and off her as she whispered, "Take your clothes off." I could not have stripped faster if my clothes had been on fire.

There is a celestial happening when souls mate. It's as if a Divine

Force uses the hips and shoulders of one lover to press into the clay of the other, leaving an imprint that no one fills until those exact shoulders, those buttocks, those legs, that belly, slide into what heaven made, and when that happens, the fit is so tight that nothing can unlock it, no amount of rolling or rubbing or kissing. For Callie and me, it was as if a cosmic glue made of sweet secretions was holding us together. We were one. So incredible was the fit that I couldn't tell up from down, or right from left, or dark from light. I didn't know which wet, pulsing orifice I was inside of. I couldn't tell if she were in me, or I were in her. The sensual sensation was so intense that I no longer knew if I was even in my body, and I wanted only never, ever to leave this blessed place. I could feel her hips thrusting into me and hear her moaning and I realized she was about to explode with the joy of it, when she pulled away from me abruptly. Pleasure aborted, my senses crashed down out of the stratosphere and onto the bedsheets.

"What's wrong?" I was breathing like a marathon runner.

"Nothing. You're wonderful. Nothing."

"It's something," I said. "Did I hurt you?"

"No, no, no." She pulled herself up into a sitting position, leaning back against the headboard, and clutched her knees to her chest, encircling them with her arms. "That's why I didn't really want this to happen," she said, and then seeing my crestfallen face, she cupped it in her hand. "I've never completely given myself to anyone...so I can't just turn it on."

"What do you mean?"

"When I was twenty, a psychic told me that I wouldn't meet the love of my life until I was in my early forties. I remember thinking, 'in another twenty years, what will I have left to give that special someone that I haven't shared with someone else?' I decided to save that one thing for the person I knew I would finally meet."

"That one thing," I repeated flatly, staring at her. "You have never allowed yourself to climax?"

"That's unbelievable to you, isn't it?" she said softly.

"No, absolutely not," I lied, all the while thinking, *Omigod, Callie Rivers is a Lamborghini up on blocks!* I put my arms around her. "So you've been with other women and you've never—?"

"I never wanted to."

"But you were with these women for—?"

"A while, yes."

"And didn't your partners ever…notice?"

"No."

"No?"

"Women can fake it so that even women can't tell," she reminded me.

I stared into her beautiful, sincere eyes. *So maybe she'll just fake it with me, or maybe she's faking everything right now.*

"So you were with other people, Tee. Did you always climax?" Callie asked. Somehow that question coming from Callie, in light of what she'd just told me, made what I thought was a normal physical reaction to pleasure seem abnormal, selfish, even depraved!

"You did, of course," Callie answered her own question, and then laughed softly.

I kissed her neck thinking, *Only some berry-eating monk could maintain twenty years of self-control.* "But it should have happened, shouldn't it? We were wild for each other. Okay, so now I'm having performance anxiety. Maybe I should have—"

"Not everything is about you, Teague," she said gently. "This one is about me. I'm just used to pulling back. It'll take time. It'll be fine. Don't focus on it, and just give me time," she said.

Callie curled up in a ball, her buttocks pressed into my belly. I wrapped around her and snuggled closer. Her scent was overwhelming, intoxicating. I wanted her, and I didn't know how many unfulfilled nights I could take without cracking down the middle like a piece of parched earth.

I should have told her I was honored that she'd saved herself for me. I should have said it humbled me to think I was the one she'd chosen, but instead, like some cop interrogating a suspect, I got bogged down in the details. *Why did Callie deprive herself of pleasure, and why does that deprivation mean so much to her?*

As if reading my mind, Callie said softly, "I just never met anyone before who made me want to let go."

I held her tighter.

CHAPTER ELEVEN

Callie awakened early. I could hear her pacing in the living room, the floorboards creaking with every nervous footstep. She'd had nightmares all night about Rita Smith, and she thought we should go over there today. I explained that stars live behind iron gates, in heavily guarded compounds, and we had no chance of ever getting within a thousand yards of Rita Smith. But Callie was so agitated, she wasn't listening. I got dressed in a pair of gray sweatpants and a sweatshirt, put my morning coffee in a thermos cup, and told Callie we should get this visit over with so I could get some work done today. Callie told me her dream on the way over.

"Two gigantic black tarantulas around a fire, and we startled them. They bit us, and we were with Rita Smith, and she died of the bite," Callie said. I told her I liked her showgirls and fifty grand dream better.

I held her hand in mine as we drove up into the Encino hills and turned in at the driveway of an iron-gated mansion. I pointed out the closed gates and the security box, telling Callie this was as far as I could take her. She hopped out of the car, walked to the gate, and lifted the latch. I waited for an intercom to come on with a reprimanding voice, or a guard to demand our identity, or for a bell to go off. Nothing happened. Callie got back in the car. Amazed at the lack of security, I drove up the driveway and parked at the foot of a long, sloping flagstone pathway leading up to the house.

Up above us, Rita Smith, her carrot-red hair flashing in the sunlight, battled the stiff Santa Ana winds, holding the door to her canary yellow Mercedes open with her hip as she tried to lift out two sacks of groceries and the dry-cleaning. I guess she could have let the servants do it, but by the time she told them what to do, it was probably easier to do it herself. Maybe it took her mind off where Eddie might be on these mornings when he wasn't taping a show or shooting on the movie lot. Maybe he told her he was at the club playing golf. Maybe she didn't care. From the looks of things, they had a great life. Why question a good thing? She might ruin it.

I'd once read an article about Rita Smith that said she was raised on a farm in Iowa. She met Eddie when they were both in college in Des Moines. The article quoted her as saying, "Who would have known that the boy all my friends said was nuts would turn out to be one of the rich and famous in Hollywood? But we love each other, and we're just ordinary people really." Not too ordinary, I thought as I caught a glimpse of sunlight bouncing off what had to be a quarter of a million dollar diamond on her left hand, and probably a fifty thousand dollar tennis bracelet on her left ankle. She could call anyone, anytime, and get them to deliver whatever it was she wanted, and oddly enough, what she wanted this morning was to pick it up herself.

She backed away from the car, then turned and shut the door with her hip and headed up the steps that ran along the outside of the mansion leading to a landing and a door that opened onto an upstairs entryway.

Callie and I were twenty yards from her, but still out of her line of sight, when Barrett Silvers stepped out from under the exterior staircase, surprising Rita and us as well. Rita dropped her packages, and they tumbled over the railing. She screamed and Barrett quickly put her fingers to her own lips, warning her to be silent. I grabbed Callie's arm and pulled her aside into the shade of a large tree. I could see Barrett trying to quiet Rita down and convince her not to go inside.

Rita Smith was incensed that Barrett trespassed the compound. She threatened her loudly with the police and the possible arrival of her husband and the idea that there were servants upstairs who would blow her brains out.

"It's too late," Callie whispered, severely upset.

"What's she doing?" I asked her.

Barrett gripped Rita's skirt, trying to keep her from scaling the steps as she continued to try to shut her up, but Rita was petrified, and the adrenaline and her superior position three steps above Barrett allowed her to kick and claw her way to the side door as Barrett clung to her.

Rita yanked herself free and pulled the door open at the top of the landing, where a man in a ski mask was waiting, and he backhanded her as one would a housefly. The force of his stroke sent her head smashing up against the doorjamb, and Rita sank to the floor, blood slowly dripping from the door handle. Barrett's eyes went wide. She hesitated only a moment in her assessment that there was nothing more she could do for Rita Smith, and in a desperate act of self-preservation, she jumped over the side of the exterior staircase, landing on the ground below. Callie and I hovered out of sight, paralyzed at what we'd stumbled on.

Barrett's endorphins must have kicked in, because she scrambled over the grounds in an attempt to escape, but two men were on level ground now—dressed ominously in black, from their black combat boots to their black ribbed sweaters and black knit ski masks—and on her like hunting dogs on a crippled rabbit. Before Callie could stop me, I darted out into the clearing to help Barrett, not wanting the guilt of having been too cowardly to at least divert them from her. I shouted for them to leave her alone, and one of the men turned and rushed me. Callie screamed as he dove on me, pinning me to the ground.

We rolled over and over trying to get leverage on one another. I caught only pieces of his face under the hood as we struggled—Anglo, older, thin—before he let out a dull moan and collapsed on top of me. Callie had liberated one of the large flat rocks that lined the elegantly manicured flowerbeds along the driveway and used it like a hammer on his head. Grateful for Callie's help, I scrambled to my feet, and we both turned our attention to Barrett.

If Barrett Silvers saw us, she couldn't have focused long enough to know who we were, because she was fighting for her life fifty yards away from us. We both headed in her direction, but it was too late. The man was pointing something at Barrett. Then came the blast, flames attacking her from all directions, engulfing her in searing, skin-scorching fire. Callie screamed for the man to stop, I screamed for Barrett to run, Barrett screamed for the pain to end.

I could smell her flesh burning, imagine her expensive gold cuff links searing into her body like a branding iron, coming to rest on her wrist bones. The pain had to be unbearable. She rolled on the ground. He shot more fire at her. She was screaming still.

My wrestling partner was already waking up. "Get those two!" he shouted, pointing his gun at us and firing bullets at our heads. We dashed through the gate in our best track time and slammed it shut behind us. We were inside the car and out of the driveway in seconds.

"Jesus God!" I backed out of the driveway and swung around the corner to a pay phone, leapt out, and used it to dial 911 so my cell number couldn't be traced. I told the female officer who answered that I thought two people had been murdered. The officer asked for my name. "Just get someone over to Eddie Smith's house, and hurry!" Tears were running down my cheeks and I could barely talk as I dialed Curtis and left word about Rita and Barrett.

"I think she's alive, Teague," Callie said of Barrett.

"Then we've got to go back and help her until the police come!" I drove the car back around the corner and pulled up alongside the curb, leaving the entrance free for emergency vehicles. This time, the gate latch on the big iron gates was locked, by the frightened servants, no doubt, and we couldn't get back in.

Callie said it was just like her dream. "The two black tarantulas were the two men in black who attacked Barrett and Rita Smith. In my dream they were around a fire, remember? And these men set Barrett on fire and then, in the dream, they bit us. You were attacked and we were both chased, which is like being bitten."

"And you said you dreamed Rita Smith died of the bite."

"I hope that part's not true," Callie said.

Paramedics arrived within minutes. The gates were opened for them by someone inside the compound. Barrett Silvers was loaded into an ambulance. The neighbors were starting to gather, walking down the street to see what the commotion was about. A second ambulance arrived and parked just below the staircase where Rita Smith lay.

A news van followed and went live from the crime scene: *Famous comedian Eddie Smith's wife Rita was attacked this morning at their home in Encino by unknown assailants who left her unconscious and bleeding on the balcony of their estate. Marathon Studio executive Barrett Silvers, also at the estate, was found badly burned and has been rushed by ambulance to a nearby hospital. The motive for the attacks is unknown.*

"We need to go back inside and tell them what we saw," Callie said.

"That two guys in black tried to kill them?" I replied. "How do we explain our having been there when it happened?"

"Just tell them the truth. The gate was open and we drove in," Callie said. I looked at her for a full fifteen seconds, letting that thought sink in.

"I know you're into truth, Callie," I finally said. "But our talking to the police won't catch those men. I've talked to the LAPD, Curtis, 911, and the APD. I've talked myself blue to the men in blue, and do you see any real help coming our way? But this crime is different. Rita Smith is a high-profile case, and the police are going to be under pressure to produce leads. I don't intend to be one of them."

Callie said nothing further, and we drove home in a state of shock.

CHAPTER TWELVE

A studio secretary from Dinallen Pictures phoned. Brenda Emory would take my pitch on the adoption story this afternoon, at three, if I were free. She was sorry for the late phone call but, the secretary simpered, "Things have been so wild here, you wouldn't believe it!" I refrained from saying she wouldn't know wild if it bit her in the buttocks, and instead graciously accepted the appointment. In Hollywood, only the deceased turn down an opportunity to pitch a story.

Barrett and Rita Smith were so embedded in my consciousness that I functioned in nearly an out-of-body state. I was dressed in my pitch uniform, standing in front of the mirror checking out my jeans and hunt jacket, almost without being aware I'd gotten dressed. I got in the car in nearly the same state. Callie joined me, saying she'd love to see how movies were sold.

"If you want to see how they're sold, go with someone else. If you want to see how they're pitched, you're with the right person. I've pitched more often than Fernando Valenzuela."

Before heading over to Dinallen Pictures, we stopped and got the Jeep back from the body shop, and it looked as if it had never been driven off a cliff at high speed.

"It's beautiful, Marty. You can do my face lift," I said.

Marty beamed. He took great pride in his puttying and painting. I envied his being able to make a living at an occupation in which he did something people actually needed.

Dinallen Pictures was always in turmoil, consolidating office space, moving office space, or building office space. Their corridors could easily be mistaken for a moving and storage locker: boxes floor to ceiling, up against every wall. Brenda Emory's secretary, who was the epitome of pert and perky with a thick mop of tight red curls and a stick-figure body, said Brenda was on a long-distance call. "Could you just hang?" she asked, and I felt the request embodied the true desire of studio executives toward producers and writers.

We sat down on a low stack of boxes for ten minutes before the secretary poked her Orphan Annie head out into the hallway again and said, "She'll see you now."

We entered a spacious office decorated Sante Fe–style with a commanding view of the ocean. Brenda Emory was a middle-aged woman in baggy jeans and a white shirt that flapped loosely over them. She apologized for the delay, saying she was on the phone with a vet in New England about her hamsters.

"Are they sick?" I feigned concern.

"Oh, no. I breed them," Brenda said. "I began with Whitey and Sam, thinking they were both boys, and it turned out Sam was a girl, so we got Lucifer and Chin-Chin." Brenda reached over and picked up a stack of pictures: close-up shots of tricolored hamsters taking a whirl on the traditional hamster wheel. She took in a deep breath and launched into the problems surrounding the breeding of hamsters. Most of which, she lamented, had to do with the size of their anatomy and their general nervousness.

Thirty minutes later, it struck me this woman was not going to buy anything I had to sell. No one who could devote thirty pre-pitch minutes to the breeding of hamsters had a life outside of hamsters, or an interest outside of hamsters, or frankly very many movies to produce that didn't have hamsters in starring roles.

"Well, I know you've got a busy schedule. We're here to pitch you a true and extremely compelling adoption story."

Brenda crossed her legs and her arms. Not a good sign. Twenty minutes later, as I wrapped up the story explaining how the long-lost adoptee finally finds his birth parents, and those same birth parents are now back together and in love after thirty-five years, Brenda let out a long sigh of boredom.

"Does he come back home and kill them?"

"Kill them?" I ask, startled.

"If he came home and murdered them, you see, we wouldn't be

expecting that, and then that would be a movie. Of course you'd want that to happen at the hour break."

"No, actually, the story has an uplifting, happy ending."

"Was he molested by them before he was adopted out? Or did he commit suicide after finding them?" she mused. "You see what I'm getting at? The unexpected."

"Well, you've been so kind to listen to our pitch, Brenda," Callie said.

I put a copy of the ten-page story treatment on her desk, and Callie retrieved it as we exchanged good-byes, sent hugs to the hamsters, and left.

At the elevator, Callie said, "She was just jerking off in there with her stupid hamster stories. Cut your losses and move on. And never leave your work behind when they've been so negative about it. Negative energy can transfer to the story and diminish its power."

I stared at Callie. Underneath this fluffy exterior lurked an iron maiden.

Callie took the car keys from me, and I got in on the passenger side, sagging against the window.

"It took twelve years to sell *Forrest Gump*. Can you imagine what you can hear in twelve years?" I did an imitation of Brenda. "There's no sex? Just this dumb guy up there for two straight hours? Does he come home and bludgeon his mother? Because you see, that would be kind of interesting. Does he have a pet hamster?"

"I should help you select places to pitch."

"I'm only depressed that I got dressed for a trip to the Hall of Hamsters."

I flipped on the radio to avoid further discussion. A newscaster's somber tone announced, *"It has now been confirmed that the woman's body found this morning in the home of prominent comedian Eddie Smith is that of Rita Smith, his wife of twenty-seven years. Mr. Smith, obviously shaken and grief stricken, has been taken downtown for questioning about an apparent burglary homicide. They are hoping he can lead them to clues that might apprehend the killer. Again, Rita Smith, wife of comedian Eddie Smith, dead following a burglary in her home. She apparently died of smoke inhalation, which occurred in a fire that was the result of the burglary."*

I flipped the radio off. "She died," Callie said solemnly.

"That makes three by fire: Frank Anthony, Barrett Silvers, and now Rita Smith. We need to get into Barrett Silvers's office and see what we can find out."

I slid my fingers into the breast pocket of my hunt jacket and felt something cold and hard.

"What's the matter?" Callie instantly caught the look on my face.

"I don't know. What's in my pocket?" I asked, struggling with the lining and the constrictions of my seat belt.

Callie reached over and freed my jacket, reaching inside the pocket and extracting a small one-by-two-inch off-white stone.

"That's the stone! The death stone! We've been marked. We're going to die. I mean immediately! Check outside. Is anyone around us? Is the door locked?"

Callie yanked on my arm with such force that it snapped my head to one side. "Calm down!"

She didn't seem to understand the peril we were in. "That's the thing the man brought to the table. The man who tried to kill Barrett."

"Is this the jacket you were wearing the day you lunched with Barrett?"

"Yes!"

"Then maybe when Barrett collapsed into your arms at Orca's, she managed to slide the stone into your pocket for safekeeping," she said calmly.

I sank back into my seat, relieved that we were not going to die this instant. "Good God. This has to be what everyone's looking for. That's why they followed me to Tucumcari and to Tulsa, why they tried to run us off the road and why they ransacked my house. This is a dangerous fucking thing to be carrying around!"

"Thank God you didn't send that jacket to the cleaners!"

"So if Barrett stored it on me, why didn't she try to get it back after she got out of the hospital? That would be the logical thing to do, but instead Barrett didn't want to see me anymore."

"Which means she planted it on you to make you a decoy," Callie said.

"No," I said wearily, not wanting to believe Barrett would set me up to be killed. I let out a deep sigh, somehow more relaxed in finally knowing what they were after. At least now I wasn't just randomly selected in some mob lottery, but instead merely had the one thing they wanted.

❖

Callie cooked spaghetti and made a large salad while I scavenged croutons off the countertop and contemplated the stone having been with me all along.

"Don't eat off the countertop. I haven't wiped it down!"

"I've been known to pick up food off the floor and eat it," I said.

"That was in your former life as a buzzard." She smiled sweetly and snatched the crouton out of my hand.

"I can't get over the fact that the stone was in my jacket in the closet the entire time," I said.

"Remember, I told you that you had something tangible they wanted," Callie reminded me.

She held up a large spoonful of spaghetti sauce for me to test. I tasted it, not taking my eyes off her, as if it were her I was tasting. "Fabulous!" I whispered and put my arms around her waist.

"More salt, vinegar, sugar?" She took a taste from the same spoon. "It is pretty good," she acknowledged without waiting for further input from me.

"Good in the kitchen, good in the bedroom…" I said.

"After last night…" she said hesitantly.

I reached behind her and deftly switched off the burners before leading her into the bedroom where I pushed her gently back onto the bed and slid on top of her.

"You're wrecking my hair, ruining my makeup, destroying my clothes…" she complained gently.

"That's precisely the plan," I said. "You'll just have to get used to it."

Callie swiftly rolled me over and grinned in delight at my surprise as I found myself looking up at her.

"You can't always be in charge." She grinned and unbuttoned my shirt and unzipped my jeans. She glanced at my feet and, seeing I was barefoot, seemed to come to a tactical conclusion. She bounced up, grabbed the hem of my pant legs, and whipped my jeans off me in one swift move, not unlike a magician pulling a tablecloth out from under the dishes without destroying a plate.

"So have you done that a few times before?" My voice became uncharacteristically high pitched.

"Were you looking for someone who doesn't know what they're doing?" She arched an eyebrow, looking very seductive.

"No, actually, this is fine…good, actually," I stammered and she knew she had the advantage.

She pounced on top of me and kissed me into a frenetic frenzy, not giving me enough breath to ask her to remove her clothes or allowing me enough space to remove them for her. She moved down my breasts, kissing and caressing and holding them in her mouth while I twisted in absolute ecstasy. Finally she slid all the way down to my thighs, peeling the rest of my clothing from my trembling body, and buried her face in me. I sucked in my breath with the first warm touch of her tongue that stroked and I followed, demanded and I gave in, thrust into me and I returned the pressure. I ran my hands through her blond hair, allowing her to do whatever she would with me, pushing deeper into me until I let out a cry and lay awash in love. She gently kissed her way back up my entire body, arriving at my lips, staring into my eyes and saying, "Now, that was so wonderful."

"My God, you're telling me." I looked at her with eyes that had seen another dimension. "I love you." The words came out before I could stop them and made me self-conscious, especially since she said nothing in return. *Why did I say I loved her? How can I even know that really? Maybe I frightened her. Maybe I frightened myself.*

I attempted to roll her over, but she slid away from me. "You just rest and enjoy. I'm finishing dinner for us," she said, amused at my groggy condition.

"No, come here," I said, but she was out of my grasp.

"It doesn't always have to be tit for tat." She smiled. "I'll be right back."

I was aware that she was still running away from me, but just like the guys, I fell soundly asleep.

CHAPTER THIRTEEN

We arrived at Cedars Sinai and went to Barrett's room, which was on the top floor. I asked the nurse guarding her door if Barrett could talk. She wanted to know who we were and furrowed her young brow for emphasis. I pulled a snapshot out of my purse of Barrett and me, arms around each other. "Her sister," I said sweetly and walked past her, knowing I had the age advantage and using it to intimidate her.

"You carry a picture of your 'sister'?" Callie hissed in a decidedly un-cosmic-like moment of jealousy.

"She can't talk long," the nurse warned, and I assured her we'd only stay a moment.

Barrett was propped up slightly, and whoever had bandaged her body probably worked in an Egyptian tomb in his last lifetime. Only Barrett's face was visible.

"I have to ask you to leave…not feeling well," Barrett muttered, almost unintelligibly.

"I'm not feeling too well myself." I yanked the stone out of my pocket and flashed it in front of her eyes. "Because ever since you planted this little time bomb on me, people have been trying to kill me. Now why is that?" I felt bad verbally assaulting a woman who had been physically assaulted, but she was the only one who could answer my questions and, after all, whatever she was involved in had made me a big target. "Start with Frank Anthony, who died clutching a death stone just like this one."

Barrett answered only because she was too weak to fend me off. "Hank Caruthers was on the Marathon board. Frank Anthony was too, but Frank had decided to resign. He knew something illegal was going on at the board level, and he didn't want to be part of it. Caruthers didn't want his old friend to resign. He knew Frank was starstruck, so Caruthers talked Frank into coming out to the studio to discuss his issues and think about staying on. When Frank agreed to come out to L.A., Caruthers called Isaacs, who in turn called me and told me to get Frank Anthony anything he wanted for the weekend. You know, impress him so he'd want to remain on the board. Turned out Frank just wanted to meet starlets for a drink, a few autographs, and a tour of Disneyland. Kind of refreshing, you know? Frank liked Egyptian stuff, so I arranged a private showing with Waterston Evers."

She pointed to a drinking glass with a hospital straw in it. I retrieved it for her. She took a sip, grimacing in pain, and collapsed back onto her pillow. "I'd phoned Frank earlier on several occasions about the prostitutes and the snuff films. I wanted someone to put a stop to it. He said it was all going to stop. The barter deals, the skimming money off the top, everything. He said he knew who was behind it. He had a list of names and some bank information. The last time I called him, he said he was going to talk to the FBI. He said if anything happened to him, to remember what he'd given me, and that the list was 'written in stone.'"

"So the names are written on this stone, like the Bible on the head of a pin?" I asked.

"I don't know, but they're somehow connected with this stone, and they'll kill to get it back." Exhausted, she sagged back into her cocoon-like bandages, in a deep sleep. I carefully opened the drawer next to her bed and searched through her belongings until I found a date book.

"Hide this in your purse," I told Callie.

"I'm sorry, she's not supposed to have visitors." The nurse poked her head into the room. "I shouldn't have let you in. My supervisor is having a fit."

Callie leaned over and whispered, "The flowers are from Sterling Hacket."

"So Sterling Hacket owes her a debt of gratitude," I mused. "You know, at lunch with Barrett, she told me she got called to a famous actor's house in the middle of the night and did CPR on this kid to save his life. Barrett said she realized it was a 'fuckin' near miss,' and she could just as easily have been on a murder scene."

"Isn't Sterling Hacket being investigated for procuring kids for sex?" Callie asked.

"Right. So maybe Sterling's deal with Marathon is that they take care of any trouble with the porn police and he makes movies at a lower fee. Whatever all these deals are, they involve more than Barrett's telling."

The nurse reappeared, even more agitated this time, and personally ushered us out of the room, leaving us only when she saw us disappear down the hospital corridor headed for the street.

When we got in the car, I checked my watch. "We can still make Rita Smith's viewing."

"Viewing?" Callie wrinkled her nose.

"As a spiritualist, I would think you would welcome any opportunity to commune with the dead," I said darkly.

"I'll have to spend a week cleansing my aura. Hospitals, crime scenes, and now cemeteries!"

In spite of Callie's protests, I popped onto the 405 north, then took the 134 east and exited at Forest Lawn Drive. We drove up exquisitely manicured hills to the southern slope of the cemetery until we were overlooking the Disney studios. Spending eternity staring at Mickey Mouse on a water tower apparently appealed to a lot of folks, since burial plots on that side of the hill were SRO.

Black limos lined the circular drive, and hordes of men and women in business suits climbed the steps to the chapel, having momentarily put show business on hold to say good-bye to Rita Smith. Inside the chapel, an organist played tear-jerking tunes about love lost as a group of well-to-do women wept loudly in the front row. Eddie was putting on quite a show. As people filed past Rita's open coffin, he shook their hands and in a trembling voice, thanked them for coming.

Callie and I took a seat in the back row of the chapel and knelt in prayer. Glancing around, I recognized a lot of studio insiders: attorneys, agents, division presidents. It did cross my mind that I'd reached a new low. First, I'd crashed Frank Anthony's wake, now I was pretending to be one of the bereaved at the funeral of a woman I'd never met!

After about fifteen minutes of mogul watching, I decided we'd better go have a look at Rita. We cued up with dozens of other people lining the east wall of the chapel alongside a parade of wreaths and flower arrangements and waited our turn to make the horseshoe curve that would let us pass in front of her casket. As we inched our way forward, Callie fingered the cards on each wreath, reading the famous names bidding Rita farewell. At one particularly huge display, she seemed to lose her balance and staggered before the man next to her caught her by the arm.

"I'm sorry," Callie said. "I'm just a little overcome; that's all." But I noticed, after she regained her balance, that the card attached to the large wreath was missing. I gave her a raised eyebrow, and she dabbed her eyes in reply. There was no time to pursue it, as Rita's lifeless form loomed, outstretched, only yards ahead of us. Apparently, Rita had indeed died from a blow on the head and smoke inhalation, and not a fire, because she looked like a large porcelain doll dressed in peach, her hair falling in beautiful curls around her shoulders, her face and hands looking a lot like marble.

After passing the coffin, I turned and shook hands with Eddie, expressing my sorrow and quickly moving on before he could ask who the hell I was. Callie and I walked along the west wall of the chapel and straight out the front door to the parking lot.

Callie flashed the stolen florist's card in front of my eyes. The big Marathon logo was embossed in one corner. It read: *Let sorrow be a gift that brings the sufferer closer to Heaven.*

"Now is that a strange thing to say or what?" Callie remarked.

"What's so strange?"

"Let sorrow be a gift. Get it?" Callie raised her eyebrows at me. "Like Rita's murder was a gift to Eddie…"

"Maybe that's what his Marathon deal was contingent on," I said. "Maybe that's what 'do her' meant."

"Could you stop and let me get a Coke?"

"Now?"

"I'm thirsty," she insisted, so I merged onto the 34 eastbound and exited again just before Highway 2, a couple of blocks from a local burger joint. Up ahead I spotted a parked car with two Latin men in it. I pulled up to the order window, then cut a sharp right, jumped the curb and floorboarded it.

Callie screamed at my sudden reversal, but I signaled her to be quiet. She paused a moment, then tried to speak again, but I waved her into silence. A few blocks away, I drove the car into the automatic car wash. Once the soap and brushes got started, I opened the driver side door. Callie shrieked as the hot water sprayed inside, soaping the seat and splattering the dashboard. Crawling out onto the metal guide rails of the car wash, I knelt down, the soap and water splattering all over me, and felt around. I located what I was looking for, ripped the box from under the car, and crawled sopping wet back inside, then reached under the front seat and yanked a wire.

"It's one thing to be followed to a fast food joint, it's another to have guys already there waiting for you. We were tapped and traced. They had a wire inside the car listening to us and a signal under the car so they could follow us," I said, handing her the tracking device.

"When was it put there?"

"Had to be at Marty's repair shop. I should have gone over the car after I got it back," I said, looking left and then right as we drove out of the car wash, relieved that we had finally lost the men trailing us.

"I've got to get home and change clothes. I'm a freaking sponge!" I yelped.

"Tight, wet clothes. Kind of sexy—except for the soap." She grinned and wiped a large mound of suds off me, tossing it out the car window.

"You're taking the fact that we're being stalked pretty cavalierly," I said.

"Sometimes you have to take charge and change the energy. I've decided to stop being fearful around the issue of our safety and just see it all working out for us."

"Good," I said, thinking she was without a doubt the strangest woman I'd ever known…and wanting her even more.

CHAPTER FOURTEEN

I was greatly relieved to know that we were no longer tied to a tracking device and I could focus now on the source of the stones.

"Waterston Evers is the collector who arranged the private showing for Frank Anthony. We need to talk to him," I announced to Callie as I pulled on a clean, dry pair of jeans and blew my wet hair dry.

Callie rummaged through my closet and found a shirt for me. "Wear this. The light blue looks great on you," she said.

"Thanks." I kissed her soft, sweet lips. "Give me a minute to walk Elmo. He's been alone a lot lately and he's feeling neglected."

Jamming my feet into my tennis shoes, I hooked Elmo up to his lead. We headed out the front door. Callie walked along beside us.

Just across the street, with her back to us, was the most gorgeous Samoyed dog I'd ever seen. She was huge and fluffy, with snow-white hair, all brushed and sparkling in the sunlight. She was obviously new to the neighborhood. Elmo stopped short just outside the front door, stricken with her beauty. He plopped his butt down on the ground, threw his head back and howled like I'd never heard him howl—a howl that bordered on a wolf whistle. He jumped up, dragging me with him across the street, and circled the dog, giving her the once over. Elmo had good taste. She was hot. Then she turned to face us, revealing a very pointy muzzle and small, squinty eyes. Elmo froze. He snorted. He turned. He did a full body shake and marched on, never looking back.

"Did you see that?" I asked Callie. "He thought she was gorgeous until she turned around and he got a look at her face. He likes gorgeous blondes with a great ass, but the front has to be as good as the rear. He's a lot like me, actually."

"Animals see beauty and judge it just like we do," Callie explained. "But I think Elmo was a little too critical of her. He should have gotten to know her before rejecting her over something as superficial as her nose."

"He's a guy. He's not going to take time to get to know her." I nodded ahead at Elmo's nicely formed hindquarters and his matching, dangling accessories. "He knows what he's got to offer. Check those chalangas! A guy like Elmo's got options, Callie." I smirked proudly, and Callie laughed at both of us.

❖

Callie located Waterston Evers's phone number in the directory, along with his address in La Canada Flintridge. With that in hand, we drove north on Highway 2, exiting up into the foothills, and wound our way around an elegant old neighborhood with houses that looked more midwestern than Californian, pulling up in front of a three-story stone-built Tudor. An elderly silver-haired man with a pear-shaped body answered our ring and admitted to being Waterston Evers. I introduced Callie and myself.

"You are the most gorgeous woman I believe I've ever laid eyes on," Mr. Evers said, missile-locked on Callie's frame. "That hair. Is it natural?"

I realized again what a knockout Callie was to the uninitiated.

"Yes, it is," Callie replied sweetly.

"Waterston Evers is just one step short of plopping down on his ass and howling," I said like a ventriloquist, never moving my lips.

"We wondered if you might have information about this cuneiform fragment," Callie asked as I produced the stone from my pocket.

Mr. Evers looked at the fragment as one might a dog that one had given up for missing, only to have it reappear years later. "It's the death stone I sold to a Mr. Frank Anthony and his people."

He stepped back to allow us inside his foyer. We followed his large derriere, like imprinted ducklings, to an overstuffed study that my nose told me was in dire need of dusting.

"Least important pieces in my collection," Mr. Evers said, lowering his sizeable frame into a well-worn leather armchair liberally stained with numerous liquids, the origins of which I did not wish to contemplate.

"You heard Mr. Anthony died," I said.

He paused. "No, I had no idea. Are you investigators or some such?"

"We're writers," I said.

"I never speak with the press." Mr. Evers tried to rise in indignation, but his was not a chassis that could swiftly throw us out.

"We're not press, we're screenwriters. A friend of ours—you met her, Barrett Silvers—was attacked recently and is in the hospital badly burned. We're trying to help find out who was responsible."

A mangy little dog snarffled into the room, clawing at the rugs as if grubbing for worms, and then deposited its body in the center of the floor and scratched. There were spots on its balding hide where it had made itself bleed, and I wanted to suggest a vet but then decided I was already interfering in enough lives without taking on Mr. Evers's psoriasis-ridden mixed-breed.

"Nice man. I'm sorry to hear of his death, and about Miss Silvers. Mr. Anthony was a knowledgeable man with a great appreciation for Egyptian antiquities. Knew more about them than most, I would say."

"You said 'Mr. Anthony and his people.' Did Frank Anthony have someone else with him the day he visited you?" I asked.

"Yes, Ms. Silvers, of course, and a man and woman not at all interested in antiquities. Mr. Anthony sat right here at this table and examined the stones with a glass while I gave his three guests a tour of the grounds. Fuji hated the man. Yeah-yus." Mr. Evers dissolved into baby talk at the mere mention of the little rat-dog's name and bent to scratch its head. "And Fuji was terrified of the woman. Don't know why. She never spoke a word, but Fuji just has a sense about people."

"Do you, by any chance, remember their names?" Callie asked.

He got up slowly and went over to a rolltop desk whose top had not been lowered in decades, if one could judge by the papers, envelopes, books, and receipts jutting out of every cubicle. He rummaged for a while as Callie and I rolled our eyes at one another over Fuji, who was blithely peeing on the Oriental rug as if that were where she routinely went. From the smell of the room, I suspected it was.

"Ah, here it is...knew I'd written it down. The two other people with him were Mr. Caruthers and a Ramona Mathers."

My eyes lit up. "Would you happen to know what the writing on the death stone means?"

"Sanskrit or Egyptian word. I looked it up when I purchased them years ago. Let me double-check to make certain before I say." He shuffled over to the bookshelf and stood on tiptoe to pull down several dusty volumes. Holding the stone in his left hand, he opened the largest volume with his right. His eyes moved back and forth from stone to book, book to stone, for what seemed like an eternity.

"Cloth," he announced soundly. "Like bathing cloth," he elaborated.

"This hot piece of evidence contains the word *washcloth*?" I asked.

"Well, that's the modern equivalent, I guess." He smiled for the first time. "What is it you were looking for?" he inquired.

"A list of names," I said.

"Well, I'm afraid it's not a phone book," he chortled.

Mr. Evers offered us tea, and before I could stop her, Callie accepted. I shot her a look that said she must be mad.

"I have an overpowering desire for tea," she whispered. "I follow my urges."

He led the way to a moldy, formal dining room, whose red velvet curtains, if shaken, would have given off enough dirt and sand to make Lawrence of Arabia feel at home. He offered us a seat at the end of a long, dark, mahogany dining-room table and poured the tea. I crossed my eyes at Callie, letting her know that pausing for a tea party was making me nuts. Callie asked Mr. Evers about his work, and he launched into a dissertation on the carbon dating of Egyptian antiquities that sent me into an alpha state.

"I'm a medical doctor, but I haven't practiced in years. My father wanted me to be a doctor, so I did it to oblige him. After his death, I returned to archeology, my first love." He elongated the word love while staring at Callie, and I realized we were invited to tea because he apparently had a crush on her.

Callie asked if he knew anything about muscle relaxants.

"Are you asking if I know how to relax muscles?" he purred. I could feel my blood pressure rising. We were moving into the dirty old man arena, where every phrase would be repeated and given a sexual meaning.

I jumped in. "She means do you have any expertise, as a physician, with muscle relaxants. Barrett Silvers collapsed in a restaurant while eating lunch, eyes frozen open, all bodily function shut down. The hospital said one of the possible causes could be an overdose of muscle relaxants."

He hated that I'd interfered with his game, but answered my question professionally. "Tubocurare, of course, is the most common, but it doesn't sound like that's what it was." Everston went to a shelf and retrieved a large reference book with some papers tucked in it. "Interesting you should bring that up. I was looking at South American tribes and their burial rites, and I came across an article on a substance the natives refer to as Batuki Tatungawa. It's a poison made from various chondodendron vines and laced with snake venom, but the piece de resistance, so the natives believe, is marinating it in poisonous toad venom. Exceptionally poisonous toads in those parts, big as sewer rats. The resulting serum in high doses, fired from a blowgun, could flatten a full-grown tapir." Evers pushed the article in Callie's direction and said he was going to the kitchen for some teacakes and would be right back.

"What's a tapir?" Callie whispered.

"In Hollywood, it's the opposite of film her. In South America I think it's a big hairy animal with hooves."

"Very funny," Callie replied, distracted by the pages she was skimming. She whispered excitedly, "Suppose I put a deadly ampoule of this stuff in a vial between my teeth, kissed you, used my tongue to force the plunger in, and shot this stuff into your neck?"

"If you did, you'd have the most agile set of lips and tongue on the planet," I purred in imitation of our host.

"Look at this picture. The bulb's back in his jaw, then he transfers it to the front between his teeth, and he uses his tongue to release the poison."

"Maybe that's why the man in the parking garage was trying to get his mouth on my neck, and why he was breathing heavily through his nose. He had something in his mouth!"

Mr. Evers was back with the tiny little squares of cake covered in almond icing. Fuji scratched endlessly beneath my feet, hurtling an infestation of fleas into my socks, or so I imagined. Infused with the idea of escaping, I downed a few gulps of tea, suddenly rose, thanked the man profusely for the information, and towed Callie to the door. Waterston Evers looked mildly distressed at losing his fantasy woman, but I was sure he'd have his pear-bottom back in the sagging leather chair in the study before I had the key in the ignition. I groused all the way to the car that I hated sexual innuendo from the unkempt.

Callie waved off my complaints, far more interested in the fact that it sounded like Barrett Silvers's attacker was South American, if one could judge from the poison.

"Who are you calling now?" Callie asked as I dialed.

"Ramona Mathers," I said, having dug her phone number out of my wallet.

❖

She answered almost immediately. "Ramona, this is Teague Richfield. We met at Frank Anthony's home right after he died,"

"You're the reporter with the glorious green eyes whom I tried to take to dinner," she said smoothly. "But you turned me down."

"Not for lack of wanting." I smiled. "You knew of course that Barrett Silvers was nearly killed, and I wondered if you could help me out as it relates to that?"

She sighed in mock petulance. "I hate it when the object of my fantasies turns out to be just another person wanting something from me. I have no idea why anyone would harm Ms. Silvers. In fact, Frank and I offered Barrett Silvers a job. She was complaining about the tawdry assignments she'd been given recently, something about procuring girls. At any rate, Frank, who was a very kind and generous man, told her to move back to Oklahoma and go to work for him."

"Doing what?" I asked.

"Frank had dozens of companies."

"Who do you suppose had the death stone delivered to Barrett Silvers?" I asked.

"Delivered? Frank gave it to her himself, right after we left Waterston Evers's house. He told Silvers that the word on the rock meant *towel* and joked that maybe it was really an ancient country club chit that gentlemen had to present to get into the baths. He said, 'Carry this as a reminder to wipe off the bullshit.'"

I sat frozen in thought. Frank Anthony gave the death stone to Barrett right after Frank purchased it.

"Are we through talking for now?" she asked. "Because I'm having a massage."

"Yes, yes, thanks so much." I hung up. "There must have been two," I blurted out and dialed Waterston Evers, asking him about the possibility of two stones.

"Didn't I mention that? Yes, two identical. He bought them both."

I thanked him and hung up.

"Two stones," I said to Callie. "And Caruthers and Mathers knew there were two stones."

"So if the stone delivered to Barrett at Orca's belonged to Frank Anthony, where the hell's the stone Frank gave Barrett at Waterston Evers's house? Maybe Caruthers and Mathers want to know that too."

"And why didn't Barrett tell us she had another stone?" Callie asked.

"Because she's got the stone that counts," I said, wheeling the car around and heading for Los Feliz.

❖

We pulled up in front of Barrett's house in Los Feliz. I checked my watch. It was early enough that her housekeeper would still be on duty. In fact, I surmised she was probably staying there to care for Barrett's dogs while Barrett was in the hospital. We climbed the steep steps to the entrance of her beautifully landscaped, fifties deco home overlooking the hills. Callie rang the bell. Merika, a pretty, slender Japanese lady, answered the door.

"Miss Tee-kee!" Her face broke into a wide grin. "Oh." Her face turned grave. "Ms. Seebers in hose-pee-tal."

"How do you know her housekeeper? Have you spent the night here?" Callie whispered.

"Just visited…a party, I think, one time," I lied.

I told Merika I'd come over to pick out a few things for her to take up to the hospital for Barrett. Signaling Callie to keep Merika busy, I flew through Barrett's bedroom at warp speed checking dresser drawers, pants pockets, jewelry boxes, attaches, and anything else that might contain the stone. Nothing. I collected myself for a moment and began again, lifting the mattress to check under the edges, checking the rim of the platform bed, looking behind books and inside the medicine cabinet. After twenty minutes, I could hear Callie approaching loudly in order to give me warning.

"Merika, I'm feeling like I would like a drink. Would it be all right if I got myself something?" Callie asked.

Merika took Callie into the kitchen. "Soda pop? Water with lemon? Coffee, tea—"

"What kind of tea does Ms. Silvers drink?"

"Very nice tea. Special kind, uh…" She searched for the name. "In here." She tapped the little canister.

Callie reached inside the canister and extracted a teabag. "Could I boil some water and make a little of this?"

"I make." Merika turned to get a teapot, and Callie held the stone up for me to see. My eyes almost popped out of my head. In fact, I could barely contain myself as the water boiled, the tea brewed, and Callie drank, making pleasant conversation with Merika and grinning mischievously at me.

❖

Half an hour later we were back in the car, and I was bouncing up and down like a kid at Christmas.

"How did you know it was in the tea canister?" I said, comparing the two rocks to see if they differed. Barrett's stone was much smoother than the stone Frank Anthony had kept for himself.

"I had this uncontrollable urge to drink the tea at Waterston Evers's house, so I knew there was something else going on, because I would never drink tea in a house as dirty as his, so I knew the tea was connected to the stone in some way. Where are you going to keep these stones?"

I pulled my shirt open and dropped one stone into each side of my bra. Callie shot me a look.

"Can you think of a safer place?" I smirked. "No one's looked there lately." Callie put her hand inside my bra and my nipples hardened.

"Really?" she said. "I guess we'll have to do something about that."

"As much as I hate to say it, stop it," I moaned and Callie laughed.

❖

I asked Callie to thumb through the pages in Barrett's date book and see if there was anything that would help us. After much searching, she found a page on which Barrett had scribbled a 213 area code and a seven-digit number alongside the words *pick up/deliver/Benny Kaye*.

I picked up the cell phone and dialed the number. A rough voice answered, "Bono's!" I asked the man what kind of shop this was, and he replied curtly, "Who wants to know?"

"We're a delivery service, and we're sending someone over to pick up an order. We need an address."

"Hollywood and Vine," the man growled and hung up on me.

"It's not Benny Kaye's phone number, but definitely a place his friends shop for him," I said.

"I don't want to go to some sleazy store on Hollywood Boulevard in the middle of the night!" Callie said emphatically.

"We don't have to go in, but this might be our first tangible proof of Marathon's barter deals with their stars. Something's being picked up there, and I'd love to know what it is."

"We could go by Bono's tomorrow," Callie offered, leaning back against the headrest and looking highly seductive, but I was already driving west on Hollywood Boulevard.

"Stop trying to distract me from my work." I grinned at her.

CHAPTER FIFTEEN

An array of street people and addicts could be seen crawling out of their daytime hideaways to prowl through alleys piled high with dirty rags and bottles, their grocery carts brimming over with the treasures they'd collected.

I looked out the car window at a barefooted black man, an army blanket pulled up around him, swearing at an imaginary enemy from his bus bench. A woman somewhere between sixty and death walked aimlessly out into the street in front of our car. She was wearing red house slippers with big fuzzy balls on the end of them, and four layers of clothing, her red hair sprouting out of her turbaned headgear like spring onions. I glanced over at Callie, who was pale and silent.

"I can't stand to look at this," she said quietly.

"You can't save everyone."

"I wouldn't try. We choose our life, and it's ours for whatever reason."

I was incredulous that Callie could believe people actually chose to live this way.

"Well, if everything's predestined, then there's no point in trying to change our lives," I replied.

"We have the power to change everything if we believe we can." Her voice seemed self-condemning.

"Makes no sense to me," I said. "But if what you say is true, then you chose this trip to the slums this evening."

"No, you chose this trip. I chose to follow you, and right now I don't feel good about it. "

I slowed up in front of a sleazy storefront with homemade lettering above the door spelling out "Bono's." There were no parking spaces available, so I had to drive around the block, which gave us a close-up look at the city side streets where drug deals were taking place out in the open. An old man was shooting a syringe into his dirty arm in full view of anyone driving by. I opened the car door.

"I thought you said we weren't going in!" Callie's voice registered alarm.

"Cops patrol this area all the time. Come on, two minutes," I said, and she jumped out of the car and followed me into the store where filthy inflatable blowup dolls with plastic holes for vaginas hung from the ceiling by a string. The wooden bins lining the walls contained boxes of dildos, edible fantasy fragrances, and large leather straps with little metal brads embedded in them. A middle-aged man with a three-day beard looked up and gave Callie an appreciative whistle.

"Honey, take it from Bono, you could be a star," he said, poking a dirt-encrusted fingernail in her direction. Callie pulled back from the offending digit as if stung by it.

"Marathon Studios pickup," I said flatly.

"You called earlier," he said. "Nobody ordered nothin'."

"Maybe it's under a different name." I turned his grimy order book around so I could see the names. He promptly turned the book back in his direction and flipped to earlier pages. "Last order picked up by…Barnett…" He struggled to decipher the name, but I recognized it immediately as Barrett's scribbled signature. He looked up. "So what do you need? Leather body harness, inflatable dolls…" His eyes never left mine. "Rainin' outside?"

Rainin'… The gears suddenly meshed in my mind. *Rain, sleet... snow. Benny Kaye is a coke head.*

"No rain…snow maybe," I gave him a resolute stare. Callie watched us as if we were crazy, and we were. Him for having it and me for asking.

Bono reached under the countertop, maintaining eye contact.

"We need to go, Tee," Callie whispered with desperation in her voice.

Bono pulled out a small plastic bag containing white powder.

"Put it on the tab," I said and reached for the package.

He gave a low laugh in appreciation of my bravado and pulled a gun from beneath the counter. "You ain't from Marathon. Into the back room!" he ordered. I glanced over at Callie. This was an undesirable turn of events, and definitely the wrong part of town in which to be towed into a back room at gunpoint. I glanced back at the door, praying some sleazeball customer would come in long enough to distract Bono, but no such luck. My mind flashed on my gun, which was safely locked in my car. Bono, his pants dangling off his skinny behind and his faded blue and white plaid shirt pungent with body odor, herded us into a closet so small that, side by side, neither of us could get our hands up above our waist. The floor was painted brown and smelled of urine. The wall, two inches from my face, had a variety of fluid stains dripping from it, colors I could see even in the dark.

"Shit," was all I could say, my heart pounding.

Outside we could hear Bono talking to someone on the phone, his voice raspy and hushed but still loud enough for us to hear. He was telling someone that we'd tried to pass ourselves off as Marathon employees. I was pretty certain it wasn't the police he was calling.

I asked Callie what she had on her, in her purse or in her pockets. "Just give me a running inventory," I said nervously.

"Keys, fingernail file, handkerchief?"

"Try to reach the file."

The next five minutes were spent wiggling around trying to get inside her purse and, purely by feel, to locate the file without dropping it to the floor. She passed it to me between her third and fourth fingers, and I got a frantic grip on it. I maneuvered myself over to the lock, sucked in my breath, and yanked my arm up, nearly dislocating my shoulder. My eyes were getting used to the dark, and I could see that the inside edge of the dirty, wooden door was chewed and clawed, as if others had tried to make their way out of this closet. If I could just wedge the file in between the latch and the battered wall, I might be able to pull the door open. I made a few quiet attempts, but the lock was sturdier than I'd originally thought.

"Fuck." I rested a moment.

Bono was at the door, his mouth pressed against it. I could smell his beer-stale breath even through the hairline crack. "He's sendin' someone who'll put the fear of God in you, believe me. Marathon don't fuck around."

I waited until he moved away from the door, and I could hear him busily straightening up the counter and opening the cash drawer as if holding people against their will were routine. It was five, ten minutes at the most, and the front door of Bono's shop swung open with such force that the bell at the top clanged in distress. Within seconds our door was unlocked and a man yanked Callie out by her shirtfront, banging her head on the door jam.

"Don't hurt her, you fuckhead!" I yelled.

"Teague!" Callie's warning came too late as another goon dragged us across the store, through the grimy front doors, and out into the street, where we were thrown into the backseat of a waiting car. The man behind the wheel sped away with us as his partner leaned over the front seat and pointed a gun at us. I realized this could easily be our last trip anywhere with our hearts still beating.

"Who are you and where are you taking us?" I demanded. The man in the front seat leaned forward and pressed the silver metal gun barrel into my forehead, the universal symbol for shut up. We were headed west toward the ocean, not a good sign. *They must be thinking of drowning us or dumping us along the forested coastline.* My mind was about to crash from overload. Should I make a stand now, or wait until I had more maneuvering room? *If I make a move now, maybe I can cause them to wreck the car and get somebody's attention, rather than have to face them alone on the beach or in the woods*. I clasped Callie's small hand in mine, sorry I had ever endangered her life and wanting only to get out of this mess and be with her.

Suddenly, the car swerved right, through the gates of Bel-Air, moving swiftly through the streets the wealthy called home. I felt relieved. Dying in a nice neighborhood seemed preferable to dying in a remote area.

The driver swerved again, this time into a large rear driveway of a palatial two-story mansion. The driver got out, leaving the door ajar, and rang the bell. Our captor spoke to someone who was apparently irritated that we'd been brought here. There was more murmuring and muttering, and finally the two men dragged us both out, holding us by the napes of our necks as a mother dog would drag small pups. I decided to find out who we were meeting before I created a stir.

Inside, we were taken to a cozy den with a fireplace and a small leather couch facing two chairs across a teak coffee table. A fire blazed in the fireplace, throwing odd shadows all around the room. Things were looking a lot less violent and decidedly upscale. I tried to steady my breathing. The men deposited us on the sofa, side by side, and backed away, guarding the door. Callie and I exchanged glances, wondering who would appear next. Moments later, Robert Isaacs in a velvet dinner jacket, looking like a Hollywood leading man, strolled into the room, his brow knitted together over the dilemma in his den. He stopped short and then gave an odd smile.

"Well, hello, Callie. Why am I not surprised to see you?" he said.

"Hello, Robert," she replied.

"You two know each other?" My breath was faster now.

"Intimately," Isaacs said. "We were married for ten minutes, isn't that right, Callie?"

I looked at Callie in utter shock, but she didn't look back.

"I heard you were traveling with Ms. Richfield. Another in a long line of your girls." And he grinned at the pain he was inflicting on both of us.

"And which of your thugs told you that?" Callie asked coldly.

He moved closer to examine the large, bloody bump on Callie's forehead. "I see someone has managed to strike you in the head. Are they still living?" he asked slyly. Callie ignored my incredulous stares in her direction. Isaacs waved off the guards, asking them to simply keep an eye out at the entrances while he talked to us. He offered us a glass of wine and assured us that, in spite of the dangerous-looking men who had delivered us to him, we were in no danger.

"Certainly not from me. Now, why are you pretending to be Marathon employees? I could, on behalf of Marathon, prosecute you, you know, but instead, I'll simply ask you to hand over the merchandise you stole. The stone." He held out his hand.

"I stole nothing, and the stone doesn't belong to you or me," I said.

"I just purchased it recently." He smiled convincingly.

"What's so important about a rock?" I pressed my luck.

"It's not necessary to know what's important about other people's property, only to know that what you have doesn't belong to you."

"I'm interested because this is the second time in two days we've been roughed up for it, but you're a day late. We no longer have the stone. Lee Talbot's men took it from us yesterday."

"You're lying," he said, and I felt the stones move inside my shirt.

"Call him!" I said with my best poker face. "Call him now." It was a gamble, but I was pretty sure Isaacs wouldn't call.

"I'll contact Talbot tomorrow. If he doesn't have the stones, I'll be seeing you again."

His refusal to contact Talbot led me to believe that whatever they were doing, they weren't doing it together. He obviously didn't want Talbot knowing what he was up to.

"The gentlemen who brought you here will give you a lift back to your car," Isaacs said.

"No thanks. We'll catch a cab." I took Callie's arm and walked past the staring goons.

"We're not through with each other yet, Callie!" Isaacs called after us.

I pulled her through the front door before anyone could have a change of heart about our departure. When we hit the street, I kept up a fast pace to Sunset, wanting to make sure we weren't being followed.

"He's gonna find out Talbot doesn't have the stones, and he'll kill us. You don't know who you're dealing with here!" Callie panted at my side.

"You married that guy! Are you still married to him?"

"Of course not," she said.

"Of course not. Well, how the hell would I know?"

"I was a kid. My friends all thought he was wonderful. I was married for ten minutes…"

"What is this 'married for ten minutes'? No one is married for ten minutes."

"A year."

"Good, now we're talking English. You were married for a year and…"

"My kid brother came out here with us to work for Robert Isaacs, his hotshot brother-in-law. Isaacs was working for Artinia Records. Drugs and the record business are synonymous."

"Incidentally, lying is bad karma. Am I right?" I said, angry over her deceit.

"Robert knew people were giving my brother drugs, and he did nothing to stop it. In fact, toward the end, he was paying my brother in drugs himself, rather than in cash. Another of his barter deals. My brother died of a drug overdose at a club on Sunset. He was so young and green and stupid that he accidentally OD'd," Callie said.

"So that's why I got the passionate kiss on the first night I met you, and that's why you wanted to travel with me. Someone who's mad about you like 'all your other girls,' and that's why you've been fine with our risking our lives to crack this story, because you knew it would lead you to Isaacs and your revenge. The word you hate, by the way!"

"Teague, I came out here to be with you, but when you told me about Barrett working at Marathon, I knew that's where Robert Isaacs was. Then you mentioned the barter system and I knew."

"Knew what? That Isaacs is our killer? Like you 'psychically' knew at the shareholders' meeting that it was Isaacs's voice behind that partition? You knew it was Isaacs's voice because you used to wake up next to it! You know, you're making it real hard for me to separate the psychic stuff from the grief-stricken, pissed-off, ex-wife stuff. And just for the record, you fucking lied to me, Callie! Lied!"

"I never lied to you."

"Okay, let's be completely accurate. You committed a sin of omission by not telling me that you were: A) married to a *man*, B) married to a man who's a *crook*, C) married to a man, who's a crook, who's trying to *kill* me!"

A cab picked us up and we rode through the darkness in silence.

"And you slept with that son of a bitch," I threw in for good measure.

"Not really," her voice drifted.

"And I suppose you never climaxed with him either?"

The cab driver's eyes darted to the rearview mirror, and the cab swung over the center line, forcing another car to swerve and honk violently.

"Quit looking back here and watch where the hell you're driving!" I yelled at the cabbie, and he cut his eyes away.

❖

Back at Bono's, our car was parked right where we'd left it, the hubcaps miraculously still attached. Two half-dazed addicts lounged across the front fender of our car. I was too hurt and mad over what I'd learned about Callie to be frightened of the half dead. "Get your fried, fat asses off the hood of my car before I blow your balls off!" I shouted at the two men, who looked at me as if I were the societal outcast.

Hollywood nightlife was getting darker by the hour, and it matched the cold, gray wind that swept across my heart. Callie Rivers had lied to me, and I didn't know how deep that lie went. Maybe it went all the way to the heart of our relationship. After all, Isaacs had touched her, had owned her, had gotten her body in exchange for his name. The rage in me was molten, flowing through my veins in a thick, angry, leadlike mass that weighed down my desire to even breathe.

CHAPTER SIXTEEN

At home, we sat in our robes curled up on the couch, having washed Hollywood's back streets off our auras. Callie sipped Swee-Touch-Nee tea, her latest Gelson's discovery, while I berated her. I couldn't seem to stop. My pride was damaged. First Barrett, then Callie. Apparently, in the lover department, I was a poor judge of character.

Callie's small, slender fingers juggled an ice pack in an attempt to keep it in place on her bruised forehead. "In choosing to marry Isaacs, I set up the entire series of events that led to my brother's death," Callie mused.

"In choosing to take drugs, your brother set up the entire series of events that led to your brother's death." I wanted to lessen her pain, but I was still feeling my own. "I guess being figuratively screwed by a crook is unforgivable, being literally screwed by one is unbearable. Just out of curiosity, how can a cosmically in-tune, spiritual psychic still have a little corner of her heart reserved for absolute hatred? According to your beliefs, isn't the cosmos supposed to take care of that for you?"

"I'm part of the cosmos." Callie's eyes glistened with tears. "The part that won't let Robert Isaacs get away." She saw my flat, emotionless expression. "Look, Teague, I know you're angry and hurt." She tried to take my hand but I pulled it away, for the first time feeling nothing for Callie Rivers.

"Don't touch me," I said.

Elmo hoisted his heavy frame off the floor, walked to the far corner of the room, flopped down against the wall, and let out a loud, forlorn groan, refusing to take sides.

The death stones rested on the coffee table looking innocently like dominoes. Who would think they could cause this much trouble? I stared at the symbols. After a long pause, I made an attempt to disassociate from my emotional state and focus on this story that had now become my work.

"Evers said it meant *bathing cloth* or *towel*."

"Same difference, I guess," Callie said, seemingly detached as well.

I picked up a pad and pencil and began doodling little squares across the top of the page. "Now how do you suppose that symbol came to be towel?" I asked. I scribbled the word Towel, then Twl, and Towl, Tal. I looked up at Callie, light dawning in my eyes. "Towel, could be Tal, as in Talbot. Maybe Frank Anthony was holding the rock when he died because he was trying to say Talbot, and not Isaacs, murdered him. I'll bet Talbot knows everything about the barter deals. He worked too closely with Isaacs not to. We've got to get into his house. He'd never leave any incriminating evidence at the studio."

❖

That night I slept with my back to Callie, not touching, not wanting. How could I have trusted that Callie Rivers wanted me? She wasn't able to give herself fully to me because the whole relationship with me was a cover-up to get her to Isaacs. It was obviously him, and not me, who held her focus. Thinking about it created a dull pain in my chest where my heart used to be.

❖

I took a chance, at nine the next morning, that Talbot wouldn't be in his office and I phoned his secretary. I told her Paramount's T. Elliott Golden had a gift for Mr. Talbot and wanted his home address. She gave it promptly.

At eleven o'clock, I stopped off at North Hollywood Magic, a prop design studio. I left Callie in the lobby to look at all the miniature motion picture props and sets while I went to a small office in the back. Peter Trayber had spent the last forty years of his life designing everything from tap shoes for terriers to cameras hidden in high heels. Rumpled and disarming, Peter rose to shake hands and gave me his big, boyish grin. I explained that I needed something replicated right away. I showed him the death stone.

"A domino?" He examined the stone.

"An ancient rock that somebody's trying to kill me to get."

"Can you leave it with me?" Peter asked, never reacting to my remark that someone was trying to kill me for it. In Hollywood, *kill* was a word everyone used but nobody meant.

"I can let you make a rubbing of the inscription, the dimensions, weight, and texture. Other than that, I've got to take it with me."

Peter smiled and said copying it would be a cinch.

Twenty minutes later, I went back to the lobby and collected Callie, telling her I'd just bought us some life insurance.

"So you'll have more stones than Mick Jagger." She grinned, trying to get back on friendlier terms.

"Cute," I replied. "Let's get some lunch."

❖

I pulled into Stanton's Restaurant on Ventura Boulevard, forced to valet park since on-the-street parking was at a premium. Inside the restaurant, the bar was packed, the acoustics were terrible, and the chairs uncomfortable, but the bread was sourdough and arrived in large, hot hunks, which was worth all the inconvenience it took to get here.

"Look, I'm really sorry," Callie began.

"No problem," I lied.

"Stop being that way."

"What way?"

"That way that says you don't trust me," she said loudly, and a woman at a nearby table turned to listen. This was my first realization that Callie Rivers liked to air her unhappy feelings out in the open, and right now, her unhappy feelings could have filled a soccer stadium.

"Just because I was married a million years ago doesn't mean I betrayed you!" she said loudly. I raised my hand, signaling her to lower her voice, but she ignored me. "I didn't *know* you! You're making a big deal out of nothing! You need to get past this!" Her voice scaled up an octave, putting us in contention for the next reality series: *Gay Gatherings Gone Bad.*

"Excuse me," I whispered, demonstrating how to argue in public places, "could you lower your voice? I don't really want all these people knowing my business."

"I don't care about these people. They're not going home with me. You are!"

"I have a right to be upset! I just learned that you were married to a despicable human being, who may be a murderer, who, P.S., fucked you. None of which, ironically enough, would have kept me from loving you had you only told me rather than pretending to be someone else! Let's just focus on the story, okay?"

I tried to calm down. "I have a plan to get us into Talbot's house to find out his involvement."

"I never pretended to be someone else." Callie refused to drop the argument.

"You'll deliver flowers. Flowers so huge they'll create a diversion that will allow me time to get inside while you're getting them situated with the housekeeper." I ripped into my sourdough like tyrannosaurus rex.

"You know in your heart I never lied to you, and I don't think delivering flowers to Talbot's house is a good idea," she said, maintaining two conversations at once.

"It's so simple it will work. If you don't want to do it, I'll figure out how to do it by myself," I threatened.

"Why do you want to put us in danger like this?"

"There's no danger. Danger is not telling the woman you're sleeping with that you were once married to a slimy crook," I said sweetly, getting the last blow in. "If anything goes wrong, you say this is your first day doing deliveries and then burst into tears and run out of the house," I instructed.

"What about you?" she asked worriedly.

"Stay on the back side of the house after I'm in and listen for me."

A tall, thin waiter swished over to us and brandished his pad and pencil. "Do you two need more time…or would that just make things worse?"

❖

Later in the afternoon, we swung back by Peter Trayber's and picked up the fake stones. He'd done a brilliant job. I asked him to rough up the corners on the two fake stones so that I could tell them from the real ones. The duplication was that good. I then put all four stones in my jeans pocket and zipped it shut, confident I could tell the real from the fake just by feel.

The next stop was a florist, where I purchased a magnificent flower arrangement the size of downtown Detroit, and I wedged it into the car between Callie and me, this time having her drive. I was barely able to keep the huge vase of flowers upright, and it occasionally sloshed water on us. She drove over the hill to Bel-Air conversing through three layers of orchids and tiger lilies, her blue eyes peering at me like some exotic bird behind the heavily scented foliage.

"I have a very bad feeling about this," she said.

"Relax. You're giving a guy this terrific vase of flowers for free!"

We drove down the 300 block of Bel-Air Canyon Road to make certain we had Talbot's house staked out. I had Callie let me out fifty yards away. Once I was in position behind a shrub, Callie pulled up in the Jeep and struggled to lift out the huge vase of exotic flowers.

A doorman was already holding the front door open for Callie, who came staggering up the walkway. She thanked him profusely, saying she was asked to deliver these to Mr. Talbot. The doorman tried to take them from her, but she said it would be easier if she could just put them on the hall table. As she was about to deposit them, she feigned a loss of balance, and for ten seconds she and the doorman were totally occupied trying to keep the flowers from hitting the marble floor. I slipped inside the foyer right behind the doorman, thanking God for the lack of hall mirrors, and hid behind an enormous oriental room divider. Callie blushed and apologized and left the doorman in a huff, thanking him for his kindness.

From behind the Chinese room divider, I checked my watch. It was 5:45 p.m. The doorman paced and tidied and dusted, as if he sensed something wasn't quite right. I wore no cologne, so that even a sensitive-nosed doorman wouldn't be able to detect my presence in the house. At 6:30 p.m. he went back to the kitchen and told the maid that he was going home. She nodded, saying she was putting Mr. Talbot's dinner on and she would be going herself soon.

Suddenly I heard the scuffling of feet, as if someone were being subdued, and then a few groans and moans. I peeked out through the crack in the Chinese room divider to see the doorman with his back to me, and the maid sitting up on a low countertop, her arms clutching him, her legs wrapped around him while he was banging and grinding away in her. She let out a series of whimpers as he quickly finished off inside her, tucked himself back in his pants, helped her slide off the countertop, and gave her a brisk pat on the bottom, in a routine they obviously looked forward to. "See ya tomorrow, my sweet," he said and whistled out the door as she straightened her uniform.

Callie's right. Never eat off a countertop until you've wiped it down.

My legs were cramping from my tenuous crouch, but I didn't dare move. When the doorman left the house, I plopped onto my butt and rubbed my legs, certain the maid would not be touring the domain.

Then I heard the kitchen door open and the scurry of toenails on marble. My worst nightmare was unfolding. Robert Talbot had a dog, and it was headed into the living room. I held my breath. Maybe he was an old dog without a keen sense of smell. But no. In less than thirty seconds, a compact Boston bulldog flew around the corner of the Chinese room divider and into my arms, snorting and licking and letting out a playful growl.

"Rockingham!" I heard the maid calling. "Rockingham, dinner."

"Rockingham," I whispered, trying to hold the squirming animal. "Go get your dinner." Rockingham wasn't leaving. A minute later, I could hear the maid shuffling into the living room searching for Rockingham and calling his name. I was frantic. I had to get the dog away from me long enough to distract the maid and to allow myself time to move to a new hiding place. The dog was making loud snorting sounds.

"Rockingham, are you behind that divider?" The maid was bearing down on my location.

I grabbed Rockingham by the snout and buttocks and rolled him out into the center of the room like a fourteen-pound bowling ball heading for a strike against the Ming vase in the corner. The maid let out a shriek, steadied the vase, and began shouting at the dog, saying he knew better than to roughhouse in the living room.

"Out, out, out!" She chased the hapless animal through the room, back into the kitchen, and outside.

Sorry, Rockingham, but it's you or me, I thought.

I made my way to the back of the house, down a cavernous corridor to a large master suite, and checked the alarm box on the wall to make sure the master suite wasn't independently armed. I unlocked and opened the window, letting out a low bird whistle. Callie came around the back of the house clutching her heart.

"My God, I thought they'd found you," she gasped, and I was pleased she was concerned.

"Had to wait for the doorman to quit boffing the maid. He's having a better day than I am." I grinned. "Didn't take long." I helped her over the window ledge just as Rockingham rounded the corner at a dead run. Callie let out a small yelp at seeing how close the dog had come to getting a piece of her leg. I put my hand over her mouth and towed her into a large walk-in closet, suggesting we make camp until the maid went home.

At 7:30 p.m. the front door clicked open and shut. I slipped out of the closet and peeked out of the large bedroom window in time to see a car pick up the uniformed maid. We were safe, but the alarm system had been set by the maid, so we couldn't open any doors. Other than that, we had the house to ourselves.

"Go through his desk drawers and his bedside table," I said.

"What am I looking for?" Callie asked.

"Bankbooks, date books, letters. Anything that'll tell us if Talbot is involved in the barter deals or skimming studio money off the top."

I booted up Talbot's computer and began going through his files. They contained a list of names and phone numbers from his last two trips to the Cannes Film Festival, an organizing list for a charity golf tournament, a host of personal correspondence, legal documents, and other miscellany.

Callie was staring intently at a photo of Talbot at a ground-breaking ceremony at the studio. "This picture has something to do with the murder. I know it psychically. I feel the hairs stand up on the back of my neck when I look at it."

"Looks like a studio ground-breaking," I said.

"I don't know, but I'm taking it," Callie replied and lifted it from the bookshelf.

We heard a sound in the hallway and looked at each other, our hearts in our throats. It flashed through my mind that no one had opened any of the doors. There was someone in the house who had been here all along. But who? Gooseflesh the size of eggs crawled along my arms as I signaled Callie to be quiet and follow me.

Chapter Seventeen

We crept down the dimly lit hallway and there, standing in the shadows at the end of the columned corridor, were two men. Even in the fading light and with the addition of dreadlocks, I could see that one of the men was Spider Eye, the man who'd brought the stone to Barrett at Orca's. Apparently, now that we were back in L.A., Raider had passed the baton and we were being handed over to the first string, honest-to-God, serious killers.

The ceilings were roughly twenty feet tall and the corridor sixteen feet wide. That said, there still wasn't much room to outmaneuver two killers, even if I had a plan for doing it, which I didn't.

"Your curiosity has killed a cat," Spider Eye said, almost getting the phrase correct. "Finish them, Gigante!"

Gigante was a short, medium-built man who had apparently received his giant name from the size of his head, which lolled back and forth on his neck as if it were too great a burden to be carried by a man of moderate frame. He headed our way.

"Get behind me," I whispered to Callie. "We've got to keep Gigante between us and Spider Eye, in case Spider Eye decides to shoot." After I said it, I realized how stupid it was of me to be giving instructions as if I knew what the hell I was doing. I was just babbling, thinking out loud in a panic, and hoping to get lucky.

"I don't think they do things with guns, Teague. Remember the poison and the ampoules in their mouths?"

Fear of being murdered on the spot in some bizarre fashion sent adrenaline coursing through my body.

"Just chant or pray or do something with white light. Not that

I'm relying on it at this juncture in my evolution, but do it anyway," I muttered with a sarcasm that masked fear.

Gigante lunged forward to grab me, and I thrust out my left leg, smashing the sole of my foot solidly into his kneecap and hearing it crunch. He bent over, giving me a momentary height advantage, and I unwound, slamming my right elbow down on his head and glancing up for only an instant to see Spider Eye stripping off his shoulder holster. *Not a good sign,* I thought somewhere in the back of my brain. *Why is he taking things off at a time when he should be coming after us?*

I yanked Gigante's head up by the hair and caught him under the chin with my knee in a pretty standard defensive combination series that hurt like hell for me. I hoped it was equally good for him. Ignoring my own pain, I was about to angle a straight-leg punch into Gigante's jaw when suddenly, as if in poetic answer to my limited kickboxing techniques, Spider Eye dropped to his knees and bounced into a handstand position, knees tucked in tight. I recognized the move as capoeira, an exotic and lethal South American martial arts technique. He vaulted toward us and launched himself into the air about ten feet above our heads in a dramatic move designed to inflict psychological damage. Spider Eye was going for the kind of terror that immobilizes.

"Oh my God!" Callie screamed as he sailed overhead. "Get down. He's trying to decapitate us with his legs!"

I shoved Callie under him as he was airborne and rolled forward right behind her. He came down in what seemed like seconds behind us and literally bounced off the floor like a gymnast, doing a one-eighty in midair and spinning toward us again.

"Grab the gun!" I shouted to Callie as we raced past the spot where Spider Eye had dumped his holster. She swooped it up, and we ran the length of the corridor and rounded the corner into the living room, both men on our heels. We dove onto the floor behind Talbot's enormous L-shaped couch. I grabbed the gun from Callie and rose up over its white brocade back and fired. Nothing! The gun had misfired.

Spider Eye smiled widely, amused that his weapon had refused to turn against him. He sprang onto the couch and reached over the back, getting a hand on me just as Callie surprised me by pepper-spraying his face. He fell back hacking and choking, the legs of the tiny tattooed spider stretching and contracting with the skin around his eye as he wheezed and gasped for breath. Desperately seeking air, Spider Eye stood up, with admittedly cosmic timing, at the split second that Gigante pulled the trigger on his gun, accidentally shooting Spider Eye in the back. He fell forward and blood splattered onto the white brocade.

"*Dios mío*!" Gigante shouted, running to Spider Eye's side, apparently caring that he'd hit one of his own.

"You're fucked, Spider Eye!" I shouted.

"Don't antagonize them any further. Let's just get out of here!" Callie shouted, and we hit the front door at a dead run, setting off the burglar alarm.

❖

We were in our Jeep and down the street before any of the alarm-immune neighbors had even peeked out through their drapes.

"The servants didn't know those guys were in the house! They must have been there to kill Talbot, because they had no way of knowing we were coming," I said as we clambered into the car.

"What if that man recovers and identifies us?" Callie asked.

"I wouldn't worry about that. Professional hit men rarely share the details of their work with cops," I replied.

"Are they acrobatic killers? What are they?" Callie asked, shaken now.

"Capoeira. An ancient martial arts technique that originated with Brazil's African slave populations, who developed incredible foot moves in response to the brutality of the slave traders. Capoeira let them fight back even when their hands were chained. They were able to practice the art because they disguised it as acrobatics and dance. That's why all the back flips, cartwheels, and handstands. Now it's been adopted by street thugs, who work so quickly and so gracefully, you can almost become mesmerized into standing still while your assailant kills you. No wonder I couldn't break away from Spider Eye in the parking garage. Nice work with the pepper spray, by the way. Where did you get it?"

"Pepper spray and perfume are the two most important items a woman can carry. Both are immobilizing." She put her hand on my thigh and left it there as we drove. I felt an invincible warmth and a strong urge to take her to bed.

❖

The aerial shots of Talbot's lawn looked like a Winnebago convention. A local news anchor was broadcasting live: *"Lee Talbot, head of Marathon Studios, has been found dead in his home this morning, victim of a possible heart attack, although he had shown no previous history of heart problems. Only yesterday, Mr. Talbot had his home burglarized, a man found shot inside. It was theorized that perhaps the event precipitated the heart attack. Recently, another Marathon executive was badly burned by an unknown assailant, and now this morning, the trouble-plagued studio finds its leader dead. Without Talbot's powerful leadership, the studio's future is in question."*

"So Frank Anthony told Barrett that the list of names and other information about wrongdoing at Marathon was on the stone she had. Her boss, Robert Isaacs, president of the motion picture division, wants the stone with the list, but he doesn't want Talbot to know he's looking for it, remember? He wouldn't call him while we were there. Furthermore, he actually believed me when I said Talbot already had the stone. Now Talbot's dead. So it's reasonable to assume that Isaacs could be behind the attempts on Barrett's life, could have ordered Talbot's death, and could be the man behind Rita Smith's murder. After all, getting Eddie Smith signed was important to Isaacs's division and the financial health of the studio. It would be weird if you were married not just to a jackass, but to a murderer." After I said it, I felt bad, but Callie said nothing to retaliate, apparently hoping my venom would soon subside.

"We told Isaacs that Talbot had the stone, and now Talbot is dead," Callie fretted.

"Callie, you weren't responsible for your brother's death, and you're not responsible for Talbot's."

But Callie wasn't listening. "Now Robert Isaacs will be after us," she said, "because we have the stones and we know he killed Talbot."

I had been certain it was Talbot, and not Isaacs, Frank Anthony had tried to finger before he died. *How could I have been so wrong? Maybe Frank grabbing that rock when he died meant nothing. Who knows what anyone would clutch with his last dying breath.*

As if she could see into my mind, Callie suddenly said, "It means something. Frank Anthony was a smart man. He went to his grave trying to tell someone his killer's name."

"Frank Anthony is killed at his gym, shot once in the head and once in the chest and then set on fire. He's wearing his gym shorts and next to him is his gym bag and towel. Barrett Silvers gets a death stone delivered to her at Orca's and nearly gets kissed to death. Then I go to Frank Anthony's house, where Ramona Mathers tells me Frank died clutching a death stone. Caruthers says he didn't, but Waterston Evers confirms he sold Frank two death stones and Ramona Mathers tells us Frank Anthony gave one to Barrett that apparently matched the one he kept. The fragments say *Tal* on them."

"Or *washcloth*," Callie said.

"That's it. Or *washcloth*....or *towel*. Mathers ticked off the items found next to Frank. Gym bag, rock, and towel. Maybe Frank Anthony was saying the answer was on the towel."

"You mean like DNA bloodstains?"

"I don't know what I mean." I grabbed the phone and dialed Wade at the police department. Miraculously, he was at his desk, where one rarely finds a police officer. He could tell by my voice something was up.

"Have you got everything that was found at the scene of the Anthony murder?" I asked.

"You think we give it away to Goodwill? Of course we've got it," he drawled.

"You got the towel?" I asked.

"Yeeeeah," Wade dragged the word out as if to say, are you going to tell me what this is about?

"Can you get it and call me back?"

"It's in the evidence locker. I can take a cell phone in there and call you back, which I'm not supposed to do, and which never happened, if you're asked."

In ten minutes my phone rang. "Holding the towel," Wade said.

"Is there blood on it?"

"Let's see, a little jock-jack, BO, but no blood." I could hear him grinning.

"You're grossing me out. Just tell me everything that's on the towel," I said.

"Not until you tell me what you're up to."

"Frank Anthony was clutching a death stone when he died..."

"No, he wasn't."

"He was, but the murderer pried it out of his hand and then

delivered it to Barrett Silvers as a warning. The fragment contained the word *towel*. At first I thought it was Talbot, but now I think it meant look on the towel."

"The only thing on the towel is a health club emblem and the words *Tulsa Health Club*."

"Shit. What does the emblem look like?"

"Bunch of scroll-y stuff with the letters *THC* for *Tulsa Health Club*."

"Okay," I sighed. "Sorry for the trouble, Wade, thanks." Hanging up the phone, I looked at Callie. "Nothing."

Chapter Eighteen

With Talbot dead, I was convinced that only Isaacs knew who was head of the whole operation, and I had devised a plan to flush Isaacs out. It required perfect timing and the hand-eye coordination of a fighter pilot. I rummaged through my closet for my cell phone scanner and took it with me to the car. Maybe I was out to get Isaacs to fill in the blanks on this story, or maybe I was just after him to punish him for ever thinking he could own Callie.

Marathon had wasted no time in announcing the promotion of Robert Isaacs to chairman, although Talbot's body wasn't even in the ground yet. In fact, his body wasn't even scheduled for the ground for another twenty-four hours, in order to allow everyone who loved Talbot to pay his or her respects at the cathedral rotunda, which would be open around the clock. Like a theme park attraction, Lee Talbot's dead body was expected to draw quite a crowd. At the cathedral entrance, massive flower arrangements rested comfortably on stands, balloons in tastefully muted colors bobbed in the wind, and little white doves trailed above the doorway. The only thing missing was popcorn and fireworks.

We entered through the thick, hand-carved wooden doors at about eight o'clock in the evening. It was dark outside, and the bon voyage for Lee Talbot had trickled down to only a few well-wishers. It felt decidedly spooky to visit bodies after dark, but I had timed our arrival to coincide with Robert Isaacs's arrival, fairly certain he'd want to be there just before the ten o'clock news, in case there was a photo op.

"What if he recognizes you?" Callie whispered.

"My own mother wouldn't recognize me. I haven't dressed like this since my senior prom!" Wearing a black dress and an auburn wig, I felt as overgroomed as a Westminster poodle. "I haven't worn a dress in years," I moaned.

"Nice legs." Callie patted my behind.

"That's not my legs."

"It's been so long, I've lost track of where everything is located."

"Are you complaining?" I asked, feeling butterflies in my stomach at the thought of her touching me.

"I guess I am. I want you and I miss you." She put her arms around me lovingly and kissed my neck. No one in the parking lot even glanced at us because we were in one of the acceptable gay-nuzzling zones. Airport terminals and cemeteries being among them. It crossed my mind that, in our culture, if women were sad, frightened, or bereaved, they were permitted whatever nuzzling they required. However, if things turned joyous, most likely authorities would have to intervene. We were interrupted by the sight of Isaacs entering the side portico of the chapel.

❖

The casket was elevated on a three-tiered circular platform in the center of the room so people could approach it from all sides. The carpet leading up to it was pale green and three inches deep, with flowers springing out of it in all directions as if it were grass. Lee Talbot's coffin was a rich, metallic mauve, shinier than a new Porsche and just about as expensive. It was upholstered in a tufted rose-colored satin with satin button studs. Three brass handles were evenly spaced along each side, and its flamboyant metallic girth rested on six fancy whitewall tires. All it needed was a steering wheel and a gearshift and it could have driven itself to heaven. I waited until half a dozen people walked solemnly toward the casket, Isaacs trailing behind them. I climbed the steps slowly and gave a surreptitious hand signal to the kid in the back of the church, who couldn't believe he was going to make a hundred bucks for doing something so simple.

Just as I reached the coffin, there was a loud crash from the vestibule. Isaacs turned to see what had happened. The young man had knocked over a flower stand, momentarily creating a disturbance.

Isaacs turned back to the coffin to pay his respects to Lee Talbot, whose dead body lay stretched out before him, lips blue, cheeks an unnatural pink against the gray skin, and one eyelid…held down by a death stone. The note, stuck unkindly into his chest, read, "You're next, Isaacs."

Isaacs's eyes widened in horror as he grabbed the death stone and the note and fled the rotunda.

"Come on!" I signaled Callie, who had carefully stayed out of Isaacs's line of sight. "Now he believes whoever has been issuing the hits is coming after him. He'll go to the source to try to stop them. All we have to do is follow him." I slipped the teenage boy the hundred dollar bill as we walked out.

"Now Robert Isaacs has the stone!" Callie seemed alarmed.

"One of the fake stones that came from Peter Trayber. I still have the other fake, and of course, the two real ones."

Her nose wrinkled up like an accordion, she fished an antibacterial wipe out of her handbag. "Wash your hands! Here! You've been touching a dead body!"

"Just his eye," I said nonchalantly.

We followed Isaacs to the parking lot and got in our car as he got in his. He immediately picked up his cell phone and dialed. I opened my glove box and took out the scanner and aimed it at his phone.

"What are you doing?" Callie asked.

"Scanning his cell phone number. It's a 918 area code." I read it off the screen, and Callie jotted it down.

I waited for Isaacs to put his phone away, then I dialed. A woman answered, "Caruthers residence."

"I'm sorry, wrong number," I hung up and stared at Callie. "So Isaacs is going to Caruthers for help. Either to tell him someone's after him, or to beg for help, or to tell him to call off the dogs."

"I think it's the latter," Callie said knowingly.

CHAPTER NINETEEN

Callie hovered over her laptop, studying the horary astrology chart.

"This is so weird." She held up the chart for me to look at, persisting in her belief that if she just continued talking to me as if I understood, one day I would.

"At the moment of Lee Talbot's death, assuming this time is accurate, Mercury went stationary direct. Mercury ruling communications. Maybe Talbot was about to tell someone about the scheme." She picked up the original horary chart. "Do you remember when I looked at the question of whether you should drop this case and Mars was Combust the Sun?"

She could see the blank look on my face.

"Combustion is derived from the myth of Icarus, who flew too near the Sun. Mars, within eight degrees thirty minutes from the Sun, is Combust the Sun. I was so busy staring at you that night," she smiled, "that I failed to realize that it was more than combust. Mars and the Sun were so close—only six astrological minutes apart—that Mars and the Sun were actually Cazimi! Heart of the Sun. The Sun strengthened the planet it was aspecting. Mars got stronger. Do you understand?"

"No, sorry."

"Well, think about it. Mars, action or violence perhaps, was made stronger by the Sun. Violence enhanced. I think that's why the number of deaths and injuries by fire has continued with more than one victim."

The thought crossed my mind that maybe I should get into this astrology thing just so I could hold up my half of the conversation.

"We've got to go to Tulsa and visit Hank Caruthers. If Isaacs called him, then Caruthers could be the root of all evil, as we are fond of saying in the Midwest."

"Okay," Callie said, "I need to get home anyway and check on a few things."

The phone rang. It was Detective Curtis. He wanted to know if I could come down to the police station in the morning and ID the guy he thought was Spider Eye. I told him I was taking a flight out in the morning for Tulsa but I would gladly cancel it.

"The DA wants him on an unrelated charge, so he's on ice for a few days anyway. You can meet Mr. Wonderful when you get back," Curtis assured me.

We agreed to meet at a coffee shop near the police station the morning after I returned. I hung up and told Callie that maybe they had the guy and he could help us fit the pieces together.

"Not the guy," Callie said quietly.

"Well, that saves me a trip," I said with sarcasm.

"Sorry, I could be wrong."

But I knew she wasn't.

As Callie continued her study of the horary chart, I phoned Wanda, my faithful dog-sitter, who said she'd stay with Elmo overnight. Then I sat down with Elmo, cupped his large head in my hands, and stared into his soulful dog eyes. "I have to go to Tulsa for a few days. Wanda is coming to take care of you. She'll feed you, give you your pills, and play with you, just like I do. You'll be perfectly safe, okay?"

Elmo flopped onto the floor in depression and Callie laughed. Kneeling down in front of Elmo, she said, "Your job, Elmo, is to guard the house while we're gone. Got it?" Her tone was crisp and businesslike, and Elmo's ears rose in anticipation of work to be done. "All creatures need a job to do. Elmo has one now," Callie said and went off to bed. Elmo followed her. A typical Hollywood animal—his loyalty was to whoever gave him work.

❖

Callie slid close to me, then pulled me over to her and kissed me. The initial meeting of tongues ignited erotic memories, but I wasn't ready to be loved by Callie and be denied loving her in return. I wasn't ready to love her only to find that she still couldn't give herself to me. I pulled back.

"Letting me love you will relax you and let you sleep so you won't worry about flying tomorrow," she said.

"I see, a purely therapeutic lovemaking. A mercy fuck."

She pulled away quickly. "Oh, Teague, you say the most awful things."

❖

Our flight for Tulsa left the Burbank airport the next morning at six o'clock. Whenever I had to fly, I tried to do it quickly without planning or forethought, so I wouldn't have time for my anxiety level to build. Unfortunately, I'd had overnight to think about it as I lay awake, electrically charged by Callie's kiss. I had worked myself into a state of tremors. It was the idea of being launched into space in a long metallic tube, strapped to a chair that could fall thirty thousand feet to the ground that bothered me. Viewed in that way, I didn't think my fears unreasonable. Nothing paralleled airline travel for claustrophobia or a sense that one was being exposed to three hundred viruses simultaneously, all compliments of the airline ventilation system. I carried the fake stone in my bra so I could get to it quickly if it came down to my life or the stone.

"Are you all right?" Callie asked touching my arm. "You're perspiring."

"Fine," I said as we watched a man remove his belt buckle and keys for the metal detectors. By now I was starting to hyperventilate, and Callie pulled me over to the side of the concourse leading to the boarding area.

"You're not going to die in a plane," she said forcefully.

"No, I'll be blown apart and die in pieces in the air."

"You will not die in any plane-related event."

"I don't even want to be scared in a plane-related event," I said emphatically. "I can't tolerate the bouncing."

"There won't be any bouncing," she said firmly.

"You can't promise me that."

"I just did."

"Okay."

I boarded the plane and took my seat behind the wing in the tourist section, that area of the plane I had decided was most likely to survive a crash. "People in first class always die," I assured Callie as I struggled to get past a three-hundred-pound man who had the aisle seat in our row. I liked sitting next to fat people. I liked to think of them as gigantic human life rafts. If we crashed, my fantasy was I would fall from the sky and be saved by landing on a fat person.

I looked up in time to see Raider pass our row and take a seat three rows back across the aisle.

"That's him!" My heart nearly stopped. "The guy in the black leather jacket, the guy I axed! Maybe he's here to blow up the plane!" It was too late. We were already taxiing down the runway. My distress over Raider overshadowed my fear of takeoff. I remembered to be upset over flying only after I felt myself being G-forced into the seat at liftoff.

"Pretend you're an angel and think of these airplane wings as your own wings, and you're lifting yourself off the ground by your own power," Callie said in a soothing tone.

Moments later we were airborne. I was a wreck the entire trip, afraid that Raider had boarded the plane to plant a bomb. I was certain at any instant we would all be nothing more than metal confetti. *Why the hell is he on the plane?* I craned my neck every minute or two for the next hour to check on him. He was drinking, eating, sleeping, and reading, just like the rest of us.

Three hours later we were descending into the landing pattern. I had to go to the bathroom. I'd insisted neither of us go, because we'd have to pass Raider, but now there was no waiting. I glanced back and saw his blanket pulled up to his ears. I unstrapped my seat belt and headed for the lavatory. The Occupied light was on, so I stood unsteadily waiting my turn. Callie had been correct, there had been no bouncing, just sort of a mild sliding side to side. I kept my back to the door so I could keep an eye on Raider's chair. The lavatory door opened, and with lightning speed, a hand reached out, grabbed my jaw like a vise and yanked me backward inside the stall, locking the door behind us. Successful attack is nine-tenths surprise, and Raider had more than surprised and terrified me. Jammed into the bathroom up against his sweaty body, I could feel the coarse stubble on his chin scratch my forehead as we both struggled.

When I banged on the side of the bathroom wall, he wrapped his belt around my neck. "I'd just as soon kill ya, really. My boss is not amused. He says the stone from the dead guy's eye is a fake and you got the real one." He reached down into my blouse, fishing in my bra until he came up with the death stone. "Bingo!" he said, holding the stone up. Then into my face he crooned, "Nice tits. Wish I had more time. Now you're going to go back to your seat and say nothing, understand? Because from where I'm sitting, I can blow a hole through both of you before you can ring for a Bloody Mary, got it? Oh, and don't try to have me searched." He took the stone, put it in his mouth and swallowed it. I marveled that anyone could pop a one-by-two-inch tile into his mouth and eat it like a piece of popcorn. The guy had to have a windpipe the size of the Lincoln tunnel! He tightened the belt around my throat, gripping it so tightly that I could feel my neck pulse, and I became light-headed.

"Stone tasted like you." He grinned. "Like your perfume and just a little salty."

I slid my hand down his pants, as if I were about to do something very pleasurable for him. He loosened his grip almost entirely with his right hand to help. I grabbed a fistful of his crotch in a viselike grip, and hoarse from his choking me whispered, "It's a shame a woman has to continually use this particular portion of the male anatomy like a time-out buzzer, but it seems to be the only thing that works. Let go of the belt, asshole!" He complied, and I opened the door and shoved him out. A man waiting to get in realized there were two of us in the bathroom and leered at me as I headed back to my seat.

"What took you so long? I was worried about you."

"Raider dummied up his seat with pillows. He was waiting for me in the lavatory," I said, showing her the belt.

"Did he attack you?" she asked, her voice alarmed. Then she saw the marks he'd left on my neck. "Did he have you by the throat?" Callie's voice rose.

"He pulled me inside, strangled me, and he got one of the stones."

Callie jerked her seat belt off. "How dare he touch you!" She bailed over the top of me on her way to the aisle. I was surprised at the vehemence in her voice, and my heart beat a little faster knowing she felt protective of me.

I grabbed her belt loop and hauled her back into her seat. "I'm okay, and the stone he's got is fake. Plus, he swallowed it."

"He swallowed it?" she said incredulously. "Well, we don't want it back, that's for sure."

I laughed for the first time since I'd boarded the plane.

"If my parents ask about the marks on my neck, I'll say you did it," I said.

But Callie was looking over her shoulder at my attacker, her eyes as cold as steel, her jaw set tight. "Whenever someone attacks the things I care about, the cosmos always takes care of it."

I chose not to pursue that comment, but made a mental note. *Don't hack off someone tapped into the cosmos.*

❖

Within seconds the wheels touched down safely in Tulsa. I was so happy I was almost speaking in tongues.

Raider hovered around the terminal, trying to decide what to do about me and periodically hoisting up his pants. I went directly to airport security and pointed him out. He vanished, never picking up any luggage, and I felt nauseated and somehow violated that he had gotten away not only with stealing, but with sticking his hand down my blouse and insulting me.

"Are you sure he got the fake stone?" Callie whispered.

"I'm from Hollywood. Everything in my bra is fake. The stone from Orca's and the stone from Barrett's tea canister are sewn into my belt. Actually, I just cut some stitching on the back side of the belt and slid them in between the two layers of leather." I bent my belt back to show her.

"You cut up your good belt?" Callie asked in alarm.

"I can get another one." I shrugged

"But that belt matches your Ferragamos."

"Yeah—"

"But now it has a hole in it! When this is over, I'll take it to a shoe repair place and we'll get it fixed. Next time, tell me when you're looking for somewhere to hide the stones and I'll help you come up with something." She sighed and headed for the rental car counter.

"If you were really cosmic," I said, "you wouldn't care so much about clothes."

"Angels are always shown in white satin or silk. The cosmos is very into look and feel," she replied.

I phoned Mom and Dad from the car to say I was in town. Mom asked how the Anthony story was going, as chipper as if it were a school project. I couldn't tell her it was going so well that we'd been put on the A-list for most likely to be found dead or missing. I hung up and laid the phone down in the butter-soft leather seats of our rental car. "Why did you rent a Cadillac?" I asked Callie.

"I like them. Why?"

"They remind me of little old ladies with chubby butts," I needled her.

"So you must be very comfortable," she said cheerily, making me laugh.

❖

From the airport, we drove downtown, where the runner-up for Miss Tetons was still manning the reception booth at the Tulsa Health Club. I asked her if we could get into the men's locker room and have a look at Frank Anthony's locker, reminding her that we were the women who were writing a story about Mr. Anthony. She gave us a furrowed look and said she "just couldn't." Normally, I would have snapped at anything that fluffy standing between me and what I needed to accomplish, but I refrained.

"Maggie." I tried to charm her by having remembered her name. "We work for a very tough editor." I was about to launch into my next ingratiating set of lies when Hank Caruthers stepped out of the locker room, ready to leave the gym. He exhibited pleasant surprise on seeing us again. Maggie quickly filled him in on our request.

"Hasn't been a woman allowed back there since the place was built in 1934. If a woman ever got back there, why, rumor has it the shower heads would fall off and the wallpaper would peel." Hank chuckled, seeming to make fun of the very rules he enforced. "It's not because we're hiding anything…'Cept the family jewels, of course!" He laughed at his own joke. "But I understand entirely about doing your job. Why don't you gals give me a call at my office and we'll talk? I'll tell you anything you want to know. I mean I was the first person on the scene, so that ought to be worth something to your editor."

Hank handed us both his card. We thanked him with big, insincere smiles and left moments after he did. As his car pulled out of the parking lot, I felt my legs go weak, and I had to lean up against the hood. Callie was immediately at my side, wanting to know what was wrong.

"Look at his card! Thomas Harold (Hank) Caruthers. Initials THC. Frank was clutching the stone to tell whoever found him to look on the towel for the murderer. The towel says THC. Tulsa Health Club."

"Or Thomas Harold Caruthers," she said. "I'm getting chills."

Chapter Twenty

I drove us across town to Maple Ridge, a historic district of ivy-covered mansions built by long-dead oil barons and the home of Ramona Mathers. I was almost certain Frank Anthony had confided in her before he died. She was so easy to talk to, and I knew for a fact that she would be the one person involved in this case who would be happy to see me.

Ramona came to the door in full makeup and a décolleté dressing gown, as if I'd phoned ahead.

"Well, look at the package delivered to my doorstep." She took a step back and surveyed me head to foot. Then, catching sight of Callie, she added, less pleased, "And you've brought a friend."

She graciously welcomed us into the stone foyer of her baronial mansion, whose hollowed halls and granite walls echoed eerily as we all clattered down them into her warm study. There was a large chaise lounge built for two by the fire, and I imagined Ramona had coaxed many a secret out of a well-lubricated oilman in that very spot.

I asked her if she knew anything about Lee Talbot's relationship with Hank Caruthers.

"And if I tell you, is there just some tiny something in it for me?" She gave me a seductive smile.

"My intense gratitude." I returned her gaze.

"Well, that's a start, isn't it? Talbot and Caruthers went way back. Hank Caruthers got Lee Talbot the CEO job at Marathon. Lee Talbot wasn't a very good businessman, which most people didn't know, but Hank felt he could shore up the financial side for him. He didn't take into account how much money Lee Talbot could throw away on one picture, and pretty soon, the studio's foreign loans were being recalled. That's when, out of sheer desperation in an attempt to shore up profitability, the barter deals started. Frank told me that he thought there was more to it than that…embezzlement, as he put it. Frank was such a conservative. He said he had a list of some sort that contained evidence of what was going on. Hank believes that if the list ever existed, it was stolen during the break-in at the Anthony mansion right after Frank's death. And that, my dear, is everything I know…well, everything I know that I can share with you in public." And she smiled. I thanked her profusely and promised to visit her again.

❖

"She's creepy," Callie said, "Coming on to you like that. Horrible!"

"At least she's being cooperative."

"Only because she thinks she's going to get in your pants," Callie said in disgust. "She's undoubtedly slept with everyone on both coasts. She probably has several diseases. I wouldn't even shake her hand, much less sleep with her!"

I reached over and took Callie's small hand in mine. "I don't have any intention of sleeping with her. As a matter of fact, I really don't have any intention of sleeping with anyone…with the possible exception of you."

Callie turned my hand over lovingly and stroked the palm and then placed it against her soft cheek and then kissed it. Callie was not a person to apologize or to take the blame, because her beliefs placed none, but this gesture came pretty close to asking me to forget the past and begin again.

"So I'm not the first," I began, referring to her sexual history, "but as the country song says, that's okay, so long as I'm the last."

She pulled me into her and kissed me, and her mouth was so hot that I was instantly turned on. She released me too soon, startling me with the question, "Why aren't you living with anyone?"

"I've lived with women." I found myself defensive.

"Not for long, though." She seemed to know without being told.

"No."

"Because?" she asked, then responded to my knitted brow, "I'm asking because a lot of women seem to know you, and yet you live alone."

"Living together gets dull, predictable. I guess it depends on whether you think highs and lows are interesting or merely a sign that you need a refill on your lithium scrip."

"Are you on lithium?"

I began to giggle. "Based on my behavior, if I were on lithium, I would say it doesn't work. Are you asking because you think I would have a better life through chemistry?"

"No, I like the way you are: spontaneous, wild, temperamental. Do you think I'm predictable?" Callie asked.

"A little. I can see trips to the mall and evenings at the computer."

"Really?" She smiled.

"Where's this going? Are you thinking we should live together?"

"Absolutely not!" she said, and hurt my feelings.

"Just checking," I said, as if I didn't care one way or the other, and I quickly changed the subject. "I'm betting Caruthers was skimming off the top at Marathon."

"Why Caruthers?"

"Because Frank Anthony said he had a list, but Caruthers convinced Ramona Mathers that there probably never was a list, and if there were, it had to have been stolen the night the Anthony mansion was broken into. Sounds to me like Caruthers was covering himself because he knows there is one. If Talbot was bankrupting the studio with bad motion pictures, then the board must have been trying to hire someone to take his place. If Talbot was replaced, maybe Caruthers's embezzling activities would be exposed. Caruthers would have to shore up profits quickly, make Talbot look good, and get the board off his back. So Caruthers hired Isaacs and got him to do the barter deals to bring in big stars for very little cash. Then to keep Isaacs in line, maybe Caruthers blackmailed him over those very deals. It might seem like a lot of trouble to go to, but just one percent of Marathon's 784 million dollar annual gross is a payday worth killing for. Maybe we didn't contribute to Talbot's death. Maybe Talbot was catching on to what was happening, and Caruthers knocked him off or had Isaacs do it."

"But what about the list?" Callie asked.

"I don't know, but I'm beginning to think we should buy vanity plates that say NO LIST, and maybe people will stop trying to knock us off."

❖

I told Mom and Dad I'd be staying at Callie's high-rise.

"Well, that makes no sense," Mother said. "You have a perfectly good bed over here at our house."

"Maybe Callie's got a better mattress," Dad said sincerely and gave me a wink.

"Well." Mother tried to salvage some vestige of caregiving. "You'll at least return that rental car right now and use your father's car. That's just an unnecessary expense you don't need." I complied, having learned long ago to pick my battles.

❖

That night, as we lay in bed, my mind retraced the events from that fateful luncheon with Barrett. Suddenly I sat bolt upright.

"Curtis!" I shouted. "I gave my business card to Detective Curtis and told him when I was leaving for Tulsa. That's how the thugs knew when I was on the highway. That's how the guy knew to follow me to Needles and Tucumcari. That's how he had my fax number. He's the one who sent me the welcome home fax when we got back to L.A.! That's how Raider knew what flight I was on. I told Curtis!"

I got Curtis's business card out and stared at it. It had a police emblem at the bottom and the words Detective Curtis on it. I dialed L.A. information and asked for the phone number of LAPD homicide. The prefix wasn't the same as the number on Curtis's card. I dialed the LAPD number and asked if there was a Detective William Armand Curtis working for the LAPD. The voice on the phone said they had no officer by that name. I hung up and stared at Callie.

"This is a bogus number he gave me."

"How does he answer when you call?"

"Curtis."

"So you could have been calling his cell phone or his home. He could be one of their guys."

"Yes, but he doesn't know I know that." I picked up the phone and dialed the number on "Detective" Curtis's card. He answered in his usual manner.

"I think I know who's behind this," I told him. "I'm on my way back to L.A. Forget coffee, I'll come directly to the station and meet you there."

"Could you hold on a minute?" He put me on hold.

I covered the receiver and whispered to Callie that he must be on another line right now asking what to do with us next. Another minute passed before he clicked back on.

"Sorry, my boss is driving me crazy. I'm on a couple of big cases, and there's just not enough of me to go around. Listen, I won't be at the station tomorrow. I'm on a stakeout, so why don't you give me twenty-four hours and I'll call you."

"Great." I hung up and told Callie he'd aborted our meeting after talking to someone on the other line.

"But he called you before we left and wanted you to come down to the police station and ID a guy. Why would he risk your driving down to the station when you would obviously discover he's not a cop?" Callie asked.

"Because he wants me to trust him, and because he believes he can lie his way out of anything—just like he did tonight."

❖

An hour later I'd almost dozed off when the phone rang. I picked it up. A voice with an accent said menacingly, "You will forfeit the stone at 12:01." The line went dead. Callie asked who called. "Just more threats saying they're coming after the stone at noon. Has to be whoever Curtis called. As far as I'm concerned, they've been coming after us at every hour of the day."

"I don't like this," she said.

Callie fell asleep immediately, exhausted. I was awake and staring at the ceiling, thinking we had pretty much pieced the mystery together. Caruthers was head of the whole operation, and like my dear old daddy was fond of saying, "Shit rolls downhill," from Caruthers to Isaacs to Barrett and somehow to the squad of goons doing the actual tracking and killing. Since the attempt on Barrett's life and Rita's murder had both taken place in L.A., we needed to get the district attorney in Los Angeles to listen to our story just as soon as we returned. I was sure Wade would call the DA's office on our behalf to lend a little clout.

❖

At dawn, I told my parents what was going on. Wade had been alerted and had assigned someone to keep an eye on them. I wrote his personal pager number on a piece of paper and propped it up by their phone. I then tried to tell them everything I could without frightening them.

My father said firmly that there was no need to worry. Any stranger who came through the front door would be shot first and questioned later. Mother listened intently to every detail, as if we'd brought a real-life soap opera into the living room, and she was delighted to be involved. We gave them explicit instructions for protecting themselves and told them the police cruiser would be coming by the house all night. Dad went to the dresser and pulled out a loaded .38. "Should have kept my .357," he said solemnly. He pulled two 12-gauge shotguns out of the closet and began rummaging through his bottom dresser drawer looking for shells.

"Where in the goddamned, mother-lovin', fanny-fuckin' hell is my—"

"Ben!" Mother called a halt to the swearing he'd managed, over the years, to elevate to an art form. To Callie, she added, "This is just a good excuse for him to do what he loves to do most, brandish firearms."

"Dad, just make sure it's not Mother prowling around in the night when you pull those guns out, all right?" I said.

"Who the hell do you think taught you firearm safety?" he growled. "Now how in the Sam Hill do you two propose to protect yourselves?"

"Wade," I lied, knowing the mere mention of a male cop would put his mind at ease.

"Wade's a good man," Dad said. "You just do what he says and you'll be fine."

Callie wanted to stop back by her condo before leaving town, so I borrowed Dad's car to take her over to the high-rise, leaving my parents to sort out who to shoot and when.

It was a shock to leave the tidy rental car for Dad's eclectic Oldsmobile. Every time I stepped on the brake, something different rolled out from under the seat and then disappeared again when I stepped on the gas: Tums, a Bic lighter, a Dixie cup. After the broken hearing aid rolled out, I told Callie to brace herself, because I fully expected to see my dad come tumbling out at the next stoplight. Callie laughed and squeezed my hand.

It was a beautiful, cool summer's day. I didn't want to leave Tulsa, and I wished I'd taken up a career as an engineer or accountant or med-tech, so I could find a job here.

I pulled the car up in front of the impressive structure and kept the motor running. Callie climbed out and headed for the gates, then paused and turned back, coming up to the car window. She seemed nervous suddenly.

"I won't be longer than five minutes, okay?" She paused and then said quickly, "I love you, Teague." She kissed me full on the mouth and gave me a big smile before disappearing. *She finally said it. She loves me. Why now?* I wondered, inexplicably happy as I watched her disappear into the building. I turned the radio up and leaned back in the seat as the DJ announced it was 10:00 a.m. Hearing the time reminded me of the phone call. "I'll see you at 12:01." *Why the hell would the guy announce his intentions? And which 12:01? Noon, midnight, tonight, tomorrow, next year?* I looked up at the towering condos beside me.

"Jesus God, 1201! The number on Callie's condo!"

CHAPTER TWENTY-ONE

I bolted out of the car and raced to the double doors of the front lobby, getting caught in a jumble of elevators and staircases as I tried the quickest route to get to Callie's condo. I hit the fire-escape doors on the twelfth floor, panic stricken and out of breath, as I raced to 1201. My mind kept up a frantic dialogue. *Why did you let her go upstairs by herself? That's why she said she loved you, because she had a premonition that she'd never see you again. Why didn't she tell me that? Because she tells you things and you ignore them or make fun of them.* The door was ajar. I pulled my gun and burst inside. There was no one there. I moved quickly through the rooms calling Callie's name, the stark white living room, once sensual elegance, now cold, white clouds of nothingness.

As I came back to the front room, I saw the blood on the white carpet, and on the wall and the doorknob, where she had held on while someone pulled her away. My heart sank. I checked the parking lot, visible from Callie's front window, while I called Wade. He responded immediately, putting out a call to all units in the surrounding area. I'd searched the parking garage and storage areas by the time Wade arrived. There was no sign of Callie or her kidnapper. I panicked, realizing how easy it was for someone to be sucked off the planet, never to be heard from again.

Wade tried to calm me down by reminding me that whoever had Callie was merely holding her to trade for the stone, since Raider had failed to do the job. Wade ordered a phone trace, and in forty-five minutes we had a man in Callie's living room with a recorder and listening device waiting for the call. Wade radioed officers and made suggestions for the search while I paced. *This is completely unlike me,* I thought, *immobile and trusting someone else to figure things out.* It was just that I was immersed in Callie, so much so, that I could not have felt weaker if someone had simply pulled my heart out with his bare hands. I was frantic to the point of being physically ill that the kidnapper would kill her. Wade came over and put his big bear paw around me. "We'll find her," he said, and I didn't trust my voice to answer.

The phone rang. I picked up the receiver at the same moment the tracer was set in motion, and now, like some bad movie, it was my job to get the caller to talk until we had located him.

"Teague?" It was Callie's slightly shaky voice.

"Callie, where are you?" I begged.

Wade looked down at the caller ID but it read Anonymous.

I could hear scuffling over the phone, and the receiver was obviously yanked out of her hand. "You have the real stone. Bring it to us. Two minutes late and we cut her up."

"Put her on the phone." I tried to sound calm and hard.

"This evening at 8:50, you will park your car across the street from the Memory Park Cemetery, walk through the gate, and stand in the shadow of the bell tower. At nine o'clock the groundskeeper will lock the gates, locking you inside. When the cemetery is clear of all visitors and it's dark, someone will approach you at the tower, and you will hand over the rock. After that, you'll walk east down the slope, then south to a marker that says Elliston. You'll find your friend waiting for you there. If anything goes awry, you'll still find her there, but in pieces."

"Let me talk to her again or there's no deal."

"I can cut her up now." He laughed, but he put Callie on.

"Teague, the Moon's in Aries at two degrees, thirty-two minutes. So pick up the pace. They mean business. The—" Her kidnapper pulled the phone away as Callie screamed in the background. The line went dead.

"Did you get it?" I nearly shouted at the cop manning the trace.

"No, not long enough."

"We can send men to the moon, but we can't do a simple trace in thirty seconds!"

Wade tried to calm me down. "What was she saying about the moon?"

"I don't know. It's astrology. She knows I can't understand it…" Even as I was saying it, I realized that she was trying to tell me something in code.

"You know any good astrologers?" I asked Wade. "I need someone to tell me what she means." Wade replayed the tape, and we both jotted down the message, "The Moon's in Aries at two degrees, thirty-two minutes. So pick up the pace. They mean business." Wade promised to track down a lady he knew and get her to decipher it. I began scrounging through Callie's bookshelves, which looked like the library on the Starship *Enterprise*: UFO books, celestial navigation, paranormal experiences, channeling, interstellar communication, and dozens of books on astrology. I opened several and put them on a reading table. This was an amazing and complicated science: charts, graphs, tables of celestial data. There was no way I would be able to decipher the message in time. *Callie knows that*, I thought in frustration, as I sat at near attention with her message in front of me. *What in the world is she thinking of, rattling off this stuff to me at a time like this?* I closed my eyes and meditated, no I prayed, "Dear God, dear guides, dear whoever you are…help me understand this now." I opened my eyes but still had no answer.

After about an hour, the two officers conducting the building search left for the station, and the guy manning the trace went to the bathroom, leaving me instructions on what to do if the phone rang in his absence. Seconds later, Wade came back, proudly waving a piece of paper with notes he'd taken from his astrologer friend.

"Okay, Teague. Got it! It means quick happenings with men." He read aloud from his notes. "She said Aries, being the first house of the zodiac, is ruled by Mars, which is action. Aries is aggressive and hard-charging."

"That's it?"

"That's it," he sighed.

"Say it again." I demanded. Wade read the note again and a third time.

Nothing. I was blank. "Aries. It's a sign, right? Like you're an Aries and I'm a Pisces, right? So what does it mean when it's a certain number of degrees Aries?" I asked, desperate now. Wade looked at me like I'd lost my mind for asking him an astrological question.

"Call your friend," I demanded. "Ask her more about Aries or Mars or something. Never mind, let me ask her!"

Wade gladly forked over the woman's phone number, and I dialed. A pleasant-sounding lady answered, and I did a quick introduction telling her how important it was for her to help with the astrology part of Callie's message. She talked to me in what seemed like a haze of mystic mumbo jumbo, which only frustrated me more.

"You said Aries is a time period, and we all experience it in general. Is that right? I'm so confused."

The woman tried again, talking for about two minutes straight. I finally stopped listening, and started praying. In the middle of all of her strange words, I heard Aries is the ram.

"Ram!" I said the first word I really understood. "Ram. Like Dodge Ram. Pick up the pace…Ram pickup!"

"Well, I guess," the woman stammered. I'd forgotten she was still on the line. I shouted for Wade. "Callie's giving me astrological clues for the cosmically impaired!" I joked for the first time. "Two minutes thirty-two seconds. That's obviously an important number like 2:32 in the afternoon or 232…"

"Partial license plate number, maybe. I'll check on a Dodge Ram pickup with plates ending in 232." Wade was on it, while I muttered about the Moon and what it meant. Maybe just nighttime. Maybe she was saying that's what they'd be driving tonight.

An hour later, two possible Dodge Ram pickups with different prefixes, but both ending in 232, were tracked to two separate owners.

"One's a 1996 canary yellow and one's a 1994 silver color," Wade said. "Any hunches?"

"The Moon is yellow, but people sometimes say a silver moon," I replied. "Wait a minute! She said 'they mean business.' Is one of the trucks registered to a business?"

Wade checked his notes, "Yeah, silver one. A lawn service."

"That's the one! It probably has a name or side plates or something that says it's a lawn service vehicle, so they could easily leave it parked on the cemetery grounds."

"Okay, but we'll put a tail on both of them just in case," Wade said in the middle of mapping out his strategy. "At 8:50 you'll be inside the gate. We'll be on the far southeast corner of the cemetery. That's where they'll probably come with Callie to stay off the main intersection." He looked at me intently for just a second, reading the anguish, sizing up my relationship with Callie in an instant, understanding what hung in the balance for me.

"We'll get her first, in case anything goes wrong," he said, "then come up to where you are. That way they can't use her to leverage the situation. I'll have a couple of guys staked out just south of you. Just stall. They'll be there when you need them."

"My parents!" I said, remembering they could be easy hostage targets.

"Already got somebody out there with them. They're fine. You got the stone these guys want?"

I nodded.

"You ready?" he asked.

"Ready." We headed out the door.

Chapter Twenty-two

At 8:45 p.m., I parked in a strip mall lot across the street on the north side of the cemetery and walked nervously across the busy thoroughfare. I entered through the large Spanish mission–style arch that marked Memory Park Cemetery, a huge expanse of rolling hills, maple trees, and headstones for as far as the eye could see. I scaled a small hill to the bell tower which, up until now, had always been a peaceful centerpiece to the park. I reached the tower and stepped back into the shadows, leaning against its cold stone wall, and tilted my watch skyward to pick up the fading light.

Eight fifty-two p.m. *Eight more minutes. Maybe they have Callie right now, safe. God, please. Will they send more than one guy to meet me here? Are they going to trade the stone for Callie or just kill her and then kill me?* My thoughts were frantic. I had to settle down. I said a prayer with my eyes open.

Nine o'clock, nine fifteen, nine thirty. It was dark. I was beginning to shiver from nerves, not the temperature. *Are they on to us? Are they phoning Callie's condo right now to say they're doing something horrible to her, or perhaps, already have?*

A voice on my left startled me. "The stone. Hand it over. I have a walkie-talkie." He poked me in the side with its thick antenna. "I radio and she's dead."

My hand went to my coat pocket for one of the real stones this time—the stone left at Orca's for Barrett. He shoved my hand away and reached into my pocket for me, extracting the small slab that had turned my life upside down. Stepping back into the light for a moment, Raider examined it and then me.

"Last stone cramped me up, bitch. So if you don't mind, I'll just put this one in my pocket." He pocketed the stone with one hand and pulled a knife from under his shirt with the other. My stomach knotted. "You hurt me real good in that airplane john. I'm gonna need to leave here feelin' like you understand my pain."

Wade, where the hell are you? I need back up! I thought.

Raider jabbed the knife at me. I jumped to one side, avoiding it. *Go with the force and create inertia,* a long-ago instructor's voice rang in my head. Raider lunged forward again, the knife blade picking up ambient light and looking almost beautiful if its mission had not been to embed itself in my gut. I took a step back with the exact timing of his jab and grabbed the wrist of his knife-wielding hand, using his own momentum to pull him forward and facedown on the ground. I dropped to the ground beside him, put my knee in his back, slid my arm under his neck, and pulled up and back on his esophagus, squeezing the breath out of him. Hearing him gasp for air made me feel better than I had in weeks. I scrambled to my feet and gave him a huge second-half kickoff to the head, ebullient when the blow knocked him out. That's when I spotted a man with a Rastafarian hairdo catapulting, capoeria style, over the hill, his dreadlocks splaying out in all directions. This was not Spider Eye, who was safely in a hospital in L.A. with a bullet in his back, so this must be Spider Eye's version of a temp: a death-dancer replacement, who was now five feet from me, putting his body into a spin that sent him into a high-speed, one-armed handstand, legs scissor-kicking into the air, headed for my head.

"Holy shit!" I yelled and rolled out of his way, banging my back on a headstone as I went. Bullets zinged into the dirt near me. I quickly rolled farther downhill to escape being hit, gritting my teeth until I couldn't roll any further from the pain. Shots rang out from the hilltop above me where I'd left Raider. He was conscious now and had staggered to his feet, blood coming from his chest and mouth. Another shot rang out, and he toppled over again. The man who had followed me to hell and gone would be trailing me no more. Raider was dead. I spotted Wade's profile a hundred yards from me, gun drawn. He was obviously the shooter and taking no prisoners.

One of Wade's officers shouted to get his attention as the capoeria temp went airborne, making a dramatic leap toward Wade. The attacker's legs sliced through the darkness like knives and came dangerously close to Wade's face, and Wade pulled the trigger again. The man came down like a punctured balloon, collapsing in a heap. Then, as if his body were rubber, he catapulted up again, wounded and bleeding, and headed for the parking lot. Wade shouted for his men to cut him off.

A younger officer appeared, just to the south of where Wade was standing, his arm supporting a small woman who looked like she might collapse. The sunlight gone and the distance great, I could only see them in silhouette, but I was certain he had Callie with him. The younger officer shouted to Wade as he carefully walked Callie up the hill. "There's only one more besides this guy, Sergeant, and we ambushed him down at the grave marker. Got him cuffed in the cruiser."

Wade nodded with satisfaction. It appeared the kidnappers were three in number and were all accounted for.

I clambered up the hill to find Callie's beautiful blond hair disheveled and her white starched shirt stained with blood and dirt. I flung my arms around her. "Oh my God, I am so grateful you're alive." I laughed and cried at the same time. Tracing the source of the blood to her shoulder, I worried, "You've been cut. I think you need stitches."

"It's okay," she said, and put her cheek on my chest and clung to me. I could feel my shirt grow damp from her tears.

"I'm personally beginning to measure okay by whether we're in each other's arms." I leaned over and kissed her and looked deeply into her eyes. "I am so grateful that I have you back safe," I said again, not caring that Wade and several cops were staring at us, slightly mesmerized.

I threw Wade a "stop staring" look that jump-started him. "Okay, gentlemen, get moving. Let's clean up this mess. Somebody scrape up these flying assholes and load them into the squad cars. Gimme your keys," he demanded of me. "I'll bring your car over here so she doesn't have to walk."

I fished them out of my pocket, my other arm still wrapped around Callie. "Raider's got the real stone in his pocket, so we want to save that one. He swallowed one of the fakes, not clear exactly where that stone is in its journey," I said.

"The guy I just killed?" Wade asked, handing my keys off to one of his men and signaling him to go get the car.

"The blond guy." I nodded in Raider's direction. "Might want to tell the coroner he swallowed it about thirty-six hours ago. I think he passed it and that's how they figured out I still had the real one, but you might want to double-check. Don't want to get the two mixed up," I replied.

"Shit." He shook his head.

"Well that's where I'd start," I said with a little protect-and-serve humor.

❖

Taking advantage of our distraction, the capoeria-temp bolted. It must have been my adrenaline, or maybe just my anger at Callie's being injured by them, but I let go of Callie and moved ten feet to her right in time to put a stop block on him that I personally felt could have made me a first-round draft pick. His chin hit the stone walkway so hard that Wade laughed and then quickly tried to turn it into a politically correct cough. I got up slowly, really moaning this time.

Wade gave me an almost imperceptible grin. "Miss your old line of work?"

Callie was horrified. "Stop that, Teague! Let the police handle it."

"Hey, that was pretty slick, gettin' us the pickup description," Wade complimented Callie, who smiled up at him. A cop complimenting a psychic in this part of the world was something one wanted to have on tape.

Wade pointed at my dad's car being driven into the parking lot on the west side of the bell tower. "Hopper will drive you down to the station so we can fill out a report and then he'll take you on back home if you want. You both look a little worse for wear."

"We should drive ourselves, Teague," Callie said.

"Come on." I towed her toward the car. "Let's give ourselves a break and be chauffeured. Wade hardly ever thinks of anything useful. I'm going to let him win this one," I said as Callie and I walked up to the parking lot arm in arm.

Given the choice, the young cop behind the wheel would probably have selected a root canal over chauffeuring two fortysomething women downtown in their dad's old car, but he pulled slowly and dutifully out onto Memorial and took a left, heading south.

"You're going the wrong way. We're going to the police station,"

I said, thinking he must be new on the force and that's why he'd gotten this duty.

"Actually, I'm going the right way," the officer said, tilting the rearview mirror to make eye contact with me.

My blood froze. "Curtis!" I screamed.

A second man rose up from the front seat. "And you remember our mutual friend, Gigante," Curtis said as Gigante pointed a gun at us.

"In case you missed the last episode, I had to give the rock up at the bell tower to Raider, one of your associates. He was shot and killed. The police probably have the stone right now." I tried to remain calm and I kept a grip on Callie's hand.

"The stones are no longer the problem. You are," Curtis said. And I began to worry that the blanket of cosmic protection Callie always promised us might be wearing thin.

I checked the street signs. We were at 211th, zigzagging toward Okmulgee, a rural farming community with lots of backwoods and vacant fields, neither of which boded well for us. Curtis checked his rearview mirror and suddenly whipped the car off the road, driving it across a leaf-strewn field, rutted and bumpy from plowing in too-damp weather. The car came to a stop under a canopy of oak trees hidden from the road. The perfect location for a murder.

Chapter Twenty-three

The police will be here in about two minutes," I lied, trying to sound irritated rather than frightened. "Just take the car and leave us here."

Curtis turned off the headlights, opened the glove compartment, and took out a pair of latex gloves. He'd become organized and industrious, not a good sign. Telling Gigante to keep the gun on us, he got out of the car, leaving the driver-side door open, and popped the lid on the trunk. I turned to watch. He removed something and snapped the trunk lid shut with such intensity that it bounced the car up and down like a rocking horse. Now I could see him approaching carrying two gas cans.

"This is going to be your transportation to the netherworld, ladies," he said happily, peering into the car through the open door.

"Why are you doing this? This could land you in prison," Callie said.

"Doin' it because I get paid to do it. Just a job. Nothin' personal," Curtis replied coolly, and I could see that Curtis was a man who had no trouble sleeping nights, because his conscience played no role in his life.

Gigante got out of the car, leaving us in the backseat, his gun still trained on us. Curtis moved quickly, dousing the ground around the vehicle in a wide circle, then he soaked the interior, splashing gasoline on me. I screamed for him to wait, and he paused for just a second. I knew we were nearly as good as dead. We had to get out of this car before it became a firebomb. It's strange where my mind went in that split second when I knew we were about to die. It went to my father, and the funny way he swore, and the clever things he said. What irony that a man who was such a fastidious dresser could leave the floor of his car in a jumble of Dixie cups and hearing aids *and old lighters.*

The gas can was in my face when I screamed, "You're missing an opportunity here! Why haven't you raped us both? The evidence of any sexual assault is going to be burned up anyway."

My remark was so bizarre and unexpected that his arm stayed suspended in midair, the gas can dangling from it. He seemed to evaluate the idea for a moment, then rejected it. "You're dying," he said, about to toss the gasoline on us.

Gigante spoke for the first time, saying something in Spanish, apparently interested in what I'd suggested. He argued his case quietly, with a shrug of his shoulders, seeming to know how to work Curtis. Curtis momentarily dropped the can to his side and relaxed his body for an instant. Gigante yanked the back door of the car open with one hand and had his other hand wrapped around Callie's arm. At least I would not see her burned. Now we were either raped or dead, and the former bought me time. Callie gave me one last resolute look, her small hand trailing across mine in a gesture that nearly tore out my heart as the man with the huge head literally ripped her out of the backseat and disappeared with her into the darkness. The idea that he could hurt her created in me an explosion that would have dwarfed whatever explosion Curtis had planned for us.

"You are one stupid fucking cocksucker!" I screamed at Curtis. It had the desired effect. He nearly ripped the car door off its hinges to grab me by the legs and haul me out feet first. I didn't go easily, buying myself just a split second to scoop up my dad's old Bic lighter from under the seat, the lighter that had bounced over a hundred roads and might or might not have any juice in it, its dusty, transparent case now resting in my palm. I landed on the ground face first to the sound of Callie's screams and Gigante's curses in the distance. Curtis straddled me, ripping at my jeans, trying to peel them off me. When that failed, he raked my leg with a knife that cut into my skin as he attempted to cut my jeans off.

My thumb scraped across the serrated wheel of the cigarette lighter: once, twice. The second time a tiny flame flickered above the gasoline-soaked ground, and then suddenly, the dry leaves went up in a whoosh, chasing the gasoline trail and encircling the car. A gust of wind, sent by angels no doubt, caused the fire to jump to the car upholstery, which burst into flames. The other gas can that Curtis had left beside the car exploded with a loud bang, launching tiny pieces of shrapnel into the air. Curtis shouted for Gigante as the fire encircling the car became a veritable wall, and I was miraculously inside that wall of fire, shielded by the flames from my would-be killer.

Griping about being interrupted, Gigante released Callie and came lumbering over, slapping at the flames that had now engulfed Curtis's shirt as he fought to get to me. A hissing sound and then another explosion, this time from the trunk of the car as a fireball shot into the air and the whole field lit up like the Fourth of July. Gigante had gotten in the path of the white-hot debris, and he was screaming and cursing. Curtis shouted for him to jump the flames and grab me.

From behind me, Curtis, shirtless now, flung himself through the flames inside the ring of fire and began pounding me, enraged that he'd been tricked. I knew he was going to kill me. Adrenaline kicked in, and I flailed at him with my arms and fists. Had I been more rested, or less battered, I might have had a fighting chance, but not now. I could hear Callie screaming for me, somewhere outside the fire ring, telling me to fight him, as she too tried to get to me. Curtis was winning resoundingly. I was winded, my muscles were cramping from holding him off, I was choking on the gasoline smells, and he knew he had me.

He wrestled me onto my back, straddling me, and pinned my arms to the ground above my head. Letting go of my left arm for only a second, he brought his fist down across my jaw in a smashing blow that opened my lip. I could taste the blood trickling down my throat. He went for a second blow. I arched my back for leverage, then yanked my knees up, butting him in the back and rocking him forward toward the fire. He jerked back to keep from being singed again and lost his balance. We both staggered to our feet. Callie screamed for me to watch my back. I turned around just in time to see Gigante lunge and then fall into the flames. I had taken my eyes off Curtis, and he flattened me. My head cracked against the hard ground one last time.

❖

I remembered hearing fire trucks approaching in the distance, then nothing. Then very loud sirens nearby, then darkness. Then the sensation that lots of hands were pulling on me. Someone was trying to unzip my pants, and I was fighting them. Callie's voice was soothing.

My body was being lifted. Somebody had my face. I felt hands on my face. I heard someone say, "Dead," and I wondered if I were.

"You okay, Teague? It's Wade. You okay?" My body was being jostled along on something white. A mattress? I was under a roof. Wade and Callie were there. I was Dorothy, back in Kansas, trying to describe her dream to the farm hands. Wade's worried face reminded me a lot of the Scarecrow's.

Callie was holding an ice pack on my mouth, and her arm was streaked in blood. A man wearing a hospital jacket was sitting next to her. She removed the ice pack for Wade to have a look, then put it back, and everything went dark.

❖

There's nothing like having someone stab your lip with needles to bring you back into focus. Numbing was the worst part, the stitching only annoying. The police filled out endless paperwork while nurses came and went. I described for Wade how Curtis had disguised himself as a member of the LAPD and had even interviewed me after Barrett Silvers's attack. In fact, he'd been so convincing as a cop, I'd kept in touch with him every step of the way, letting him know where I was. That's undoubtedly how Caruthers's boys knew where and how to get us. I suggested Wade phone the LAPD and warn them about Curtis.

"I guess you were out during that part," Wade said, glancing at Callie.

"Curtis is dead, Teague," Callie said.

"The Gigante guy is too," Wade added.

"How badly did he hurt you, Callie?" I asked.

"Curtis interrupted Gigante before he could rape me," Callie answered.

"Good. That saves me digging the sonofabitch up and beating him to death," I said with bravado for Wade's benefit, but deep down I was just grateful and relieved Callie had escaped him. "Did we find out who he worked for, or any of the details?" I asked, and Callie shook her head.

"He was banging your head into the ground and Callie was on his back, trying to pull him off you, when we arrived. One of my guys jumped him and went a couple of rounds before it got ugly and we had to put him away."

❖

My parents came through the emergency room doors looking frantic. Callie had called them and assured them I was all right, but after seeing my lumpy face, they weren't convinced. I told them there was good news/bad news. The good news was that we were alive. The bad news was their car went up in smoke.

"That's okay, honey," Mom said sweetly, "we didn't really use it that much," which made me laugh, which in turn hurt from my waist to my teeth. While day-to-day events baffled my parents, crisis was their finest hour.

The ER doctor wanted to keep me overnight for observation, but I insisted on going home with Callie. I also demanded that Callie rebook our flight for the next day, which seemed to provide a mild source of amusement for those in charge. Horizontal people have less clout than vertical ones.

❖

That night Callie brought me liquids to drink through a straw and kept the ice packs frozen. My lip was now throbbing and I was feeling pretty cranky. Callie fluffed my pillows and reminded me that due to the concussion, she had to keep me awake for a few hours to be certain I wouldn't lapse into a coma, a state I felt could only be an improvement over my current one. When I finally fell asleep, I was unconscious until noon, arising to feign total wellness, although my body parts were so sore I could happily have become a drug addict. It was a solid week before I began to be able to tell one day from another.

❖

It was late evening, eight days later, when Wade drove us to the airport at Mach speed, gesturing with both arms and steering with his knees. It was a perfect prelude to flight. He recounted how he and his men had located the silver pickup and Callie, trussed up like a turkey, down below the hill. He'd given his man Hopper hell when he found out someone had kidnapped us right out from under him at the cemetery. As it turned out, the young cop had been tricked by Curtis into forking over our car keys. However, Hopper redeemed himself slightly when he followed up on a hunch about the reported explosion on 211th. Wade said when they arrived on the scene, I was unconscious and Callie had bitten a hole in Curtis's hand the size of a silver dollar.

Callie interrupted Wade to say she still wanted to know how Caruthers or Isaacs knew the stone I'd left on Talbot's eye was fake and that the stone Raider swallowed was fake.

"You left a stone on a dead guy's eye?" Wade grimaced.

"Long story," I said. "Bottom line is there's something about those stones that we don't know yet. The bad guys seem to be able to tell 'em apart like kids."

❖

At the airport, we hurried off to the gate. I waved over my shoulder to Wade with tears in my eyes from sheer gratitude at our being alive, but also from the pain of lifting my arm up above my waist.

Fifteen minutes later, we were taxiing down the runway, which always gave me the shakes. I'd had thrust/drag ratio explained to me, the physics by which objects the size of buildings are able to float on air. But rationally, it made no sense, and I was convinced that, at any given moment, the physics and mathematics behind the whole dubious process would finally be proven false and I would simply tumble out of the sky. I mentioned this to Callie, who put a headset on me and cranked the volume up to glass-shattering levels.

I signaled the flight attendant to bring me a drink. Callie cancelled my order, reminding me I'd taken pain medication. When we were up in the air, surrounded by a black void, I began to relax. I could no longer look down and see how far there was to fall. I was able to think of the darkness as something solid, a metaphor for life, maybe. Callie leaned up against me reading her book, and for a moment, everything seemed like it would finally be all right. Callie's safe return to me was, I had come to realize, the most important thing in my life.

I watched her put on her reading glasses. She propped them on the end of her straight, aristocratic nose, and I thought she looked smart and sexy as she studied her book about interstellar communication with spiritual entities. I just wanted to be with her like this, our bodies touching, even peripherally, as we moved through life.

"What?" she asked sweetly, feeling me staring at her.

"I like you in glasses. You look—I don't know—sexy."

"It's the drugs, honey." She patted me and went back to reading.

She's funny, I thought. *I've spent so much time just lusting after her that I never realized she has a very funny wit.*

"Are you starting to like more than my ass?" she asked, never looking up from her book. I laughed at being caught thinking just that.

❖

We drove directly to the police station from the airport. Detective White stood ready to make notes, having been contacted by Wade. We began with Orca's, moved on to the murder of Frank Anthony at the Tulsa Health Club and the barter system at Marathon Studios, the prostitution and drugs that escalated to heavy-duty pornography and murder. I explained how Isaacs had been turned into Caruthers's personal puppet and Caruthers was probably behind the murders of Rita Smith and the attempted murder of Barrett Silvers. When Frank Anthony threatened to report the studio's nefarious activities, he was shot in the forehead, compliments of Hank Caruthers, whose initials were on the health club towel, and it was Hank Caruthers's goons who had just tried to light up our lives in Tulsa.

Detective White scratched his head, obviously sorry we'd brought this high-profile Hollywood mess to his division.

"Where was the gun you say he always carried in the gym bag?" White asked us.

"We don't know that," I said.

Detective White seemed pressured, if one could judge by the sweat rings under his neatly pressed shirt. "Marathon is a huge studio and it employs thousands of people. To tarnish a company and its management like this, you need hard evidence. What you've got would make a good TV show, but it doesn't make an arrest. Rita Smith's death is on the books as a robbery homicide. Talbot had a heart attack. Now you're telling me all these people were murdered by a bunch of studio executives who needed to attract stars at any cost. That's not a motive. That's the problem half a dozen studios out here have: attracting stars at any cost. I'm sorry, but it's not enough."

I told the detective I thought Spider Eye should be questioned about the possibility of his having been sent to Talbot's house as a hit man and not a burglar.

"Maybe even do a little checking on his background in South America to see if hit man comes up on his resume," I said, only half joking. I could tell from White's expression that none of what I was suggesting was on his to-do list.

Callie stood up, letting me know it was time to cut my losses. "I think we should go to Cedars," Callie whispered, "and talk to Spider Eye ourselves."

CHAPTER TWENTY-FOUR

Outside hospital room 6632, I whispered for Callie to stand guard. "He's staying in a very nice hospital room. Must have good insurance," I quipped.

"Maybe the studio takes good care of its own," Callie replied.

I walked slowly up to the bed where Spider Eye lay recuperating from his gunshot wound. He looked a lot less terrifying stretched out with a large hole in him. He'd been hit in the back and was obviously on heavy medication for the pain. Helpless, Spider Eye looked up and saw me standing in the room. I thought he'd need a transfusion to bring back his color. He started to yell for someone, but I put my hand over his mouth. He looked as if he thought I'd come to finish the job.

"Spi-dah, Spi-dah, Spi-dah." I said it with the inflection Cary Grant had used when he spoke Judy Garland's name. "You try to kill me and my friend for no reason. Now, I can kill you, or you can talk to me. I want to know who hired you. I will lift my hand off your mouth, and you will say two words. The man's name. If you say any other words, I will pull my gun out and I will kill you. Are you ready?"

He nodded. I removed my hand, and he tried to call for help. I clamped my hand over his mouth and pulled the gun out of my pocket, tapping him on the forehead with the barrel in a manner that would not have been very painful to a healthy person but did nothing to improve Spider Eye's condition. He moaned.

"Now we're going to try it again, only this time, notice that I have the gun under your throat. Who hired you?"

"Talbot," he muttered.

"Talbot's dead," I said.

"Talbot." His eyes pleaded with me to believe him.

Callie stuck her head in the door and said a doctor was coming.

"Keep this visit just between us," I said.

Callie and I beat a hasty retreat down the hallway.

I told Callie that Spider Eye said Talbot hired him, so maybe Talbot was involved after all. But Talbot was dead, so why didn't everything come to a halt?

"Let's go wake Bare up and ask her."

❖

It was nearly midnight when we knocked on Barrett's front door. She answered after a few minutes. I was shocked to see the scar across her Greco-Roman features, as if the Roman statue had fallen over and cracked but the damage had not been total. She was still handsome. She opened the door slowly, with an arm that was still bandaged.

"It's late," she said, "I really don't—" She tried to close the door on us.

I planted one foot inside her door. "Why in the frog-friggin' hell did you turn me into a walking decoy by planting that stone on me when your stone is the one they want? A young blond hood in Tulsa is dead and his Rastafarian buddy wounded. Curtis, a would-be cop, bit the dust in Okmulgee, but they're just barnacles on the boat. We're looking for the boat. Now you either help me, or maybe the police would like to talk to you a little more in depth."

"The day Frank Anthony bought the stones at Waterston Evers's house, he spent about an hour there going over Evers's collection. Mathers, Caruthers, and I were gone for a while looking around the grounds. I think that's when Frank took the list and put it in the stone. He knew a lot about death stones and—"

"In the stone?" Callie interrupted.

"Frank did his homework on death stones. Certain stones, recognized by their smoothness or eloquent carving, are death stones. Used on wealthy people—princes, kings. Expertly carved, they contain a passageway inside where the family could write a special prayer to the gods, stick it in the stone, and be sure that it would pave the way for their loved one on the other side. Frank put the list in that stone and gave it to me for safekeeping. He knew they were trying to kill him, but he was a courageous guy. He said if anything happened to him, to get the stone to the FBI."

"So when the death stone was delivered to you at lunch..."

"I knew Frank was dead and that someone was telling me I was marked."

"Who was telling you?"

"I don't know. When I got out of the hospital, I was going to get the stone back from you, but then I learned they were going to kill Rita. I had to try to stop it, and they got me. I figured if they knew I had the real stone and I was flat on my back in the hospital again, they'd come and finish me off. Self-preservation. I left you to fend them off until I could get out."

"You're out, but apparently coming forward and talking to the authorities has kind of slipped your mind," I said sarcastically.

"Did you take the real stone from my house? Merika says you were here."

"Yes and yes," I said.

"Good, because I want nothing more to do with this!" Barrett closed the door, and I could hear the dead bolt slide shut.

❖

That night at home, I was working on another script, trying to take my mind off the Marathon mess that I'd now almost grown accustomed to, like an annoying rash. Elmo had his huge jowls resting on my bare foot, and his big floppy, soft lips were comforting.

"I missed you, Elmo," I told him, and he sighed, letting the full weight of his head sink onto my foot, confirming he'd missed me too.

Callie smiled at us and drank her tea. She continued to stare at the photo she'd taken from Talbot's house and absently twirled the last remaining death stone, obtained from Barrett's tea canister, around and around on the coffee table.

"No seams," she said of the stone. "How could a note for the dead get put in this stone?"

"Maybe the note is somehow written on it," I said absently.

"How's your lip?" She reached up and gently touched it with her fingertips.

"Stitches dissolved. All is well."

She leaned in to take a look and then gently kissed me. "Does that hurt?"

"No, it feels good," I breathed, as she took the script out of my hands and tossed it onto the couch.

"Now is this a sympathy thing?" I whispered.

"This is an I'm-crazy-about-you thing and I-thought-I'd-lost-you thing." She slipped my shorts and T-shirt off me and shrugged off her own.

"My favorite things." I pulled her onto the couch and we lay wrapped in one another's arms. I reached down her small, firm thighs and rested my hand between her legs. I was void of expectation, wanting only to be near her. I closed my eyes as she snuggled closer and slid gently onto my fingers, allowing me inside her. I held my breath, not wanting to want, but that was impossible. She clutched me more tightly now, uttering soft sounds of pleasure, and began slowly pressing her body into mine. Blood rushed to my groin and to my head in sudden recognition of this moment, and my mouth devoured her, creating a wet, hot, rhythmic kissing that matched the rhythm of our bodies. Her fingers dug into me, as if she were afraid I'd let go of her before she had let go. The heat from our bodies was so intense that we were wet inside and out; her skin hydroplaned across mine, arousing in both of us a frenzy that was out of control. Unable to hold back any longer, Callie stiffened and thrust herself into climax, moaning wildly and collapsing against me, her damp hair lying on my pounding chest as I kissed the back of her neck.

"That was phenomenal," I said.

She began to cry softly.

"What's wrong?"

"Nothing," she said.

"It doesn't seem like nothing." I wiped away her tears. "That was magical."

She held me tighter, her arms encircling my waist, and said nothing for a long time.

"Can you talk to me a little bit?" I asked.

"It's just…I don't know how to describe it…" She broke off the words and became quiet again. "It's as if I kept this coin—this gold coin—like the currency of my resolve, and I wouldn't spend it on anyone until I knew that person was worth it. Then I met you…" She stopped and I buried my lips in her hair, holding her, smelling her, touching her, and waiting. "Then I met you, and I knew that you would take care of me, of my love and my emotions. I made a decision to give myself to you physically, but more importantly, to give myself to you emotionally. When you're physically naked, your body is exposed. When you're emotionally naked, your soul is exposed. And there is nothing more vulnerable than that."

And suddenly, I felt something deep inside me shift ever so slightly. As if there had been an energy transfer of sorts between us that even I could feel. She had entrusted me with her vulnerability, the most fragile part of herself, trusted that I would do my best not to hurt her—me, the most jaded, blunt, sarcastic of people—entrusted with her, the most loving, joyous, and light-filled person. My job was not to dim the light, but to give it space to glow. *And what if I fail at that? Callie was afraid, on the front end, to give it up, but I'm afraid on the back end.*

I sucked in my breath and said, "I'm not really what you deserve, Callie. You're so pure and trusting and cosmic, and I'm just…not. You saved yourself for this perfect person, and I don't want you to think that's me. I don't even come near being perfect. I mean, if it's true that I was promised to you, then somebody might be playing a cosmic joke on you. I'm not ethereal, spiritual, cosmic…I just don't want you to expect too much. What I'm trying to say is that I don't want to disappoint you. I mean, you waited twenty years, for God's sake, and you got me? Just the surface stuff could drive you nuts: I swear, I'm moody, I eat food if it drops on the floor, and I'm on my best behavior right now! Imagine what I'm like when I'm comfortable and not trying!" I was tearing up trying to get the words out, afraid of what she would think or say.

I saw the love dancing in her eyes. "You're right, you're not perfect…but I think you're perfect for me," she said gently and kissed away any further protest from my lips.

She made love to me slowly and deliberately, maintaining eye contact, letting me know she loved me as she moved inside me with each stroke, teasing me with her luxurious kisses, and then finally laying across me, her body in rhythm with my own, in a timeless orgasmic dance that left us further soaked and sated.

We lay in each other's arms, breaking the silence with nothing but our breathing. Had I been able, I would have merged my very being with hers, in one skin, and one soul, and one mind, so that this moment would never end.

❖

At dawn, I held Callie in my arms, savoring her softness and the light on her hair while Callie studied the photo of Talbot. With her other hand she stroked Elmo, who had managed to work his way into her heart and onto our bed, albeit on a separate sheet Callie laid out for him and washed daily.

"You weren't married to Talbot for ten minutes, were you?" I asked. "You're obsessed with that photo of him."

"It just gives off the strangest vibes," Callie said, and Elmo chimed in with a low sob. I went back to kissing her neck. I'd looked at the photo before and far preferred looking at Callie's naked body. The photo was a shot of Talbot in the foreground, his foot resting on a shovel as he broke ground on a new film archive building on the Marathon lot. In the background, a throng of people who played a role in making the building possible stood around, smiling and applauding.

Callie got up and wandered over to a desk retrieving a magnifying glass. "Tell me who that is," she said, putting the 8x10 glossy on the bed and laying the magnifying glass over a group of faces.

"From their uniforms, I'd say maintenance men, maybe gardeners."

"Third guy from the left."

I sighed and looked again, far preferring just to look at her.

"And the guy to his left," Callie persisted.

My jaw must have gone slack. "Spider Eye! And the guy to his left is the Rastafarian who was shot in Tulsa at the Memory Park Cemetery. My God, two rows back, it's Gigante and Curtis! Studio maintenance guys are the hit men responsible for all the attacks!"

"Teague, do you remember when we went back to the studio guard gate, and there was this man they called over? He was a supervisor."

"Aaaarnold," I said, imitating the guard who'd summoned him.

"The guard said he had friends in high places. That line stuck with me, and he had this little trickle of blood on his chin. His skin was so thin you could almost read a paper through his face," Callie said. "But his upper face, his forehead, seemed okay."

"What are you saying?"

"My dad once told me that welders get thin skin like that from having the flame hit the lower part of their face and cheeks. If they've been doing it for years, their face is like paper. That guy was welding a metal sign when we drove onto the lot."

"He would be good with a blowtorch!" I exclaimed.

I felt a cold ripple of excitement traverse my skin as I called the studio guard gate and asked for landscaping and maintenance. The operator said no one would be on duty until the five a.m. shift.

"Who's on?" I asked casually, as if I knew them all.

"Just Talbot this morning."

"Talbot," I said casually. "You know, I always wondered if he's related to the deceased Lee Talbot."

"Yes, ma'am, sure is. Arnold's his son," the voice replied.

I hung up and shrieked, "Spider Eye was telling the truth. Talbot did hire him. Arnold Talbot. You were right. A man who isn't powerful but has power."

"It's like the chart said. Combust the *Son*. The horary was telling us that the son was at the root of the murders, and the murders involved fire! And, oh my God, it was Cazimi—the heart of the Sun. Maybe the son had no heart when it came to his father, or maybe the father had scorched his son's heart," Callie marveled. We both sat staring at one another, knowing we had gotten to the source. Arnold Talbot was definitely the man we had to talk to. He obviously answered to Caruthers and Isaacs, and he probably did the torch work himself or deployed whoever did it. Callie and I were so nervous neither of us could sleep.

I took the stone out to have one last look at it. "I'm feeling like things are heating up. Somebody could knock us in the head and take it. How do we protect it? There's no bank vault open at this hour."

"If I get knocked in the head again, the last thing I'll be worried about is that stone," she said, holding out her hand for it. We missed the hand off, and the stone clattered to the tiled pavers along the hearth as we both held out breath. Callie reached down and quickly grabbed it. "Barrett's stone has a crack right across the face. Was that there before?"

"We cracked it?" I was incredulous. "The thing makes it through fifty centuries and we crack it on my fireplace? Let me see it."

I pulled a light over to have a closer look and used the magnifying glass to examine it. "This crack is perfect. I mean, it goes all around the edge of this petroglyph, like a diamond cutter did it," I said.

"Let me see." Callie edged in closer to share the magnifying glass.

"Teague, it's not a crack. This thing opens up, just like Barrett said. Get my fingernail file and a razorblade."

I hustled around gathering equipment like I was working for Dr. DeBakey as Callie kept staring under the light. When she had all the tools assembled on the coffee table, she placed the razor's edge inside the cracked line.

"Here, hold the stone steady," she ordered. "I need something to tap the end of the razor. Never mind, I'll use the end of this file to tap it. No wonder we couldn't find out how this thing opens. We were looking along its edge, expecting it to swing open like a book, when it literally breaks in half like a cracker along this hieroglyphic symbol."

Three taps and the stone fell open into two perfectly fitting halves. We both squealed. A tiny sheet of paper jutted out of the hidden compartment, the writing so precise and so minute, we had to put it under the magnifying glass.

"Will you look at this," I breathed. "We have the list, and Hank Caruthers is right at the top. Why all this killing because you're on a list made by a dead guy who couldn't testify against you anyway?" I wondered.

"It's not just names," Callie said. "Safety deposit box number 737 at the B.H. bank, box combination 24-57-16-32. Records verifying embezzlement."

"So Caruthers needs to destroy those records," I said.

"We should make a copy of this note and hide it in the house, so it's safe while we're gone." Callie scanned the room.

"They tore this place apart looking for the stone. They could break in again and maybe beat us to the bank. It's safer to keep it with us," I said and handed it to her.

"I can't wait for the day when the only thing I have on me that someone wants is a great tan," Callie sighed.

CHAPTER TWENTY-FIVE

At four a.m. I kissed Elmo good-bye and told him to "guard the joint and think good thoughts." Callie and I drove by the North Hollywood Hotel and loaded half a dozen hotel planters into the backseat of the Jeep, Callie doing the bulk of the lifting because my ribs were still killing me. Callie insisted we call the motel office later and pay for them. Theft was bad karma. I promised her we'd take care of it. It was just that no nurseries were open at this hour.

At five a.m. we drove up to the Marathon guard gate where the late shift was still on duty. A sleepy-eyed man stuck his head out the window.

"Muirfield with a delivery ordered by Arnold Talbot," Callie said.

"He's a maintenance supervisor," the guard said, staring at the flowers.

"I don't know what he is. I just know who I am, which is the person told to deliver plants if they get ordered. Talbot said they needed to be here by 5:15 a.m., so I've been up since forever."

The guard punched a buzzer trying to reach Arnold as Callie held her breath. Finally the guard said, "He must be walkin' around. Drive up to that building, go right around Soundstage Two, and his office is the maintenance building to your right."

Callie pulled into the lot and parked behind a large van. In minutes we were standing in front of a door with a gray plastic nameplate. The white letters read: Maintenance Supervisor Arnold Talbot.

The door was unlocked, so I pushed it open a few inches. No one was in the office, which was entirely concrete except for a small window behind a wooden desk that looked out onto a brick wall. Arnold came around the corner dragging a fifty pound bag of concrete.

"Mr. Talbot, could we talk to you a minute? I'm Teague Richfield and this is Callie Rivers."

At the mention of my name, Arnold Talbot's eyes widened like a horse's in a burning stall, and he leaned up against the wall, I assumed to brace himself. I asked if we could go inside. He moved hesitantly through the doorway and walked around behind his desk, imposing a barrier between us. He reached for his desk drawer.

"Is there a gun in there?" I asked amicably. "I have one too. Why don't we just talk? Here's the way we figure it. See if we're close. You hired South American thugs, brought them here, where they readily fit into the Latin population, and put them to work in the studio's landscaping and maintenance department. Only these guys have serious criminal records in South America and could be sent back or jailed here if anyone knew that, which is how you control them. You sent one to Orca's—that would be Spider Eye. You had the blond-haired boy we call Raider track us on the highway. Spider Eye and Gigante tried to kill us at your father's estate. But after Isaacs threatened you backstage at the stockholders' meeting, you didn't trust your guys with the Rita Smith job, so you and your handy blowtorch accompanied them. You killed her and torched Barrett Silvers. In fact, I think Callie rocked you to sleep on Rita Smith's lawn."

Suddenly the door behind us opened, nearly giving me a coronary, and there stood Hank Caruthers, his Southern charm all but drained.

"What timing you two have! Of all mornings! You've interrupted some very important business. Haven't they, Arnold? You never called me, Miss Richfield. This does change the script. Get him, Arnold." Arnold moved to the small closet on the right side of the room, opened the door, reached down onto the floor, and dragged out Robert Isaacs. He was hog-tied, his roped legs pulled up behind his head and his mouth taped shut, a scene I'm sure Callie could have enjoyed more under other circumstances.

"We were about to give Mr. Isaacs, our former friend and associate, a new home with an ocean view, but your arrival has changed all that." Isaacs's eyes darted pleadingly to Callie, and for a moment I felt sorry for him.

"I'm afraid we're going to have to make this look like a love triangle," Caruthers said.

"That makes no sense." I was stalling for time.

"I was in the process of scaling down my operation, you might say, the night my men were at Lee Talbot's Bel-Air home. You interrupted them and then escaped. Your friend Callie left prints in several places in Mr. Talbot's mansion, which will allow me to prove that she was there to see Talbot and ask for his help with Isaacs. She was distraught and furious that her ex-husband, Robert Isaacs, with whom she was still desperately in love, was having an affair with her best friend Teague Richfield. She came to the studio to confront Isaacs about your affair and found him, alas, once again with you. She killed you both, and herself, in a mad lover's rage. The stuff of which movies are made. I've always been big on plot."

"And how does Arnold Talbot figure into all this?" Callie asked.

"Ah, Arnold. Imagine having a father who was head of one of Hollywood's largest studios and he throws you the scraps by making you, his only son, head of maintenance. We weren't sorry to see Lee Talbot die, were we, Arnold? Unfortunately, most of Arnold's staff is now dead as well. Therefore, he's a liability, drawing too much attention to us."

This was apparently new and disturbing information to Arnold, who ran for the door just as Caruthers nailed him in the back. He sagged to the floor, blood flowing from his body. "Silencer," Caruthers said, explaining the lack of sound.

"You killed Frank," I said, and tried not to look at Arnold, bleeding on the floor, a reminder we could be next.

"Frank looked at every company as a takeover opportunity, so he couldn't be content with just an outsider's view. While we were working out at the club, he said he knew some pretty shady things were going on at Marathon, and he cited Barrett Silvers's call about the bartering of controversial items and services, and of course the money skimming. Frank wanted me to go with him to talk to his friend at the FBI, since Marathon was a publicly held company. I couldn't let that happen. Looking back on it, I should have skipped Frank Anthony, a good man really, and I should have merely killed Barrett Silvers. She was the one stirring up all the trouble." Caruthers stared at me, but his eyes signaled a mental drift, as if his mind were having to leave his body in order to avoid witnessing what his trigger finger was about to do.

"You shot Frank Anthony with a silencer and then removed his gun from his gym bag," I said, trying to force him to focus on me. "But why the torch?"

"Workers were fixing pipes in the locker room showers and had left an acetylene torch lying there while they took a break. I fired Frank up to kind of muddy the trail."

"But what about his shoes in your locker?" I persisted.

Caruthers suppressed a laugh. "Why is it that the near dead are always so curious? Frank had already taken off his gym shoes. I took his gun out of his gym bag and slipped it into his shoes, storing them in my locker. In the chaos of discovering the body, I slipped his gun and mine out of the building, but left his shoes in the locker. An oversight on my part, of course."

"So your men broke into the Anthony mansion after Frank's death and broke into the antiquities looking for the real stone."

"Right you are." He grinned with glee.

"The trouble was always with the missing stone. I knew Frank had two. I'd seen him buy them at Waterston Evers's. He said he carried them on him for luck, but of course we only found one—the wrong one. Then it dawned on me that he must have given Barrett the other one for safekeeping while we were at Evers's estate. I pried the stone out of Frank's hand, yes. Ramona was right, Frank was clutching the stone when he died. I sent the stone with the man you call Spider Eye to visit Ms. Silvers to warn her that she'd better fork over the other one, but alas, things went awry. And since you had interjected yourself, we felt you had them both for safekeeping. Then you got very creative and began manufacturing fakes, and well, things just got very messy."

"Look, we know where the financial information is that implicates you. We'll take you to it, and you'll let us go. You destroy it, and it's anyone's word against one of the most powerful men in Hollywood."

"There's a quicker fix. Just give me the stone." He held out his hand for it.

I paused and Callie said quickly, "Give it to him, Teague."

I pulled it out of my pants pocket slowly to assure him that I wasn't pulling a gun on him. He snatched the stone out of my hand and pulled it apart, knowing immediately how it worked. He tore the vault numbers off the bottom of the paper, then struck a match and set the list on fire. It burned to ashes in seconds. The list we had unknowingly, and then knowingly, risked our lives for. The list that could bring about the downfall of Marathon Studios. The list that would end the seedy barter system and serve as a warning to other studios about the consequences of embezzlement now no longer existed.

"Well now, that's all just hearsay, isn't it?" He grinned and raised his gun to my eye level, the huge silencer staring into my face.

"I'm a spiritualist," Callie interjected with her head bowed. "Would you allow me one small ritual before I die?" I couldn't believe she was actually suggesting some voodoo ceremony at a time like this. Caruthers seemed amused and asked what it entailed. She said it would only take a second and asked permission to reach into her purse for the cards. Caruthers kicked her hand aside and upended her purse, tossing the cards on the floor at her feet. She picked up the cards and with trembling hands shuffled them. I was about to crawl out of my skin, my eyes darting to every possible escape. I could lunge at him, but now he had the gun barrel flat up against Callie's head. I was panic stricken that he might shoot her.

She carefully placed the cards in a strange pattern, praying, "My life is placed at the four corners of the earth." She stretched her hands up above her head, her eyes closed. "To the sacred spirits who have guided my life. I pray for guidance at this hour." She swung her arms down slowly. "And I offer up these orbs…" Callie raised her arms up swiftly and secured a death grip on Caruthers's crotch, at the same time trying to escape the gun barrel at her head. I grabbed the gun, deflecting the bullet that Caruthers fired reflexively as he writhed in pain and fell forward on top of me. I poised my right hand in the air, forming a hook with my index and middle finger, and brought my hand forward into his face, striking his eye. Between his eyes and his crotch, Mr. Caruthers was pretty much in agony from head to toe. Callie rang the guard gate, and in five minutes we had enough Marathon people in that office to shoot a movie. I shouted at the security people to take Caruthers into custody.

"Touch me and I'll have you fired!" Caruthers bellowed. The guard hesitated and then backed away. I had underestimated the power of the studio executive. On this lot, Hank Caruthers was one of the studio gods, and lesser folk trembled in his presence.

"He shot Arnold Talbot and he's a killer!" I shouted at the nervous guard, who saw his retirement plan teetering in the balance. He stood immobilized as Caruthers stumbled by him and out the door. I made a move to go after Caruthers, but the guard blocked the doorway.

"We've called the police," he said as if I were the problem.

Another guard helped Isaacs up, untaping his mouth and untying his legs. Isaacs rubbed his arms to bring back the circulation and managed to get Callie in a position where he could talk to her.

"Thank God you came here when you did," he said. "I was pretty terror stricken."

Callie looked at him, her eyes seeming to pierce his skin, and said coldly, "Then you must know some of the terror my brother felt before he died." Isaacs tried to say something, but I guess he couldn't think of anything. Truth sometimes has a way of rendering one speechless.

❖

Detective White arrived on the scene, more interested this time in what we had to say. He put out an APB on Caruthers.

Paramedics were working on Arnold Talbot. Isaacs was dialing his attorney, and I called Isabel Anthony in Tulsa, who promised me her story rights. And in Hollywood, "a verbal" is as good as "a written." Like everyone in Hollywood, we'd all hit the phones at the first break.

After an hour of filling in Detective White and his promising to call us for more details, we were released. We stepped out into the main parking lot into a blur of news vans broadcasting, camera shutters clicking, and reporters screaming, "Over here! Talk to us!"

We got in our car, locked the doors, and drove through the crowd.

"I can't believe while people were bleeding and being untied, you were phoning Mrs. Anthony for her story rights."

"Isn't that why we did all this? Make a great theatrical, and only we know the whole story? Speaking of unbelievable, how about your final ritual with the orbs?"

Callie shot me a shy grin. "Well, I rarely use spiritual rituals in vain, but I do think this was an exception. And besides, I learned it from you."

"It's interesting that you wanted to see Isaacs dead and you ended up saving his life," I mused.

"I thought about that. He and I obviously had unfinished business from another lifetime," she said, very matter-of-fact. "I have some unfinished business with you also," she said, letting me know she had plans for our evening. "This will be the first night since I met you that no one is chasing you but me."

❖

I awoke wrapped around her, both of us naked, the sheets down around our legs, our own body heat having kept us warm. I was so in love with her that I could never bear to be without her. I liked the smell of her, the look of her, the way she talked, the way she walked, the way she dressed. I was, as the Shakespearian bard said, besotted with her. I kissed her sleepy face into recognition of the dawn, and she opened her eyes, looking lovingly at me. "It's possible that I could fall in love with you." Her voice had a teasing lilt to it.

"Too late. You already have." I grinned.

"You are a little too cocky." She punched me. "I have to tell you something." And almost before she said it, I caught a glimpse of a suitcase on top of the dresser, partially packed.

"What's that?" I asked, my heart in my throat.

"I have to go back to Tulsa in a few days."

"Okay, I'll go with you," I said.

"Me, not you. I live there."

"You live with me now," I said, and she laughed.

"Why would I live with you? You're not tidy and you're spoiled." She smiled lovingly at me.

"And your point would be?"

"Seriously, Tee, we barely know one another. In fact, I would say you really don't know me at all yet. We have to spend time together."

"My point exactly. Which is why you can't leave."

"I have to go home and take care of some clients, but I'll come back."

"No!" I said, and Elmo chimed in with a well-placed howl.

"Have to. We'll meet in Vegas." She was upbeat.

"Meet in Vegas? You think I just want to meet you places. No, I want to live with you! I'm going to live with you. In fact, if you leave and go back to your condo, I'll just show up, and we'll be living together there."

She pulled me into her. "I've made a hotel reservation in Vegas for us two weeks from Thursday. We'll meet there and we'll gamble."

"That's right, you're a gambler," I said sadly, knowing she was indeed leaving me for some mysterious reason she would not, or could not, explain.

"Only a gambler would contemplate falling in love with you, Teague Richfield. And I'm betting as time goes on, you'll be happy with the outcome." And Callie Rivers rolled on top of me and began kissing me. I didn't know if she'd keep her word and show up. I didn't know if we'd ever live together, but I did know that whatever this woman wanted from me, she was bound to get.

About the Author

Andrews & Austin are pen names. The authors are life partners and live on their ranch in the Central Plains with their horses, dogs, cats, Austin's mom, and an occasional assortment of friends, family, and stray animals. They are avid writers, riders, and lovers of wide-open spaces.

Their upcoming works include *Stellium in Scorpio: A Richfield & Rivers Mystery* (February 2007).

[illegible] the Author

The Traitor and the C[illegible]

them, Tovi and Jemery [illegible]

traitor and retrieve the c[illegible]

([illegible])

[illegible]

Erotic Interludes 3: Lessons [illegible]

Seaman. Sign on for a class [illegible]

take us to school." (1-933110 [illegible]

[illegible]

Books Available From Bold Strokes Books

The Traitor and the Chalice by Jane Fletcher. Without allies to help them, Tevi and Jemeryl will have to risk all in the race to uncover the traitor and retrieve the chalice. The Lyremouth Chronicles Book Two. (1-933110-43-0)

Promising Hearts by Radclyffe. Dr. Vance Phelps lost everything in the War Between the States and arrives in New Hope, Montana, with no hope of happiness and no desire for anything except forgetting—until she meets Mae, a frontier madam. (1-933110-44-9)

Carly's Sound by Ali Vali. Poppy Valente and Julia Johnson form a bond of friendship that lays the foundation for something more, until Poppy's past comes back to haunt her—literally. A poignant romance about love and renewal. (1-933110-45-7)

Unexpected Sparks by Gina L. Dartt. Falling in love is complicated enough without adding murder to the mix. Kate Shannon's growing feelings for much younger Nikki Harris are challenging enough without the mystery of a fatal fire that Kate can't ignore. (1-933110-46-5)

Whitewater Rendezvous by Kim Baldwin. Two women on a wilderness kayak adventure—Chaz Herrick, a laid-back outdoorswoman, and Megan Maxwell, a workaholic news executive—discover that true love may be nothing at all like they imagined. (1-933110-38-4)

Erotic Interludes 3: Lessons in Love ed. by Radclyffe and Stacia Seaman. Sign on for a class in love...the best lesbian erotica writers take us to "school." (1-9331100-39-2)

Punk Like Me by JD Glass. Twenty-one-year-old Nina writes lyrics and plays guitar in the rock band Adam's Rib, and she doesn't always play by the rules. And oh yeah—she has a way with the girls. (1-933110-40-6)

Coffee Sonata by Gun Brooke. Four women whose lives unexpectedly intersect in a small town by the sea share one thing in common—they all have secrets. (1-933110-41-4)

The Clinic: Tristaine Book One by Cate Culpepper. Brenna, a prison medic, finds herself deeply conflicted by her growing feelings for her patient, Jesstin, a wild and rebellious warrior reputed to be descended from ancient Amazons. (1-933110-42-2)

Forever Found by JLee Meyer. Can time, tragedy, and shattered trust destroy a love that seemed destined? When chance reunites two childhood friends separated by tragedy, the past resurfaces to determine the shape of their future. (1-933110-37-6)

Sword of the Guardian by Merry Shannon. Princess Shasta's bold new bodyguard has a secret that could change both of their lives. *He* is actually a *she*. A passionate romance filled with courtly intrigue, chivalry, and devotion. (1-933110-36-8)

Wild Abandon by Ronica Black. From their first tumultuous meeting, Dr. Chandler Brogan and Officer Sarah Monroe are drawn together by their common obsessions—sex, speed, and danger. (1-933110-35-X)

Turn Back Time by Radclyffe. Pearce Rifkin and Wynter Thompson have nothing in common but a shared passion for surgery. They clash at every opportunity, especially when matters of the heart are suddenly at stake. (1-933110-34-1)

Chance by Grace Lennox. At twenty-six, Chance Delaney decides her life isn't working so she swaps it for a different one. What follows is the sexy, funny, touching story of two women who, in finding themselves, also find one another. (1-933110-31-7)

The Exile and the Sorcerer by Jane Fletcher. First in the Lyremouth Chronicles. Tevi, wounded and adrift, arrives in the courtyard of a shy young sorcerer. Together they face monsters, magic, and the challenge of loving despite their differences. (1-933110-32-5)

A Matter of Trust by Radclyffe. JT Sloan is a cybersleuth who doesn't like attachments. Michael Lassiter is leaving her husband, and she needs Sloan's expertise to safeguard her company. It should just be business—but it turns into much more. (1-933110-33-3)

Sweet Creek by Lee Lynch. A celebration of the enduring nature of love, friendship, and community in the quirky, heart-warming lesbian community of Waterfall Falls. (1-933110-29-5)

The Devil Inside by Ali Vali. Derby Cain Casey, head of a New Orleans crime organization, runs the family business with guts and grit, and no one crosses her. No one, that is, until Emma Verde claims her heart and turns her world upside down. (1-933110-30-9)

Grave Silence by Rose Beecham. Detective Jude Devine's investigation of a series of ritual murders is complicated by her torrid affair with the golden girl of Southwestern forensic pathology, Dr. Mercy Westmoreland. (1-933110-25-2)

Honor Reclaimed by Radclyffe. In the aftermath of 9/11, Secret Service Agent Cameron Roberts and Blair Powell close ranks with a trusted few to find the would-be assassins who nearly claimed Blair's life. (1-933110-18-X)

Honor Bound by Radclyffe. Secret Service Agent Cameron Roberts and Blair Powell face political intrigue, a clandestine threat to Blair's safety, and the seemingly irreconcilable personal differences that force them ever farther apart. (1-933110-20-1)

Protector of the Realm: Supreme Constellations Book One by Gun Brooke. A space adventure filled with suspense and a daring intergalactic romance featuring Commodore Rae Jacelon and the stunning, but decidedly lethal, Kellen O'Dal. (1-933110-26-0)

Innocent Hearts by Radclyffe. In a wild and unforgiving land, two women learn about love, passion, and the wonders of the heart. (1-933110-21-X)

The Temple at Landfall by Jane Fletcher. An imprinter, one of Celaeno's most revered servants of the Goddess, is also a prisoner to the faith—until a Ranger frees her by claiming her heart. The Celaeno series. (1-933110-27-9)

Force of Nature by Kim Baldwin. From tornados to forest fires, the forces of nature conspire to bring Gable McCoy and Erin Richards close to danger, and closer to each other. (1-933110-23-6)

In Too Deep by Ronica Black. Undercover homicide cop Erin McKenzie tracks a femme fatale who just might be a real killer...with love and danger hot on her heels. (1-933110-17-1)

Stolen Moments: Erotic Interludes 2 by Stacia Seaman and Radclyffe, eds. Love on the run, in the office, in the shadows...Fast, furious, and almost too hot to handle. (1-933110-16-3)

Course of Action by Gun Brooke. Actress Carolyn Black desperately wants the starring role in an upcoming film produced by Annelie Peterson. Just how far will she go for the dream part of a lifetime? (1-933110-22-8)

Rangers at Roadsend by Jane Fletcher. Sergeant Chip Coppelli has learned to spot trouble coming, and that is exactly what she sees in her new recruit, Katryn Nagata. The Celaeno series. (1-933110-28-7)

Justice Served by Radclyffe. Lieutenant Rebecca Frye and her lover, Dr. Catherine Rawlings, embark on a deadly game of hide-and-seek with an underworld kingpin who traffics in human souls. (1-933110-15-5)

Distant Shores, Silent Thunder by Radclyffe. Dr. Tory King—along with the women who love her—is forced to examine the boundaries of love, friendship, and the ties that transcend time. (1-933110-08-2)

Hunter's Pursuit by Kim Baldwin. A raging blizzard, a mountain hideaway, and a killer-for-hire set a scene for disaster—or desire—when Katarzyna Demetrious rescues a beautiful stranger. (1-933110-09-0)

The Walls of Westernfort by Jane Fletcher. All Temple Guard Natasha Ionadis wants is to serve the Goddess—until she falls in love with one of the rebels she is sworn to destroy. The Celaeno series. (1-933110-24-4)

Change Of Pace: *Erotic Interludes* by Radclyffe. Twenty-five hot-wired encounters guaranteed to spark more than just your imagination. Erotica as you've always dreamed of it. (1-933110-07-4)

Honor Guards by Radclyffe. In a wild flight for their lives, the president's daughter and those who are sworn to protect her wage a desperate struggle for survival. (1-933110-01-5)

Fated Love by Radclyffe. Amidst the chaos and drama of a busy emergency room, two women must contend not only with the fragile nature of life, but also with the irresistible forces of fate. (1-933110-05-8)

Justice in the Shadows by Radclyffe. In a shadow world of secrets and lies, Detective Sergeant Rebecca Frye and her lover, Dr. Catherine Rawlings, join forces in the elusive search for justice. (1-933110-03-1)

shadowland by Radclyffe. In a world on the far edge of desire, two women are drawn together by power, passion, and dark pleasures. An erotic romance. (1-933110-11-2)

Love's Masquerade by Radclyffe. Plunged into the indistinguishable realms of fiction, fantasy, and hidden desires, Auden Frost is forced to question all she believes about the nature of love. (1-933110-14-7)

Love & Honor by Radclyffe. The president's daughter and her lover are faced with difficult choices as they battle a tangled web of Washington intrigue for...love and honor. (1-933110-10-4)

Beyond the Breakwater by Radclyffe. One Provincetown summer, three women learn the true meaning of love, friendship, and family. (1-933110-06-6)

Tomorrow's Promise by Radclyffe. One timeless summer, two very different women discover the power of passion to heal and the promise of hope that only love can bestow. (1-933110-12-0)

Love's Tender Warriors by Radclyffe. Two women who have accepted loneliness as a way of life learn that love is worth fighting for and a battle they cannot afford to lose. (1-933110-02-3)

Love's Melody Lost by Radclyffe. A secretive artist with a haunted past and a young woman escaping a life that has proved to be a lie find their destinies entwined. (1-933110-00-7)

Safe Harbor by Radclyffe. A mysterious newcomer, a reclusive doctor, and a troubled gay teenager learn about love, friendship, and trust during one tumultuous summer in Provincetown. (1-933110-13-9)

Above All, Honor by Radclyffe. Secret Service Agent Cameron Roberts fights her desire for the one woman she can't have—Blair Powell, the daughter of the president of the United States. (1-933110-04-X)

BOLD
STROKES
BOOKS